Covert Commando

A Sam Harper Military Thriller

Thomas Sewell

Dedicated to our sheepdogs in the Armed Forces.

And to the readers who pre-ordered this book,

whose interest and patience made me keep writing it.

And as always and forever, Christi.

Without her support, I probably wouldn't be done writing it
either.

For a current list of related books and short stories, please visit SharperSecurity.com.

Email subscribe@catallaxymedia.com for news about future books.

Cover Design by Aaron Leavitt.

ISBN 13:
978-1-952242-02-1 (Paperback)

Published in the United States of America

Catallaxy Media, Charlotte, NC
http://CatallaxyMedia.com

Contents

PART ONE
MANILA MAYHEM

Chapter One: Shooting Rooftops

Urban battles suck. Especially during a muggy island afternoon in Manila. We roasted beneath a mottled gray sniper hide on top of a blazing skyscraper's roof.

Reflected all the heat right back at us.

My fogproof M151 spotter scope fogged up. Or maybe that was just my drippings. Sweat pooled in the corner of my eyes. I shook my head and scattered perspiration in bulbous droplets across my civvies.

My *disguise*. Shorts and a tourist t-shirt.

How could Schnier stand it? He just rested there behind his rifle, comfortable in old jeans, and claimed the humidity is even bigger back in Texas.

Rather be surfing off Point Loma. A cooler wet.

Schnier and I took turns observing the lectern the local government raised on a platform, plus the government-center buildings and civilian spectators which surrounded it.

The Speaker of the Philippine House of Representatives sure riled up that crowd.

Two plainclothes police guarded him.

My MI team warned us of an Abu Sayyaf sniper team, local jihadi militants, so I don't know why the locals hadn't deployed more men. Perhaps they'd also placed counter-sniper teams in nearby buildings?

If so, I hoped they didn't spot ours. We'd be tough to explain.

A high-velocity bullet tore one of the bodyguard's right arm from him with a thud.

Red blossomed across the guard's flowing-white embroidered baróng shirt. He spun at the impact. Collapsed on the platform above the crowd of demonstrators.

Dude! Only two-feet from the Speaker of the House.

Boom. The shot's echo reverberated from Manila's skyscrapers. Shattered the crowd's calm.

The ShotRadar app on my issue sat phone pinged. Displayed a satellite map of the area surrounding *Batasang Pambansa*, the Philippine House of Representatives complex.

Sound waves impacted known ShotRadar listening posts. Based on the muzzle blast's audio intensity, the expert system automatically tagged them as a gunshot. Triangulated the location of the shooter.

Flashed a red dot onto the map.

The Speaker's other white-shirted guard tackled him. Dragged him behind the bamboo lectern.

Drew a pistol from under his loose dress shirt. Pointed it randomly and ineffectually into the air.

Protesters screamed. Dove. Hid.

Milled in swirls of confusion, like a disrupted whirlpool.

I pivoted my spotting scope away from the lectern. Toward the red dot's real life location.

"Contact. Two tangos. Parking garage. Four o'clock." Glanced at the rangefinder. "640 meters. Black van. Three ... no four floors down from the top."

Captain Schnier swung his Stoner SR-25 rifle across the tar and gravel roof. "Set, Harper." He let the black-camo blanket over the barrel flap in the wind. Settled in the tripod. Lay prone again. "Contact".

"Go to glass."

He twisted his Houston Astros ball cap backward around his red hair. Sprawled his legs to absorb the recoil. Peered through his scope.

"Two on roof of black van. Sniper and spotter."

Dude always has been vain. "Sniper is your target. Check parallax and mil."

He adjusted a nob on his scope. Aimed at the parking garage. "Ready." Paused his breathing.

"Check level. Hold over, two point four." Just enough for the bullet drop from our height to theirs to impact on target.

"Ready."

I gave him my final correction. "Wind left point 6."

Barrel flash from one of the two figures laying on top of the van.

Too slow to prevent another shot.

My TCAPS earbuds dampened the peak of the 7.62 cartridge blast from Schnier's rifle. That shockwave combined with the boom of the enemy's shot.

ShotRadar pinged again. Two red dots.

I ignored the app. Watched the track of Schnier's projectile.

Air turbulence swirled off the supersonic bullet as it cut through the summer heat. Van's windshield exploded. Rear-view mirror tore off.

Shards scattered across the van's interior.

"Six inches low. Four left." Just missed the figure firing the sniper rifle.

The Speaker's lectern exploded.

The windshield below Raven shattered into a web of safety-glass cracks. She rolled off the roof of the van. Slammed into the concrete of the parking garage deck.

"Oof." Knocked her breath out. Dirtied her black cotton shirt. Took forever to hand-wash it. At least her modest tan pants didn't show dust.

How inane.

Omar flopped off the van's roof like a wounded bat. Hit the pavement on the far side. Clutched his rifle. "Move!"

Her first firefight. Don't flip out. Don't flip out. She couldn't afford for Omar to see her as flaky.

She filled her lungs. Crawled around the back of the van. Stood. Sprinted across the garage's parking spots.

Wished she still owned Adidas running shoes, instead of these Filipino clunkers.

Yearned for a lot of things from her old life. Freedom, for one.

Omar ran with his rifle held across his chest.

It slowed him down. He fell behind.

She led him down a circular ramp meant for cars.

He gasped for air. Panted behind her. "Secondary firing location."

She nodded as she stopped. Slammed her hands into the door of the beat up silver sedan they'd stashed in a parking spot ahead of time. Absorbed her momentum.

Yanked the car door open. Slid into the driver's seat. Fired up the engine.

Pressed in the clutch. Ratcheted the gear-shift into first.

Facing outward. So easy to drive away without him. Steer for the exit. Floor the accelerator.

Make him dodge.

But the girls back at their island mountain camp would pay for his anger. She'd continue to go with the flow.

Look for her opportunity.

He caught up. Shoved his rifle onto the back seat. Jumped up front. Yelled.

"Drive, wife!"

Slammed his passenger door on her dream of escape.

After the first shot, plainclothes Special Action Force (SAF) Captain Larrikowal tackled the Speaker of the House.

Pulled him across the dais. Behind the bamboo lectern.

"Stay down!"

The soft wooden stand concealed ballistic armor. Thick fibers designed to give and spread shock while solid plates prevented penetration.

It'd have to do. Safer here than running.

His top sergeant just lost an arm, but his duty for now was to protect the Speaker.

Larrikowal drew his 9mm service pistol. Pointed it at his best guess of where the shot came from.

Somewhere above them. In a building.

Where were the counter-sniper teams responding to the ShotRadar the defense ministry installed for just this situation?

The lectern exploded into bamboo shards. Left the black ballistic armor exposed, but not penetrated.

Another pair of shots. Different locations.

Protesters screamed. Dove. Hid.

Police Central would summon reinforcements and an ambulance, but they'd take forever to fight through this crowd. Too long to reach them.

He pulled the flexible armor back and down. Covered the Speaker's entire head, plus his chest past the waist.

Confused people milled around, unsure of what to do. Others with better ideas ran. Didn't want to remain near a target for gunfire.

Not that he could blame them.

Nothing else to do, but to lead their horses to water. He edged closer to the smashed lectern. Pulled its thin dangling microphone down to his mouth.

"Please *walk* quietly and calmly to the nearest exit from the plaza. Additional emergency services are on their way. You are not at risk. If you are injured and can walk, please exit with the others. If not, stay here. Medical services will arrive shortly."

Distorted, but fathomable, his words reached the crowd. Beginning at the edges, they picked their way toward the streets leading between buildings. Out of the plaza.

"For everyone's safety and so medical personnel can reach those injured, please depart quietly and in an orderly fashion. Calmly. Ensure no one else is injured."

The crowd pressed away from the center of the plaza. A little strain where the mass filtered down to a narrower flow at the exits, but they'd clear out soon enough.

From above, another high-powered shot rang out.

He flinched. The crash echoed.

No nearby impact.

The crowd ran. A woman carrying a sign tripped. Fell. Then a man wearing a city maintenance uniform stumbled over her.

Disaster.

Chapter Two: Shooting Cars

Ranger Captain Buck Schnier paused his breathing again. Waited for one of the pair of tangos sprinting along the line of cars to cross his optics.

"Rushin' like all git-out."

Tangos fled on foot. One wore baggy tan pants. Long sleeve black shirt. Flowing brown hair.

No obvious weapon.

Centered her in his cross-hairs.

Dad-gum it! Schnier wasn't fixin' to shoot a fleeing woman in the back, no matter how dangerous.

He was the herd's bull. Here to protect, not to murder.

Well, also to party. Party and protect. His Manila motto.

Someone began making announcements on the plaza's public address system. Schnier blocked out their words. Harper would tell him if they had to leave.

That's what intelligence subordinates were for. Real-time tactical info.

Through his rifle scope, he watched her slide into the driver's seat of a silver sedan.

Car's running lights flashed on. Male ISIL terrorist in the passenger seat.

Harper packed his spotting scope into their hard case. Folded his tripod. Gathered their gear. Swept loose Orange Fanta, Cherry 7-UP, and energy drinks into a black duffel bag. Left the hard-case open for his rifle.

Ready for pursuit.

"Radio chatter. SAF coming. Time to go."

Schnier ignored him. Shifted his point of aim. Prepped the trigger.

The woman drove forward. Out of her parking spot. Swung her car around to face the down ramp. The exit.

Faced directly at Schnier. He pressed his delicate trigger. Set in motion a brief explosion.

Recognized her face.

Raven?

She turned right into the path of his next bullet.

Their car's front grill caved in. Hood popped up three inches. Caught on a twisted latch.

Raven recoiled from the impact.

Steam exploded out of the radiator. A shot cracked from outside. Echoed across the parking garage walls.

Not one of theirs. Enemy sniper again.

She desperately needed to escape to somewhere safe. Protected.

But for now, she'd settle for survival. Her white knuckles gripped the steering wheel.

Omar commanded in Tausug-English pidgin. "Ignore the radiator. Go!"

He curled up below the windshield. Behind the dash. Protected by the bulk of the engine.

"Always looking out for number one." She'd pay for her comment later, if he remembered. If he understood her expression.

He growled.

She shoved down the accelerator. Their wounded sedan lurched forward. Freaking out wouldn't help.

Shifted into second. Accelerated down the concrete ramp. Followed the black and yellow stripes painted on each edge.

Summer heat reflected from the pavement beyond the flimsy exit gate.

She aimed the car at the red and white boom barrier. No time to stop and pay.

At least it couldn't damage their radiator more than it'd

already been destroyed.

How far would they get before the engine seized from the heat boiling up?

Police Central shouted in Larrikowal's ear. Difficult to make out over the screams of the mob rushing the exits. Something about teams arriving.

Weapon out, he scanned the skyline. Expected another shot any second. One that could make him look like his sergeant, moaning on the dais.

"Repeat."

"Assault teams reached the two buildings identified by ShotRadar. Proceeding to clear the locations."

Two buildings?

He turned away from the lectern. Activated his throat mic.

"Confirm, shots from multiple locations? Different buildings?"

How organized were these guys, to have a backup team? No wonder he'd heard so many discharges.

They'd been lucky.

"Yes, Captain."

The anguish on his sergeant's face as he clutched the remains of his shoulder prompted Larrikowal to try again.

He leaned back toward the lectern's microphone. "Please. Slowly and calmly. Everyone will get out. Emergency personnel will be able to get in and help."

Stupid politicians, to insist that once everyone was searched for weapons at the entrance, no crowd control officers were needed in the Plaza itself. They'd just inflame the masses.

After all, it was a friendly crowd, right?

Not entirely. Not anymore. People were hurt out there.

His sergeant rolled toward him. Trying to get help? An attempt to help cover the Speaker from further shots, despite his injury?

The man was obviously still in shock, but what bravery. Courage. He'd see he got a medal. Perhaps even a good disability pension.

Larrikowal glanced at the Speaker. What a waste.

Still, he did his duty. Kept him safe.

Chapter Three: Shooting Away

Out of time.

I shoved my multi-tool into a cargo pocket on my shorts. Everything else packed, I tapped on Schnier's shoulder. "No more time, dude. Officially not here, remember?"

"Don't pitch a hissy-fit. Might could've had 'em."

He levered himself up with his elbows. Crouched on the roof. Folded up the tripod on his rifle.

Needed to depart the building's roof before we blew the covertness of our mission.

"Still gotta go."

He grunted. Seemed distracted.

I tapped my electronic map, updated in real-time by my MI platoon in support. It showed the spread of our nine sniper teams across the area, the tango's last known position, and the Philippine National Police response.

"Local forces less than three minutes out."

He settled his long gun into its padded hard case to protect the scope's zero.

"Michelle's gonna kill us if the SAF catches up to us, but those hombres won't get far in a wrecked car."

I helped him lock down the case. Slung half our gear onto my back. Not usual officer work, but we'd stretched Schnier's platoon thin to cover this whole Manila government district without detection.

"Got three teams vectored in from the other side. They can't escape."

Schnier looked pale. Like he'd seen a ghost. "Ever wonder if what you see in a scope is real? Or if yer just imagining it?"

"Sure. Our minds play weird tricks sometimes. Not going loony on me, are you?"

I hustled over to the roof access door. Pulled it open for Schnier.

He flowed through. Carried his rifle case. Concrete steps became minor speed bumps.

"Plumb loco. For a second, thought Raven, that hippie chick I dated in college, drove the tango's getaway car."

I followed him down the emergency stairs.

We needed to exit at ground level before the SAF followed their own urban shot trackers to our location. When it came to the area where the second in line to the Presidency was almost assassinated, they'd lock it down like a shark bite.

"Too much of a coincidence. Just your imagination. You've been looking for her everywhere since we got here."

"Dunno."

This dude needed to focus on the job at hand. "Your mind formed a familiar pattern on the face of someone with similar looks."

"Yeah, must be it."

Schnier didn't sound convinced.

Raven cycled through the gears. Dodged around trucks and mopeds.

Turned right from Batasan Road onto a wide street. Four lanes. Commonwealth Avenue. The swarm of late afternoon traffic escaping the protests would delay pursuit, but didn't help their situation.

Car's temperature gauge swung into the red. Limited time before it flat out died.

Omar pointed at an elevated metro train platform atop concrete pillars. "Leave it."

She shrugged. He was in charge. She parked on the right edge of the street. In a bus zone in front of a five-story building.

A queue of people waited behind waist-high portable fencing for the next shuttle bus home.

Omar grabbed her arm. Squeezed hard. "Stay with me, Songbird."

She gulped. Nodded. Not frantic. Laid back.

He released her. Opened his door.

A police officer blew his whistle as he ran toward the rear of their illegally parked car. Sounded like a furious football referee.

Omar removed a gunmetal gray 9mm pistol from the glove box.

The officer arrived at Omar's open door. Gestured a command to move on.

Omar lifted his pistol. Shot him twice in the chest.

Pop. Pop. So little noise to end a man.

Stood over his body. One final bullet to the face.

Tucked his pistol behind his belt. Under his untucked shirt.

Winced more at the heat of the weapon's barrel than he had during his murder of the officer.

The crowd waiting for the next bus heard the shots and looked around for the source. A few of the closest turned and jogged away, head on a swivel, either down the street or up to the train platform.

Why didn't more notice? Realize what had happened?

Raven left the engine running. Didn't matter now. Hopped out. Almost got knocked over by a motorcycle weaving through traffic.

Ran around the front of the car.

This time Omar ran ahead of her. He'd left the sniper rifle behind. His pride and joy.

Must really hurt.

He pushed through a crowd of people carrying home-made signs to the protest, "Umuwi ka na ang China."

China go home already, she automatically translated. Pulled her niqab veil from beneath her headscarf. Covered her face as a cheap disguise.

She jogged in his wake. Followed him up a staircase. Across the pedestrian walkway over the street.

He ran as if late for a train. He'd bribe the station security if stopped for a search. Foreign money went a long way here.

Surely their path was too obvious? Too constrained?

Maybe the police would catch them.

If it weren't for the other women back at their mountain camp, she'd hope so.

Larrikowal took off his loose shirt. Exposed the armored vest he wore underneath. Didn't matter now.

His sergeant had made it close by. He whimpered in pain.

They'd stuffed their medical supplies in bags behind the dais. Larrikowal didn't dare leave the Speaker unshielded to hunt for them.

He rolled his shirt into a make-shift bandage. Stuck a shard of bamboo into the middle to use as a windlass. Wrapped the whole thing around his sergeant's upper arm.

Not much left of his lower arm. No easy place to apply direct pressure, just attempt to cut off the flow from above.

He tied the make-shift shirt-rope off. Wound the stick. Took up all the remaining slack, and then a bit tighter.

Felt his sergeant's artery below his tourniquet. No pulse. Bleeding slowed. Stopped. Good.

He checked the time. Medical would want to know. Improvised a strap from his sergeant's boot-lace. Tied down the stick so it wouldn't move.

From now on, his team would carry their combat tourniquets with them even on quiet civilian protection assignments. Materials out of reach weren't useful.

Two more of his SAF team, both in uniform, finally pushed through the flow of the thinning crowd to reach the plaza.

It'd only been a few minutes, but he took a long and deep breath to quiet his pulse.

Reinforcements.

The radio in his ear crackled.

"Both ShotRadar buildings are secure. No snipers. Repeat. No Snipers. Captain, you're clear to move the Speaker."

Chapter Four: Shooting Execution Style

Michelle paced a semi-circle around her hut. Flipped the hemline of her locally sourced black cotton dress out of the way of her stomping knees.

One of the floor's nailed-down bamboo strips creaked every time she stepped on it.

She'd made her bed up hours before with a sleeping bag. Her bed filled the center of the woven thatch wall opposite the ladder down, hence her semi-circle.

Her nipa hut, raised on house-posts against storms in the South China Sea, combined home and office.

West Philippine Sea, she corrected herself. Wouldn't do to slip up on the name with her outside voice.

She'd rented a group of isolated nipa huts next to the ocean with the Agency's cash. The walled resort compound perfectly contained the two platoons of Rangers assigned to assist her mission while keeping nosy neighbors away.

As far as anyone was concerned, this was just a corporate retreat, keeping to themselves.

Not to mention being the ideal location for their mission. She'd claimed this frond-thatched hut for herself.

It alternated between nice and a nightmare to be surrounded by so much testosterone near the water.

After the last visiting forces agreement treaty with the Philippine government broke down, they were *supposed* to be hidden visitors here.

Deniable. Under civilian cover. Covert commandos.

Sam and Schnier asserted the privileges of rank to split the largest hut as their headquarters. Maybe she should use it, instead of her cramped quarters.

They certainly weren't there right now.

No, she couldn't remain near Schnier's shooters and Sam's Military Intelligence platoon.

Too many ears. Might overhear her boss reaming her out.

She descended the bamboo ladder. Each rung complained as her steps stretched the leather straps holding the cross-pieces to the poles.

Strode across the sand to the foot-thick, rubber-coated communications cable. It led from farther inland, across the beach, and then vanished into the sea.

The reason for their presence here.

Far enough.

She punched the saved number on her secure sat phone. Best to get this over with.

After they exchanged guarded greetings, CIA Assistant Director Edward Metcalf's deep bass voice boomed out of her phone's speaker, "I'm cutting you off. Pack everything up. Get those rangers in Manila to the embassy, where they can hide out with the marines until this blows over."

She took a deep breath. She'd promised herself she'd be more diplomatic with lackadaisical Langley losers.

Honey caught more flies than vinegar, after all.

That's what Sam claimed, anyway.

"Sir, the Philippine's Special Action Force hasn't caught up with our men. They'll evade and regroup. Nothing to worry about. It'll be like they were never there."

"You set Ranger counter-sniper teams in a ring around their legislature. SAF was already on alert for sniper threats."

She could hear his disbelief and exasperation through the phone, but couldn't insert a word in edge-wise.

"Your, how did you put it, 'fresh local intelligence' told you all about the sniper threat, but it didn't occur to you that if the SAF caught your teams in place after shots were fired, they'd decide the United States Army was planning to assassinate their legislative leadership?"

Michelle grimaced, glad he couldn't see her. "Yes, sir, but one of our teams also disrupted ISIL's assassination attempt. Forced them to flee. We have teams closing in now."

"Call them off. Return to the embassy. We'll arrange a flight, or perhaps a slow boat on its way from China, to bring you back to CONUS."

Pretty sure he was joking about China. The Seventh Fleet anchored itself in Japan.

She'd dedicated her life to her career. Clawed her way to the top. To her posting as Station Chief here. Now Sam's reckless do-gooding had burnt her position to the ground.

Destroyed her reputation for competence.

"Our original mission remains intact. The Chinese are a threat to the undersea cable network. Huawei isn't going away. Let us remain and we'll protect both the Speaker and the network. We can't just ignore the remaining risk to an allied power."

"Sure you can. Allow me to demonstrate how ignoring a professional liability works."

Her phone blanked as he hung up on her.

Either they gave up on stopping the terrorists Sam's MI platoon had gathered electronic intelligence on, or remained truly on their own.

She wished Sam was here for her to curse out, instead of roaming Manila with that hot-head Schnier and his platoon.

If she just had enough power, she could aim it at the evils present everywhere.

But she already had few enough friends left.

Spaced out, Raven stared through the half-open window of their elevated train car. The painted concrete walls of Quezon City's crowded people jungle flew past outside.

Faded red. Pale blue. Algae green.

She'd never gain Omar's easy comfort with death.

The resident's wall colors looked like they'd given up on life.

Omar snored behind her, drained after a night of waiting to shoot and the adrenaline of their escape.

Supposedly, she watched for signs of pursuit, but her mind

flew to the other side of the world.

Back in Texas.

This wasn't what she'd signed up for. Her sociology professor made life as a rebel sound so fulfilling.

Fighting for The People. Helping the poor.

Pure motives. Passionate for a cause.

Those weren't enough.

She'd horrified her traditional Texas family by converting to Islam. She'd thought of herself as submitting to the will of Allah. That made clear she would no longer submit to her parents. To their expectations.

Their abuse.

It'd been simple. Proclaim the Testimony of Faith. Get accepted into a new global family.

Travel to the other side of the world. Fight western capitalist oppression.

Join Omar's band of freedom fighters. Help the resistance of Allah.

But somewhere, it'd gone wrong. She'd screwed up.

Just still wasn't sure exactly how. Bummer.

Worthless.

Omar, the Wrath of Allah for The People, shifted in his sleep.

She flinched. Didn't want him to awaken.

Ever.

That wasn't the peace she'd sought. Had she been this murderous in her thoughts before joining him?

She should pray, but instead she stared at the jungle canopy wrestling the edge of the city.

Omar's phone rang. He snorted and awoke. Clawed at his shirt pocket. Answered.

Shouting from the other side of the conversation.

Omar ignored security to argue. "There were other bird watching teams in the trees. Our agreement held no warning of tight quarters."

Alone in the train compartment, speaking in code, it wasn't *too* risky.

More noise. More subdued. More conciliatory.

"No." Omar frowned. "The deed was done at substantial risk.

Compensation must be increased."

Something about checking with someone. Wanting to preserve their relationship. A strange accent. Almost sing-song.

"Do that, but deliver soon."

Omar growled as he stabbed at the phone to disconnect the call. Glared at her.

She ignored him. Stared out the window at the passing jungle. She was strung out. A nervous wreck.

His mood would pass. They almost always did.

Larrikowal worked with a team of five more of his men to surround the speaker. Escort him off the platform. Indoors. Back into the Batasang Pambansa Complex.

Away from any potential physical threat.

All things considered, the Speaker had remained remarkably calm throughout the attack. Larrikowal shrugged. Hard to tell in advance how someone will deal with stress.

A paramedic team carried away his sergeant. He'd visit him in the hospital later.

Larrikowal paced down the BP Complex's long corridors toward Police Central.

Right now, he needed to report to his superiors. In a political matter such as this, they'd need to brief the Secretary of National Defense.

Lelfin Dorenza headed up more than the military. His cabinet department also encompassed the nation's police forces.

Larrikowal respected Dorenza, but preferred not to enter his notice for a negative event like this.

Careers, even lives, had been ruined for less.

At least Dorenza and the Speaker were political enemies, both in the running to replace the current President, ineligible to run again in this election.

Maybe the thought of his rival being so unpopular to be at risk of assassination would put him in a good mood.

Unless he needed a scapegoat to make it clear to the people he wasn't involved. That Dorenza hadn't deliberately allowed the Speaker's security to lapse.

To fail.

No, Dorenza had a reputation among his subordinates as a fair man. He wouldn't throw Larrikowal to his enemies, would he?

The light security had been the Speaker's decision. His insistence, in fact. Larrikowal had an email trail from the Speaker's office declining any additional security inside the Plaza, or in the surrounding buildings.

They'd stated publicly that they trusted their popularity with the people. They didn't need protection from their own supporters.

How'd that turn out for them?

Larrikowal preferred not to be the one answering for that.

He approached Police Central. Squared his shoulders. Plastered a grim smile on his face. Blew past the sergeant at the front desk. Headed for his boss's office in the back.

Either way, this wouldn't be a pleasant conversation.

He smacked his head. Dumi! He'd forgotten to call his girlfriend. Tell her he was fine. She'd have watched the speech on television.

That chat wouldn't be fun either.

Chapter Five: Shooting Information

Schnier furiously refused to think about Raven while they returned to base. He managed to delay his call to Major Williams for all of 15 minutes after they arrived at their beach headquarters.

Truckin' secure communications into their raised hut made the autonomy of this, his first independent command, a fond, but distant memory.

Williams never beat around the bush. "Whiskey Tango Foxtrot did you think you were doing splitting your platoon into sniper teams to scatter across Manila?"

Schnier resisted the urge to stand at attention while on the secure sat phone in his own hut.

"Harper's platoon developed tactical intelligence which indicated an immediate threat to allied local government officials, sir. We needed to act immediately to prevent a jihadi assassination."

"You're supposed to be in charge over there. Reigning him in. Instead, Harper's a dangerous influence on you."

Schnier tried not to give Sam, playing with his laptop at his flimsy desk, an earful. "Yes, sir. No excuse, sir."

"Don't feed me that. Shooting up the city while you're supposed to be covert is bad enough, but how the hell did you blow your entire operational budget already?"

Bull-dung. He'd momentarily put that little snafu out of his mind. "Human error, sir. My new clerk inadvertently transposed two digits in the National Stock Number for the requisition. Instead of 1375-25-119-7872 to order a case of fuse cutouts, he typed 7782. Limpet mines are more expensive than fuses, sir."

"I don't care about the details. Fix it before they arrive. What's a ranger platoon going to do with a dozen limpet mines?"

A mine magnetically attached by hand to a ship underwater and then detonated later? Not much use to a land unit.

"We'll get it straightened out, sir."

"Better, you signed off on it. That leaves you with no remaining budget for bullets and beans. Quit screwing up your command, Captain."

"No excuses, Major."

After his CO hung-up, Schnier stuck his head in his hands. How could he prevent other people's mistakes from tearing his command away from him?

The sparse hut furniture reinforced his sense of isolation. Sam tapped away at his keyboard.

That hombre always looked cheerful.

Annoyin'.

Well, no use crying over spilled fuses.

He heard a rattle and clack from the base of the ladder into their hut. Knew that sound.

Finally, someone who wouldn't spend their time dressing him down for today's action.

Michelle raised her head over the top of the bamboo ladder. Ascended into the room.

He'd always appreciated her movement, especially in that flowing black dress. Fine as horse hair split eight ways.

She glanced around, as if to be sure only officers were present.

Frowned at him.

"Agency is pulling the plug. Operation's toast. Prepare your rangers to depart as soon as the Navy can arrive. I'll clean this place up after you leave."

Well, didn't that news beat a rodeo clown to death!

Lieutenant Pahk Geon hung up the old-fashioned handset tied into the Chinese Destroyer's satellite link Voice Over IP

(VOIP) phone line.

Admiral Hu, the Fleet's political commissar (PC), pushed open the white bulkhead door into Pahk's tiny shipboard office.

Did Hu hear his conversation with the ISIL terrorist, Omar?

Pahk stowed his thin black metal desk into the wall to create room to stand at attention.

Under the Chinese Communist Party (CCP)'s system for the People's Liberation Army Navy (PLAN), a career admiral was the military commander, but not the person in overall charge.

The PC's political heft generally won if he and the military commander disagreed on a course of action.

At least back in Korea, the military and the political class were better integrated. None of this separate duties nonsense.

Either way, the "Party commands the gun" as the CCP put it.

Admiral Hu, the PC in question, cleared his throat. "Your pet terrorist becomes a liability."

Clearly, he *had* listened to their call.

A premature end to Omar would also terminate Pahk's mission to deniably coordinate with the terrorist. Potentially fatal consequences would follow.

He'd need to walk a tight rice furrow here.

"Omar will expect a double-cross right now. Better to pay him off with some cheap weapons, make him believe we have more work for him, then set a later trap."

"Perhaps. It doesn't escape me that your idea extends your useful life to the PLAN. Perhaps your actions will reflect well on me, or perhaps not, but your family's health still depends on how well you handle Omar."

Pahk ground his teeth, but then forced a smile. "Of course. I'm confident I'll ultimately resolve the situation to your satisfaction."

"See that you do." Hu pointed at Pahk. "Surprises can be deadly. I don't like this sniper team that shot at Omar. We need to be ahead of the Philippine President's information loop, not behind it, if I'm to maintain our influence over him."

"I'll have the Comment Crew investigate." The PLA's Unit 61398, the elite Chinese military advanced Persistent Threat team known informally as the Comment Crew, had already infiltrated the local government.

One more information request wouldn't strain their talents, nor their access.

Hu grunted in deniable agreement. Clanged the bulkhead door shut behind him.

Pahk unfolded his desk out of the bulkhead. He'd need to arrange for a new batch of weapons for Omar.

Good thing the Chinese armorers were excellent craftsmen. Arranging a suitable payment would be more enjoyable than listening to the Chinese Navy threaten his family.

Once he had the weapons in hand and Comment Crew seeking new intelligence, he'd have a long boat ride ahead of him to Lubang Island.

After a sandpaper consultation with his superior, and with her superior, Larrikowal wrote it all down to send upstairs. Attached the email chain from the Speaker's office.

Having covered his rear that way, he changed into his black and gray urban camo. Loaded up his hard plates. Hung his carbine over his shoulder. Tucked his sunglasses into the center of his shirt.

Arranged his black beret.

The paramedics had taken his shirt tourniquet along with his sergeant, but now he was SAF official.

He'd need to intimidate a bit at the sniper locations, anyway. Best way to impress a bunch of city cops was to look like he was ready to shoot them at any moment.

After all, with his sergeant in the hospital, he was ready to shoot *someone*.

He could use the travel time to explain the day to his girlfriend, Sheila. Call her on his mobile phone from the back of the police car.

Reassure her.

His driver didn't need him to navigate within Manila. Officers get used to locations in the areas they work, even if without a strict system of street numbers they needed additional knowledge to translate which particular building was located where.

"It's okay. I'm safe."

"I saw on teevee. You were there."

He frowned at the accusation in her voice. "It's my job, but no one was gunning for me. They were after the Speaker."

"That doesn't help if you take a bullet for him. How can I live without you?"

"Sheila, I'll come back to you. I always do."

"Don't dismiss my worries. You always say I'm too emotional, but I have a right to my feelings. Why can't you move to an office job, like your cousin?"

"My cousin is a *putanh in mo*. He lives off bribes. Doesn't help anyone."

"Don't speak of your aunt that way. Besides, he bought his wife a house outside the city, how about that? I could use some of that kind of help, if you ever marry me."

"I get it. You're worried. I appreciate how much you care about me, but this is my job. You need to accept that."

"Why must I accept you getting yourself killed by some random bullet?"

"Won't happen. I was never really in any danger."

"Your sergeant. Was he in no danger?" She let out a low moan. "Is he even still alive?"

"In critical condition, but the doctors say he should pull through." Maybe he could spin it as a good thing. "*He* gets to retire."

"If you ever get killed dead, don't come running to me. I won't have it."

Not everything was within his control.

"Yes, my flower. Now, I have to get back to work."

"More shooting?"

"No, just looking over a crime scene."

"No more shooting."

"Okay. Okay."

While they said their goodbyes, his driver smirked at him in the rear-view mirror.

Smirked!

Really, he could've been killed. But Sheila didn't need to worry about that.

The skyscraper roof was a bust. Empty as a wallet left in a Naga city bar.

No new information, except they were obviously professionals, to clean-up so thoroughly while dodging our assault team.

He left the crime scene team attempting to find a print to lift, or some DNA or fiber trace, but wasn't optimistic.

His driver wiped the smirk off his face for their second trip, but only because of a department casualty. A traffic officer near a train station.

Shot and killed from close range. Abandoned car nearby.

Larrikowal frowned.

Connected? One of the sniper teams escaping?

Around the block, across the way from the skyscraper roof, the cordoned-off parking garage told a different story.

Wrecked black van windshield displayed a bullet hole. They'd found a high-powered round embedded in the back seat.

Fired from above.

Shrapnel in the driveway from what the techs guessed was a torn radiator, judging by the pool of coolant surrounding it.

The sniper team on the skyscraper roof hadn't aimed at the Speaker. They'd been shooting at this team.

Trying to stop them?

But the SAF didn't have anyone up on that roof until the assault team arrived, well after all the firing stopped.

So who were they? Had the speaker hired private security? Is that why he'd been so calm while lying exposed on the dais?

Something smelled. Dumi!

Chapter Six: Tracking Bits and Bytes

My MI platoon's earlier success penetrating the Philippine government's innermost secrets just whetted my appetite. In this environment, I hungered after more information like a shark looks at dangling chum.

Despite the captain and his lady, both intent on interrupting my work with their bickering.

I gave Spec 4 Watkins, standing next to my desk, a look to pretend he didn't hear them.

Not ideal for his career.

I spun my mouse's wheel to find more to show him. Dragged it across the hut's table. Scrolled through intercepted emails on my thickly hardened green issue laptop.

Scanned through documents captured by keyword search algorithms.

My platoon had trained expert systems to filter the mass of information pouring through undersea fiber optic cables.

Those cables connected the Philippines to the rest of the Internet.

I showed the process to Watkins, a lanky Boston kid among Schnier's shooters. He loved electronics, and I wanted to see if I could talk him into a future switch to intelligence.

Currently, looked like a triathlete on vacation, hiding in plain sight like the rest of us.

"It's a simple enough process. My rangers dug through captured data. Rated it as interesting or not. Thumbs up. Thumbs down."

"Wicked! Even I could do that. It's like Tinder for intel."

"MI has all the fun. We used those manual ratings to train the computer system. Get it to create millions of rules to determine which documents were interesting. It tried out all those possible rules. Kept the ones which gave results similar to the team's manual ratings, tossed the rest."

"How does it know what to do with new documents, though? Ones not like the data you trained it on?"

Kid was smart, I'll give him that.

"Ran them through its rules based on that training, and then my team rated those results to give feedback. It adjusted itself to compensate. Used the second round of feedback to judge it's first round attempts. Through self-reinforcement, improved itself over time. It's a computer. Can afford to run a billion tests while we're all sleeping."

"Right. So then what, you just dump more data in?"

"We have it hunt through every electronic communication in the country. Produce virtual needles out of the local haystacks. Makes our intelligence production a billion times faster."

"That's killa mint."

He spoke techno better than I spoke Boston. "Is that good, dude?"

"Ya huh!"

I leaned back to show him today's intelligence take. My cheap thatch office chair squeaked.

Our island headquarters held a hodgepodge of locally acquired products and the military procurement we'd either brought with us or received from regular supply runs up the beach from the Seventh Fleet.

Modular electronics contrasted weirdly with a nipa hut constructed from bamboo and palm fronds, but the locals knew what they were doing.

Besides, we wouldn't be here long enough to get comfortable.

Instead of a lowly spec 4 on his first deployment with Schnier, what I really needed were my TCAPS earbuds, so the screeching lovebirds didn't disturb my concentration on figuring out the reactions to this morning's sniper attack.

Michelle sighed somewhere behind us. "Captain, you're here

at the behest of the Agency I represent. I've argued with D.C. all night. They order your platoons to pack up and go home. The Navy will be here in a few hours to drag you out of bed."

It's always a bad sign when she calls Schnier by his rank. I glanced at Watkins. Held my finger to my lips and then mimed slicing my throat.

He nodded, eyes wide.

"Look, honey, we evaded the SAF. Stopped the assassination of a major government leader." Schnier gave as good as he got. "Probably prevented the protests from turning into riots. Kept Manila from burning last night. They could cut us a break. Call 'em back. We're safely home now. Situation has changed."

"The overnight crew in Langley don't have the authority to countermand anything. The Assistant Directory left an hour ago. I'm not calling him at home again."

We pretended to ignore them. I flipped through a few more summaries to show Watkins what the system output.

Interesting, the President didn't seem surprised by the assassination attempt on his political ally. In fact, his press secretary emailed about pre-written obituaries for key government ministers just yesterday.

Schnier wasn't done. "Give us until the end of the day. Our mission isn't complete. We have at least sixteen hours until your boss is back. We can take that long and still be moving when he arrives in the morning."

She stuck her hands onto her slender hips. "What can you hope to accomplish? We can't locate the ISIL cell and do anything about them in less than a day. Besides, our mission is information gathering, not direct action."

"Direct action is what rangers do, babe. You know that."

Michelle pointed at me, "Not his guys."

I shook my head, "Leave me out of this. You two love-birds are doing fine on your own. Besides, I may have found something interesting."

Of course, rather than ignoring me as requested, they crowded around, one looking over each shoulder.

Their presence pushed Watkins away, around the table.

I give up.

"Michelle, you remember Watkins, right? I introduced you at RASP graduation. He was on my team during ranger selection."

She glared at him, as if he represented the worst of me and Schnier both. "Of course."

I winked at Watkins. "We can pick this demo up another time. Our allotment of the fourth dimension shrinks rapidly."

He nodded. "Sirs. Ma'am. If you'll excuse me?" Headed for the ladder down without waiting for a response.

Schnier cocked his head. "Fourth dimension?"

"Never mind. He got it. I'll explain later, when we have more time." I pointed at my screen. "Why wouldn't the President warn his top political ally in Congress about an attempt on his life?"

Schnier shrugged.

I expanded another email from the President's chief of staff. "Read this. No coincidences. His inner circle obviously knew all about it."

Schnier glared at Michelle. "Maybe they had a falling out. It happens, even between the closest of people. Maybe even especially between intimate partners."

Michelle ignored his insinuation. "Or maybe the sniper meant to miss. Did you geniuses ever consider that you weren't quite the big heroes you thought you were, saving the day?"

A false flag operation. Something to turn the politicians in power into *almost*-martyrs. Flip the protests against their corrupt administration into disgust for the evil assassins. Perhaps even justify another round of martial law to crack down on their political enemies.

Had we been worked?

Schnier's wheels didn't quite turn fast enough. "At least we dodged the bull's horns this time. Hot damn."

Michelle scowled, like she did when a bully back in high school hit on her and she preferred to punch him.

"You got lucky. There's a reason this entire mission is covert. Just knowing we're operating here would piss off the locals. The ones who already dislike America. Imagine if they had caught you with a sniper rifle near the assassination attempt? Would've justified their entire campaign to cancel our base leases. Lead to war if they didn't know they'd lose."

I tried to save him. "We had actionable intelligence of a credible threat. Couldn't just sit on our boards watching the wave, doing sigint while ISIL operated in Manila. What's the point of developing intelligence if you don't use it?"

She shook her head. Huffed. "My point exactly. What's the point of your intelligence if you don't use it? Let me spell it out for you. That's not our mission. Leave it to the locals. It's moot. We're going home anyway."

Maybe she was right. What if the Filipinos didn't want us here? Their government certainly didn't, so we hid our presence. Do we really have the right to stay and pursue our own ideas of morality if it conflicted with the local's choices? Get some people killed as collateral damage? Their arm blown off, like that bodyguard whose image appeared every time I closed my eyes?

Schnier wasn't much for retreat. "Harper may be here to collect intelligence, but my guys are strictly the kick ass and take names variety. Point us in the right direction and we'll take care of it. Not our fault we've had yet another intelligence failure."

My laptop emitted a soft ding. A priority update.

I flipped it up on the screen. Read.

Michelle stalked to the door. Evidently, ready to go call in the Navy to have us escorted out of her territory.

"Wait." I pulled up a map. "Come back." Zoomed in. "SAF reported a dead cop next to an abandoned car with a bullet hole in the radiator. Got a good image of the dude with the sniper rifle from a train platform camera. Omar Yousef. AKA, the Wrath of Allah."

She stopped. Looked back. "So?"

"My team ran the image through facial rec. Analyzed the local video feeds. Got more hits. Followed Omar onto the train. Tracked his female companion, although she covered her face, so no identification there. They got off the train near a ferry stop. Ferry runs to Lubang Island. Omar and Abu Sayyaf must be based on the island. No other reason to leave the train at that stop."

Schnier grinned like a shark tossed a handful of bloody fish. "Less than ninety miles. Plenty of time to check it out."

I shook my head. "We'd have to wait for naval transportation, and they're planning to take us in the opposite direction, north to Japan and Seventh Fleet HQ. No, it's going the long way, but we should take the ferry. Might even be able to track him from the dock on the island."

Michelle shook her head. "You two won't be happy until you've started a war, will you?"

We needed to appeal to her well-worn sense of self-preservation.

"If we go home now, your mission will be a failure, but if we take down ISIL in the Philippines, any issues along the way become, what did you say before? Moot."

She tilted her head. Pursed her lips.

Finally, rolled her eyes and sighed.

"Find them and get back in less than sixteen hours. I'll blame a storm or the tide or something for the delay."

I gave my best mock salute. Attempted a serious look.

"Yes, Ma'am. They call us Recon Rangers for a reason. I'll find them, then Schnier's platoon can come destroy them."

Now it was my turn to receive one of his Texas glares.

"Be reasonable." I grinned. "You can't go hiking through the jungle looking for their base while also organizing your platoon to come along and mop them up. You're in command here. Have duties. Responsibilities."

"I *came* here to party, not sit back in camp."

"You'll get your shot. Just let my team guide you in."

"On a buckin' bronco with the rope down to it's last thread." Schnier let out a growl, but then shook his head. Stomped past Michelle. Out the door to get a warning order off to his men.

Michelle gave me a stare-down. "I mean it. Back in sixteen hours. Don't go playing hero again."

"When have I ever let you down?"

I mean, a couple hours on the train. Couple more on the ferry. A while tracking through the jungle. Should be able to get there and back with plenty of time remaining, right?

Now to download a better map of Lubang Island. Could

spend the train ride reviewing likely terrain features.

Terrorist camp, here I come.

Typical female driving.

Pahk banged his hand on the PLAN Houbei class missile boat's console. A wave of salt water sprayed across the forward-looking windows.

Would the PLAN's lady pilot bounce the boat all the way to Lubang? The type 22 was supposed to be a wave piercing stealth design, but surely its camouflage worked better at slower speeds!

Besides, he needed to read his tablet computer. Her small craft piloting didn't help.

Pahk scrolled through his messages with one gloved hand. Grabbed onto the boat's console to steady himself with the other.

Publicly, the Philippine government took credit for driving off a terrorist attack with only minimal casualties. They pronounced the disarmed sergeant in critical condition a national hero.

Privately, his contacts and Comment Crew's report on their internal security emails showed mass confusion. They didn't actually know who had interfered.

Comment Crew was pursuing a theory, though. The Americans had various presences in the Philippines.

What if western imperialists shot at Omar?

That could change everything. Omar and his entire group, along with their link to Pahk, might quickly become a liability to the Chinese government.

Liabilities to the Chinese government rarely lasted long. That went double for a man just trying to stay in their good graces long enough to establish a new home for his mother and sister after being disgraced in Korea.

Unless he could use Comment Crew's information to turn the tables. Flip things on the Americans.

Set a trap.

The idea appealed to his own special forces background.

Pahk replied with a request to analyze every American

special operations sniper-capable unit in the region and verify their current location.

Some group would be missing soldiers. That would tell them who was behind the attack on Omar and what to expect next.

Knowing your opponent is half the battle, after all.

Larrikowal took a deep breath. Straightened up outside the steel door to the Mayor's Command Center. Smiled at the Philippine National Police (PNP) guard in a powder blue uniform stationed at the entrance.

CCTV cameras covered all of Manila's streets, mostly hanging from traffic signals. Every public space around the government buildings had them, including public transit.

Now Larrikowal just needed the images they recorded. The facial recognition records near his crime scenes.

Normally he'd email a request to the Department of the Interior and Local Government (DILG) and they'd pull the requested video locations and times from their Chinese-financed equipment for him.

Nothing in the bureaucracy processed fast, but his Special Action Force (SAF) had enough pull to get top priority. They worked cases such as hostage rescue, critical incident response, and attempted political assassinations, after all.

Not this time.

They'd refused his request. Not just a delay. Outright refusal!

Couldn't possibly be a bureaucrat looking for a bribe, could they? From the SAF?

That would go too far.

He stared at the guard. "I need to see the camera coordinator."

A PNP junior sergeant, the guard took in the Captain's rank and his SAF uniform and nodded. Pulled the door open for him.

Larrikowal strode through the doorway, into a semi-circular room oriented around a giant screen no one watched. It displayed monitoring from the Public Safety Answering Point (all calls answered within four minutes), the DILG (something about utility truck response times), the PNP (a map of current incident locations), the Bureau of Fire Protection (Just a scattering of red dots to indicate flames), and the Bureau of Jail

Management (All prison systems nominal).

Useful for touring politicians, the inhabitants of the room used the two monitors on their desks and ignored the big screen.

He made his way over to where the bureaucrat who ran the CCTV network sat, conveniently next to a PNP lieutenant designated to coordinate with others in the command center in the event of an actual city-wide emergency.

The older, ashen-faced man who controlled the camera systems stood as he approached, as if to not be intimidated by Larrikowal's five foot eight inch height. "Captain."

"So, you know why I'm here. I'm investigating the incident earlier in which assassins critically wounded a PNP. Why don't I already have all relevant video footage available for my team?"

The PNP lieutenant cocked his head, as if this was the first he'd heard of the denial.

Mr. CCTV gulped. "I'm sorry, sir, but it's out of my hands. Policy from the Interior Secretary. With the Supreme Court's recent privacy ruling, our privacy department must review all police requests for video. Any which worry them regarding the legalities will need a court order instead of just a request."

"But we've only requested footage of public spaces? How can there be privacy concerns?"

"This is the first time I've seen a request denied by them." The bureaucrat shrugged. "You must get an order from the Metropolitan Trial Court before we can release any footage."

"Well, who's in charge of the privacy department?"

"Because of the number of requests, they're more like contractors following policy and procedures. We outsource the work to a company the Interior Secretary personally selected."

Meaning a company who'd paid him off for the lucrative contract. Maybe even another of his Chinese buddies, wrangling their way into the country via investments in key infrastructure functions, like the CCTV network.

"Where do I need the order delivered?" He'd need to contact the city prosecutor's office. Maybe he could get one of his staff to follow-up on it.

"They can send it here."

Larrikowal turned to the PNP lieutenant. "I'll have my staff email you the order as soon as they obtain it. I expect you to hand deliver it to this... gentleman, as soon as it arrives, no matter the time of day."

"Sir."

Turning back to face the door, Larrikowal added, "And if you don't want me to arrest you, have the responsive videos ready to transfer to the SAF the moment you get that order. I want every possible camera angle from the nearby streets."

The bureaucrat's neck and cheeks turned bright red. "I'll protest to the Secretary about this high-handed treatment."

"You do that."

Great. All he needed was to make more enemies in the bureaucracy, but this time they'd gone too far.

Almost as if someone purposefully attempted to delay his investigation.

Naw.

He couldn't let paranoia set in. The normal bureaucratic screw-ups were enough to drive an officer mad.

Chapter Seven: Tracking Behavior

I needed a better disguise to ride this bus.

An average Filipino male is four inches over five feet tall. I'm eight inches taller than that.

Unless they dye their hair, and none of the dozens of men around me on the bus rumbling down the Calatagan-Lian Highway were citified enough to color it, it's brown.

Not blonde. Not even my dishwater blonde.

So even in a tourist disguise, complete with oversized baróng shirt to hide the SIG Sauer M17 tucked into a concealment holster under the waistband of my cargo shorts, I stood out in the crowd.

The bus I rode stopped in front of Elvan's Bakery. A ramshackle collection of corrugated aluminum panels converted into walls and ceiling.

They sold small loaves of bread and little juice bottles. Political advertisements plastered the shop's walls.

Even way out on the western coast, Presidential politics attracted supporters and detractors.

After a half-a-mile jog down Talisay road, a glorified alley past beach resorts, I reached a hundred-meter long creaking wooden pier with a pair of sailboats anchored inside the bay it created.

The only ship tied up to the pier in the setting sun was a flat two-story ferry. An outrigger ship with an elevated deck for observation and control.

Suitable for light ocean work, they tied tires to the front and back to allow it to bump safely up against the dock while loading and unloading.

Center of the floating dock supported a combination ticket seller and customs shed. A lone security camera viewed the pier itself from atop that shed.

Not exactly the height of vigilance.

I ignored the local's stares at the obvious tourist. Waited in line to speak with the clerk working the shed.

He spoke the Filipino version of Tagalog to everyone else, but tried out his English on me. "Ferry 27 US. Show passport?"

"How long does the trip take?"

"Four-hour trip."

I winced. An enormous chunk of my 16 hours.

Held out my sat phone, with a zoomed-in photo of the terrorists from the train security camera displayed. "I'm supposed to meet some friends of mine. Have you seen them?"

He stared at me. Didn't glance at the phone. "You want ticket? Show passport."

Covert, I needed to avoid any official records of my passport, if possible.

"Perhaps if I find my friends?"

He gestured me away angrily. Told the next in line to approach his counter.

Maybe I should've bribed him, but at least I had one alternative for confirming the terrorist's visit. A bribe would've cemented my request in his mind.

I walked around to the back of the shed for privacy. Pretended to stare alternately at the anchored boats and my sat phone.

Stayed out of sight of the ferry and it's mingling passengers.

Searched for wireless networks. Found the one the shed's camera was on. Cloned the MAC address of its gateway router. Pretended to be the server it was authorized to talk to.

Dug through its on-board video storage; good for a week. Rolled back to just after the terrorist's train would've dropped them off locally.

Scanned forward at 4x speed. Watched the crowds ebb and flow across the pier.

Found the woman's distinctive veil and headscarf. Made it easy to locate Omar nearby.

Holding her arm. Tugging her along.

Bingo. Confirmation they'd taken the ferry, rather than hole up locally.

Even better, which ferry, the early one to Bayan ng Lubang, essential to tracking them on the other side.

Sent the video I'd found to my MI platoon. Added a note to pass it on to Schnier. It'd reach them over the encrypted network eventually.

After deleting the camera's video, I tucked my water-resistant/shockproof phone away in a carry pouch. Now, how to get across the water myself without leaving a trace?

The ferry would depart soon.

Could find a local to pay off. Get them to buy me a ticket under their passport.

They'd remember that for sure, though. The tourist who paid extra to not use their passport.

The type of stories men tell when bored fishing, or at a bar.

No, that wouldn't work.

All alone. No one currently in sight. Everyone busy getting ready to push the ferry off the other side of the dock, or gawking at those departing.

I took three long, deep breaths to store oxygen.

Nothing ventured, nothing gained.

Lowered myself into the water beside the dock. A final deep breath to hold.

Ducked under.

Warm, clear water streamed past as I swam below the customs shed, under the dock, beneath the ferry.

Surfaced. Gasped. Hoped the sound went unnoticed.

Ducked under to swim along the hull.

Poked my head up below the shadow of the outrigger where it's painted wooden beams met the hull.

Reached up. Got a grip on a beam. Chose a spot where they'd turned a smaller boat, more like a large canoe, upside-down and laid it across the outrigger beams for storage.

Pulled myself up onto the outrigger's arm.

Nestling inside the canoe would hide me until I could decide to either ride the whole four hours concealed, or else sneak over to the deck itself and hope no-one noticed the giant blonde tourist suddenly appearing.

I *really* needed a better disguise.

Raven hiked from beneath the jungle canopy to where their dirt trail opened up on a circular rock pond.

Her favorite part of this bad trip.

Omar followed her steps toward the thirty-foot waterfall. It splashed down a cliff's edge into the pool.

Too far out of the way for tourists, the locals periodically came to pick the water lilies, really hyacinths, which covered about a third of the pond with ponderous green leaves.

Her sociology professor would've been proud of her botanical knowledge, but she needed to become as bold as their tall purple flowers.

The locals dried the leaves to weave into baskets, matting, rope, or even paper. They'd visit with carts once a month. Swim and harvest a fresh supply of the fast-growing plants.

Otherwise, everyone knew to leave the waterfall and pool alone.

Omar passed her on the trail as she gawked. Couldn't help it. This place remained beautiful to her.

Despite the horrors it hid.

"Come on." He didn't stop to wait for her.

She trailed after him. Head held high beneath her head covering and veil.

The path turned from dirt to rock as they reached the basin's edge. They followed it around the outside curve.

Another trail worn into the rock continued farther up the mountain's face, but they turned off to the side.

Climbed across stepping stones behind the waterfall to a cave entrance. Water carved the gap decades before. Out of sight, beyond the crashing flood, they approached a steel door wedged between rock.

Omar gestured at the door. "You know the story?"

She did, but also that explaining it improved his mood. "Tell me, wise master."

"This door, this camp, remains from the Japanese occupation."
She nodded.

"During the last World War," he cleared his throat, "a small group of Japanese soldiers, led by an intelligence officer, Hiroo Onoda, were ordered to surrender under no circumstances.

"They destroyed the airstrip. The pier. Hid in these mountains. Harassed the locals. Didn't believe it when told the war was over by their enemies. Thought it a trick."

"How long?"

He spit into the waterfall. One of his nasty habits. "Never captured. A retired Japanese Major, Onoda's commanding officer, returned to properly relieve Onoda of duty in 1974. They fought for 29 years in this jungle."

"A long time."

"I keep Onoda's sword to remind us to persevere despite our enemy's claims. If we remain true to Allah, we can easily remain even longer, but we won't need to with our allies."

He wiped sweat off his brow. Pounded on the steel door. Waited for the guard to open it.

She needed to cool it. As much as he lived as a rebel terrorist, Omar was the establishment here in their camp. She couldn't let her hang-ups about him stop her from surviving.

Prevent her from ensuring all the women here lived.

Really wished she knew how to accomplish that.

Larrikowal leaned back in his desk and stared at the over-sized SAF badge hung on his office wall. An upright scimitar with wings for cross-guards and the motto *By Skill And Virtue, We Triumph.*

When he'd completed the Commando Course and gotten his black SAF beret, he never imagined he'd be here behind a desk as a Captain.

At least he still got out of the office regularly as the scene commander and for their high-profile assignments. Wasn't a pure desk-jockey just yet, no matter how much Sheila would prefer that role for him.

His computer chimed with a new message.

Court order delivered, his team worked the video feeds. Searched for anyone suspicious near the crime scenes.

Found video of two tall military age white men. One blonde, the other red-haired. Military short hair.

Conspicuous. Carried black luggage. Waited to cross the street.

Just outside the skyscraper. Timed just before the assault team arrived.

The men who'd fired at the assassins?

His team submitted a follow-up request for more video. For tracking them to their source and destination. Using facial recognition to follow them anywhere they'd been in the country. Identify any vehicles they'd used.

The SAF would find them.

Chapter Eight: Tracking Enemies

My outrigger ferry rammed itself to a stop by planting its bow into the sand next to Tilik Seaport.

Apparently, they didn't believe in docks on Lubang island ferry runs, despite the nearby perfectly good concrete pier run by the port authority.

Maybe they charged extra for its use?

A seawall rose above the beach to protect a ramshackle collection of homes from errant storm waves. Each home also contributed a glass-shard-topped security wall around its yard for additional protection from seaside invaders.

Four locals dragged a boarding ramp on puffy sand-tires across the beach. Labor must be cheap.

The legal passengers crowded forward to be the first to depart.

A pair of customs officers in light-blue uniforms followed the ramp. One checked paperwork as each local descended from the boat while the other supervised the procedure.

Could tell he was in charge by the way he ignored the work and by the relative size of his belly.

I'd need another path.

Easing my way from under the canoe lashed to the outrigger beams, I lowered myself like a jungle cat into the water.

Warm. Comfortable. A home away from home.

The supervising official must've caught movement out of the corner of his eye. He pointed.

Adrenalin flooded into me. I ducked underwater. Pushed off

the hull for a fast start.

Transparent water didn't work to my advantage.

Swam as far as I could toward the end of the concrete pier. Surfaced right at the corner of the end. Glanced back to shore.

The paperwork official blew his whistle for reinforcements. His supervisor sprinted along the beach. Reached the 20-meter wide ramp where the pier connected to land.

No escape there.

I hauled myself up onto the pier. Scraped my forearms and legs. Jogged across it to a white fishing trawler alongside.

Recovered some of the breath I'd expended swimming.

The supervisor sped down the pier. Fast for such a robust eater.

Couldn't shoot him just for doing his job.

I let him get most of the way to me. Climbed up on a yellow metal safety fence. Dove back into the water. Swam for the shore around a corner of the seawall.

Scrapes reminded me that open wounds don't go with salt-water.

He turned to run back.

Couldn't outswim his legs, but because a walled yard surrounded every building, he not only had farther to run, but would need to pick a gate and demand entry to reach the seawall.

I stroked past several smaller outriggers at anchor. Presumably belonged to the homeowners.

Should I borrow one?

No, even if I found a paddle and cut the anchor, I'd have to return to shore eventually. He could track me at leisure in a government vehicle.

First, I'd make him guess where I left the water, but second I'd need to then hide somehow.

Couldn't exactly blend in while towering over a crowd.

Homes might also be occupied. I'd attract attention in their yards.

No other choice.

I picked a yard with three lines of clothes hung across it. Plenty of concealment.

Scaled the seawall. Scrapes complained again. I told them to shut up.

Shouts from a home toward the pier in Tagalog. Probably the supervisor arguing with an occupant.

Needed to avoid that, myself.

Pulled my shirt off. Doubled it up. Used it to protect my hands from the glass shards and razor-wire embedded in the top of the block wall around the yard.

Dropped low. Out of sight from the other side.

At least they weren't rich enough to own a dog.

Ducked between the clotheslines. Bright yellow sheets pinned on the outside. Female women's wear hung from the center line. Muslim styles in black.

Muslims made up ten percent of the island's population. Just my luck to find myself in their literal backyard.

What if they supported the ISIL tangos?

I grinned. Grabbed a full flowing black dress. Pulled it over my head. Donned the headscarf and veil. Took me three tries to tie it right.

After all, I needed a better disguise.

No reason they couldn't support me at the same time.

Arms folded, I minced along with a hunch to pass as shorter and fatter. Headed out a gate to the street. Turned back toward the port, opposite of where they'd think to look for a fleeing fugitive.

The customs supervisor bounced right past me on the street, hopping up and staring over yard walls toward the water.

Once out of his sight, I sat on a landscaping rock preventing vehicles from ramming someone's banana stand near the street corner and transmitted a message to Schnier.

He'd have to find a different way besides ferry-boat to get his platoon and their weapons to the island.

Now how would I locate Omar's group?

Pahk's tablet showed a new message from Comment Crew, but he'd need to wait for calmer seas before reading it in detail.

He preferred command to riding as a foreign passenger. Former Korean Special Forces first lieutenants should get more respect from Chinese sailor women.

The green mass of Lubang Island grew at high-speed to fill the horizon.

He imagined each wave crossing the bow of their torpedo boat was aimed at him deliberately by the pilot in her protected cockpit. That turned his bouncing struggle to stay upright on the fast-moving craft into a fierce battle for supremacy.

Not a game he was winning. Seawater drenched his clothing.

Pahk knew the covert boat needed to get in and out before anyone from the local navy noticed them, but did that process require rattling his teeth around?

As the PLAN boat approached the shore, their speed dropped to where conversation was possible against the wind. They motored toward the mouth of a small river, barely wider than their hull.

"We're going in there?"

The witch at the wheel glanced back. "You want to meet your group's truck, don't you?"

"Yes, but we don't need to wreck in the process."

She looked ahead. Pushed the throttle forward again just enough to bounce them across a shallow spot where the sea met the river's mouth. "The truck is inland."

He stared at the back of her navy blue digital camouflage uniform. Arrogant, as well as a crazy driver. Almost like a fighter pilot.

She throttled back as the river narrowed.

He checked his tablet. Comment Crew sent a list of American units in the Pacific Region with unknown whereabouts.

The hacking unit also included images of various sniper teams taken from traffic and business cameras in Manila during the incident.

Definitely Americans, despite their civilian clothing.

The boat's pilot pointed ahead. "Your dock."

A faded orange truck waited, backed up to a four-foot jetty along the right side of where the river widened. The truck's bed made up for its short length with tall walls and rear-gate.

The sort of thing two-dozen Filipinos would pile into the back of for a free standing-room-only ride into town.

This one came with four grim-faced ISIL soldiers idly smoking.

Good, they'd need help with transferring the weapons he'd prepared as payment.

She cut the engines, spun the wheel, and coasted the boat up to the pier. Barely tapped it, but managed to spin around in the process to leave the rear facing it.

One sailor jumped off the stern. Another tossed him a coil of rope, unspooling through the air. He wrapped it around one of the landing's wooden posts.

The Chinese always were efficient, at least. It was how they'd come to rule this part of the world.

While the sailors and ISIL soldiers hauled weapon crates across to the truck bed, Pahk flipped through the rest of the security camera photos Comment Crew had emailed.

He stopped at a photo of two military age men, one carrying what looked suspiciously like a hard-case for a sniper rifle, the other a pair of black duffel bags.

They faced the camera while preparing to cross a street. Checking for cross-traffic.

Pahk knew them. Recognized them.

Had lost his career, his homeland, to this particular pair of Americans.

That changed everything.

Could he be sure? Checking the missing units list, he found their ranger platoons reported as having vanished from Seoul, destination unknown.

His intentions shifted.

He'd deliver the weapons to Omar, but then it would be time to plan an ambush for his two friends from the old country.

A deadly trap.

Larrikowal stared at the report on his computer. Omar Yousef. A jihadist extremist known as the Wrath of Allah. Responsible for over a dozen terrorist bombings. Three dozen shootings.

Hundreds of murders.

Add the traffic officer near the train station to his tally.

They had him on video from the rail platform nearby. He jogged as if late. Pressed cash into the hand of the security guard responsible to search everyone who entered.

The guard would pay for that mistake.

But Omar was a dangerous man. Unlike him to miss a target, but there was still the other team. The one who'd fired at him. Drove him away ahead of the assault team.

Facial recognition tracked Omar south from the train to Talisay Road. Near the Lubang ferry. He'd made a mistake. Led them closer to his hideout than ever.

Unfortunately, the video recording from the customs shed on the dock was missing. Not a malfunction, because more recent footage was recorded.

Another cover-up? Or a stupid mistake by someone?

After all, it left a trail. Video didn't delete itself.

Tracking the second team had gone better. No facial recognition hits, somehow they'd avoided airports and other public transit locations, but they'd found them exiting a vehicle outside the building with their sniper nest on the roof.

Followed the vehicle back in time to the west of Manila. To a vacation resort on the coast. A collection of nipa huts, the entire complex recently rented by a shell corporation out of the Bahamas.

Very little in public record about it, just owned by yet another shell. A front for some nefarious organization.

But they had the resort complex.

Time to prepare a raid. Propose it to his boss.

Catch the bad guys asleep in bed.

Chapter Nine: Tracking Paperwork

Michelle wondered if her relationship with Schnier could survive their working together. He didn't take orders to pack up and go home from his girlfriend very well.

She lifted and clacked two of the shells on her necklace together. Helped her think.

Of course, Sam was just as bad, and he was supposed to be her best friend. He'd rather roam the islands to lead the way looking for terrorists, though.

Men.

Even worse, Army Rangers!

Schnier soared up the bamboo ladder into the boys' home/office combination nipa hut. Ignored her to dash over to his laptop computer.

Ugly thing. Green and clunky.

The laptop, not Schnier.

Well, he had a strong jawline and lean muscle for days, anyway. Plus red velvety hair everywhere.

Not all bad.

Despite his job-obsessed rudeness.

"Something new?"

Schnier looked up. Shook his head to clear it. "Sorry, forgot you were waiting there. Sam tracked the tangos to the Lubang ferry. His platoon sergeant passed on video of them buying tickets."

"That's good news, right?"

"Sure, but, well, Sam says there's no way to get my platoon

across on the ferry, so I need to find an alternative. Maybe a boat?"

She shook her head. "Any boat ride you get from the seventh fleet at this point is going to end in Japan."

"I'll get the MI guys working on finding a local charter boat for us. Should be something along the coast."

Sometimes as dumb as hitting on nineteen in blackjack, though. She made a production out of checking the time on her sat phone.

"That going to happen in the ten hours you have left until D.C. wakes up?"

He sighed. Began typing a message to Sam's MI platoon, designated to support his. "We'll hire a charter bird instead."

Her last helicopter ride ended up with her parachuting into the Pacific Ocean. "Well, I'm not going with you, then."

"Who said anything about you going? This is a combat reconnaissance, search and perhaps destroy, not a spy mission."

Despite all his confidence, Schnier could be a real jackass sometimes. Or maybe because of?

"If a microscope man like you can handle it, I'm sure I could. Besides, I'm in overall charge here, remember?"

Could he take a joke? Remember the reference to how they'd met?

"The agency may have you running things in-country, but that doesn't put you in my military chain of command."

Apparently not. What was she still doing with this jerk, anyway? Her stomach tightened.

"I may not write your performance evaluation, but your assigned mission is to support me."

Not that he shouldn't already be supporting her, rather than running off to chase terrorists with Sam.

Didn't he realize her career was on the line here?

He grinned. Speared her with his intense blue eyes.

"I'm sorry, but did you forget this is my first independent command? It's not just *your* career at stake. How will the Army trust me with company command if I can't pull off leading two platoons on an allied island? After what happened in Seoul, Sam isn't exactly the major's favorite, either."

Selfish. That's what he was. Egotistical. Narcissistic. Just wrapped up in himself.

She'd have to stroke his ego a bit, but that didn't end this.

"You're doing fine in command of your rangers." She reached out. Slid her hand down his bicep. "You know I want you to succeed here. We all want to succeed together. Just remember the actual mission."

He leaned back in his chair. Exhaled loudly. Deeply. Tension vanished from his body.

"Thanks. Need to step back. Work the problem."

"You do that. I'll catch up on my own messages."

He nodded. Stared back at his laptop.

A girl wants a little romance, you distracted muscle-bound jerk.

She walked over to his bed. Sat on the end. Scrolled through the messages on her agency phone.

Should she drop Schnier? There were plenty of other men around, although not as many with the right clearance to know what she actually did for a living.

No, not one of those embassy boors.

For the millionth time, she wished things had worked out between her and Sam. They'd broken up after high school. Drifted apart when they went to separate colleges. Her to Berkeley, while he remained in San Diego.

They'd stayed friends, but it didn't make sense at the time to not date others. Eventually, they each found someone local they liked.

A long-distance friendship, until the tech demonstration of his eSurfboard and her orders to get him to Seoul.

That'd worked out alright. At least for her career prospects in the agency. She'd parleyed the win into this assignment as station chief in the Philippines.

Well, that and a little judicious leverage of her boss back in D.C., who made the assignments she wanted.

With Sam out in the field, out of touch much of the time, she should check his email. Just in case something needed to be dealt with to preserve his covert cover.

She switched to his mailbox on her phone. No parents to

write him. Terrorists killed them when he was a kid.

A couple of group messages from the BOQ office in Seoul. Bunch of Army procedure updates spam.

Unanswered email from Hyo-jin, that volleyball scientist Korean girl he met in Seoul. Only knew the cover story, that the ranger platoons were off on a training mission in New Zealand.

Probably private. Should she read it?

Most likely person to blow his cover, after all. She'd expect to hear back from him. No one else would think anything was wrong if they didn't get a response right-away.

She shifted on the bed. An invasion of his privacy? Naw, they were close friends. He'd already told her a lot about their relationship.

It wasn't as if she didn't already know they were together.

Better read them. Just in case.

The messages were stuffed with mush. Ugh.

That brat didn't deserve Sam.

Even if she claimed to miss him more than a thousand sunsets.

Why did that cause her eyes to tear up?

Michelle blanked her phone. She wouldn't reply to Sam's girlfriend with enough gushiness to make a response believable.

Maybe if her roll of the dice with Schnier came up craps, she'd have to see if Sam was a better prospect instead.

After all, they were already best friends. Worked together. No reason they couldn't go back to having more benefits.

She stood up. Marched over to the ladder. She'd return to her own hut. Figure out how to save this fiasco in the making.

At least from the agency end.

But what could she do about Hyo-jin?

Raven collapsed with exhaustion once they finally reached the portion of the cave complex reserved for living quarters.

Dead to the world.

Waking, she arched her back. Stretched her arms wide, like she was preparing for her gymnastic floor routine. Crawled off her sleeping mat. Knelt at its foot. Rolled it up with the bedding inside. Leaned it against a deep green cave wall, next to the LED lantern she'd brought from Texas.

She'd grown used to the light aura of dampness on every wall and floor of the cavern complex. Like tears flowing from the mountain above.

She repressed her own weeping inside.

At least Omar didn't make her sleep next to him in his private section of the men's quarters. Probably afraid she'd stab him while unconscious.

Or interfere with one of his concubine's visits.

She shuddered. Donned a robe and head covering for warmth. The next prayer would begin soon.

Time to go prepare food for him. She couldn't risk being caught unready. The last time she couldn't provide a meal when he wanted it, he'd stripped her down and beaten her with a wooden rod. The stave he kept specifically for that purpose.

For beating his wives. Concubines. Slaves.

He enjoyed their screams. They excited him. He called her his songbird, as if it were an endearment. A compliment on how well she howled in pain to please him.

She'd believed she was preparing to join his jihad. After converting to the religion of peace, she'd followed her professor's exhortations to unite with her new people.

Make a difference. Follow ISIL. Fight for the down-trodden against the corrupt west.

They'd sent her to a finishing school for potential brides in Manila. She memorized Koran passages. Passed the test given by the Shaheed in charge, an older woman, wife of a martyr.

Earned her red slip, which proclaimed her ready for a husband.

At the end of the selection process, when the ISIL warrior beat her while naked, she'd been afraid, but told herself it was a test to see if she could resist pain and endure humiliation for her duty.

Now she knew the truth. It was to see if Omar was pleased with the screams of his potential bride.

His new songbird.

Now she existed, along with the others, to feed him. Clean his quarters. Supply sex. Scream.

That's how she tried to think of it. As a transaction. He was her husband, and she was to obey him. To give him everything he might need to sustain him in their fight.

In reality, to give what he demanded in order for her to survive.

Her break-through was to convince Omar he needed a female spotter to provide better cover. A male and female couple looked more innocent than two men.

Unlike the other women, it allowed her out of the cave complex.

For training, at first. Now for an actual mission to Manila. It helped she could drive. That growing up in Texas, she'd grown familiar with rifles as a teen.

Now, he expected company. The unbeliever he'd spoken to on the phone.

She'd hurry to prepare their repast.

Why can't bosses just listen once in a while?

Larrikowal stood across the desk from the SAF Major in command of his district. He'd presented his paperwork requesting approval for a raid on the west coast resort they'd identified by tracking the counter-snipers.

She'd spent the last two minutes reviewing in excruciating detail with him how much negative political impact there'd be if he screwed up in a high-profile way just before the election, especially right after being involved in an assassination attempt on one of the two major candidates.

"Ma'am, if you'll approve the movement out of our district and over to the coast, my team can set up surveillance of the complex. Gather more information on who these people are. Perhaps even determine what they want. Make the decision about an assault clearer."

"I don't like that they're *mga puti*. What if they're American, Australian, or British spies? What a mess."

Should he put his cards on the table? "If they're allies, they should've let us know of their presence. Requested permission. They're most likely private contractors, hired by the Speaker because he doesn't trust the ministry run by his chief political opponent to protect him, but doesn't want to admit it."

She rubbed her short hair. "That just makes it worse. We're dealing with presidential politics here. Way above my pay grade. What are the implications for the defense minister if we catch these guys and they're tied to the Speaker? Is it worse if we don't? Either way, my rear-end is on the line."

"Make it Dorenza's problem? That's what he gets paid for as the political head, right? He can hardly blame us later for what he decides now."

"You think so?" She laughed. "As much as I appreciate our current Secretary of Defense, and I'll even vote for him to be president, but politicians look for scapegoats when bad things happen. It's the way of the world."

"He also won't thank you if you sit on the request. Might be argued later that you were impeding the investigation into the Speaker's attempted assassination for political reasons. To help him against the Speaker somehow. Our best bet is to follow wherever the leads take us and let the politicians make the political decisions. Let the pigs eat the slop while we milk the cows."

"Whatever that means."

"Everyone does their own job, that's all."

"Load up your team and head out. Surveillance only. I'll send the request for a raid up the chain of command. They'll cover themselves by bucking it up further. Forward any new relevant info you develop to me. I'll keep the request updated in the system with the latest."

Victory over the bureaucracy! He'd won this battle anyway, although not yet the war.

"Thank you, Ma'am."

He turned on his heels and strode out of her office. Now he just needed to call Sheila and explain that he'd be going out of town for work, but that he couldn't tell her why.

Maybe he'd get his team going with a warning order first to grab their NODS and lasers and pack for a night surveillance mission followed by an assault on what would presumably be a well-defended complex.

That'd be safer than phoning Sheila. He could talk to her on the way, safely out of reach and surrounded by well-armed commandos.

Chapter Ten:
Tracking The Wrong Tea Tree

I sprinted away from the barking dogs. Across the dirt path. Through muddy fields.

Did every rice farmer's hut on the island keep a pack to detect strangers? My only solution was to get away. Circle around their territory.

Hunting for a way to find the tangos, I'd tried to avoid the roads, but that wasn't working.

No clues, but maybe I could deal with the dogs.

I stopped. Pulled out my sat phone. A nice piece of expensive equipment, with all the latest miniaturized bells and whistles.

Called up an audio tuning app. Pumped up the volume. Set the frequency to higher than human hearing. Blasted out an unheard tone at 35 kHz.

Like a dog whistle.

The barking stopped. A whimper.

For now.

Local canines were annoyed. At least confused.

I paused. Stared at my phone.

That's it!

Sent a message to my platoon. Told them to look for cell tower pings from devices which connected at the shooting site, the train station, and near the ferry terminal.

If the tangos had a mobile phone, even a burner, as long as they kept it on them, powered-up, it'd leave a trail.

At least until service ran out in the wilderness, but that'd get me close.

I jogged between the rice furrows to find a place to rest up and wait for their reply.

Maybe get something to eat before we tripped over our deadline from the Agency and the Eleventh Fleet.

Pahk squatted at Omar's table. Paint flecked off the oak door set on a pair of raw pine crates.

No chairs. Instead, dark woven mats for seats.

Not the classiest dining room he'd ever seen. A grotto carved out of the mountain's marble and granite, complete with a single bare bulb dangling from the center of the low ceiling.

Presumably, wired back to a silent generator out of sight. Hydro-electric, embedded in a mountain river?

Omar gestured generously at the bowl of fruit and pot of rice in the center of the door-turned-table.

"Enjoy a feast with me."

His American wife bowed respectfully. She rested a platter with roasted chicken next to the rice.

Pahk wouldn't mind taking her out for a spin. Omar had offered other girls among his followers during past overnight visits to cement their deals, but his prize wife was probably off limits.

She represented his ongoing domination of the imperialist Americans.

Pahk smiled. "Your wife. A good omen."

"Yes." Omar grinned back. "She brings me luck. Did you know the enemy sniper knocked the rear-view mirror out right below us? Another few inches higher and you would dine alone."

Was he fishing for more of a reward than the additional weapons Pahk just gave his group?

"With the missiles I've delivered, you can take your revenge on whoever you believe responsible."

"Finding them is the problem. The enemy hides far from our lands."

Set the hook. "Perhaps not as much of an issue as you might

believe. My organization not only has excellent weapons but also many intelligence resources. They were American soldiers, not Filipino."

Omar's eyes narrowed. "Americans? The government wouldn't stand for that."

"Covert. Not here legally. Would lose much face if caught. Or found dead in suspicious circumstances. Would drive a further wedge between the President and the westerners. Perhaps even force them out of their remaining bases here."

"Find them for me and we will destroy them."

Pahk chewed on a piece of pineapple sugar-apple. Spat out one of the flat black seeds. The Muslim leader was right where he needed him to be. Ready to fight.

Not that it took much to bring Omar to a boil.

Raven brought a covered pot of hot tea with a spout and a pair of plastic cups. Set them on the table.

Poured.

That was a concession to him. A sign of respect for his recent payment in gold and weapons. Omar's group didn't normally drink tea.

"What if I told you they were coming here?"

"Here?" Omar laughed. "You mean the island, correct? No one who might betray us knows our base of operations. The previous occupants hid for decades without discovery."

Pahk pulled out his tablet. Unlocked the screen. Held it up and turned it around to display the photograph of the American rangers. "These men. Look well so you'll recognize them."

Omar leaned forward.

Raven glanced at the tablet. Shifted the spout of the teapot forward. Splashed it on the table. "Oh!"

She startled backward. Sloshed hot tea onto Omar's exposed wrist.

He backhanded her across the face. "Stupid whore. Fetch water. Now!"

She fell backward. Scuttled away, bowing. Muttered an apology for her clumsiness.

"Send me the photo." Omar grimaced. "I'll distribute copies to my men. To my observers in the villages and ports. If they come to this island, we will see them."

Pahk persisted. "They will come here. Perhaps in the night. In the surprise of the early morning. It is the American way."

"Don't attempt to teach me the fighting ways of western armies. We've survived more than a decade of combat against them. They must locate us before they can attack us. The damp granite of the mountain is impervious to their infrared tracking. To outsiders, we vanish."

"I know these men. They're resourceful. Special Operators. Engineers. We must take them seriously if we are to defeat them. Don't underestimate our enemy."

"I have spoken. It is enough."

Raven scurried back into the dining cave. She carried a pitcher of cool water from the nearby mountain stream.

"Give it here, woman."

Omar poured the water on his arm to relieve the pain of the burns he'd refused to recognize while they spoke.

"They are like your burn." Pahk leaned forward. "Ignore it and it will continue to hurt you, but pour bullets into them and their lives will be washed away in their blood to trouble you no more."

"What more would you have of me?"

"Let us arrange ambush sites along the jungle trails. If they can't track you here, there is no harm, but if they come this way soon, your men will be prepared to stop them, to eradicate them, before they locate these caverns."

"Very well. It will be good training for them. Get them used to the new weapons. After all, if they bring their helicopters, we can now deal with them, thanks to you."

"We are in agreement, then."

Pahk's payment of surface-to-air missiles would be perfect against typical American jungle tactics.

Raven's face turned paler than usual. Made her look almost Korean, with her dark hair, if it weren't for her deep blue eyes.

Probably anticipating how Omar would retaliate later for his burns.

Pahk dug into the meal. Finally, an opportunity for revenge on those who humiliated him. Who cost him his home. His country.

It would be a good night, even if he didn't manage to borrow one of Omar's spare women later.

Secretary of National Defense Lelfin Dorenza leaned his chair back and puffed on a Fighting Cock cigar, the extended wings, screeching beak, and sharp talons on the label ready to defeat Philippine's enemies.

He approved of the cigar brand's symbolism for his duty.

Should he approve the SAF's proposed raid, or not?

Would the recent violence in the capital see him elected as the next president, or cause frightened people to rally to elect the current President's hand-picked successor, the Speaker of the House?

This was the first time it appeared an incumbent President would actually abide by the constitutional term limitations.

It helped that Dorenza, the President's primary political opponent, controlled the military and police. Part of their deal to prevent violence after the irregularities of the previous election.

His senior naval aide stepped up to the edge of the polished walnut desk dominating Dorenza's office.

"The Americans have communicated they will send one of their LCS ships to the West Philippine Sea. They've calling it a freedom of navigation exercise, but it's unscheduled."

Dorenza stubbed out his cigar on a bauxite ashtray the Prime Minister of Australia sent to commemorate Dorenza's tenth year in office.

He straightened his chair. Faced the white-shirted aide who'd interrupted his pondering. "Why the demonstration? Has there been an uptick in Chinese *fishing vessels* recently?"

The aide pointed to a working map posted on the wall. It showed their beloved country surrounded by its sea moat and was covered in magnetic unit markers. "Our best estimate is a response to this Chinese naval squadron circling the airstrip they built on Pagasa."

"Estimate? Guess, you mean. Only a handful of ships there now. Nothing like the 200 we chased off a few years ago."

He traced one of the deep scar lines across his cheek with a thumb. Really, the Australians and Americans chased them off, but Dorenza was happy to take credit for the couple of old frigates his ministry had contributed to the effort.

"We know of nothing else of interest to them in the area and the American 7th fleet are remaining tight-lipped allies, as usual."

"One ship? Not nearly enough. Perhaps they plan for a reconnaissance mission. An American LCS carries a full complement of drones. They could track the Chinese from over the horizon."

"That must be it, Mr. Secretary."

The last thing he needed was another yes-man. It might be time to send this aide back to a line command.

"Send 7th fleet our best wishes and an offer of any support needed."

His aide paled to match his shirt. "May I remind—The President's orders..."

Dorenza waved him away. Maybe not a total yes-man. "You have your orders from me. The President won't want to risk a confrontation this close to the election. Not when I can show our people the Chinese Navy in the Spratly Islands. Besides, I'm exhausted with his kowtowing to Beijing. His tame foreign minister makes us look weak enough already."

"Sir." His aide took a deep breath. Gave a brief bow. "I'll pass the word as you command, Mr. Secretary."

Interesting. How could he use this recent gesture of support from the Americans, despite the well-known wishes of the current Filipino president, as evidence it was time for a more western friendly regime?

He re-lit his cigar and leaned back in his chair. Propped his feet up on the corner of his desk.

The Americans had a poor history, according to Filipino public perception, but they'd voluntarily granted them independence.

The Chinese sought more control than that.

He picked up his desk phone. It automatically connected to his secretary.

He'd be seen to publicly do something about the recent attack, the recent violence, at the risk of it turning into a disaster.

The SAF was competent enough. Captain Larrikowal wouldn't make a mess of the raid.

"Tell the SAF I approve the resort mission. Once the on-scene commander believes he's gathered enough intel to keep his force safe, assault the complex."

Chapter Eleven: Tracking Allies

Not a literal deadline; The Agency wouldn't execute us if we crossed it, but as dusk encroached on Lubang Island, light would rise in the D.C. skies.

My MI platoon sent me a string of map coordinates. A line where the tango's mobile phone had checked into cell towers.

Their path led away from the coast. Off-road. Up a river that snaked across rice paddies.

Into the jungle humidity. Away from any offshore breeze of relief.

Great.

I found a rusted-out boat with an ancient outboard motor. Pulled the starter string. It buzzed like a rusty machine gun on the third try.

No night vision, just my Muslim female civilian disguise. Shouldn't raise any alarms, right? Lone lady in the wilderness?

Farmland near the coast. Tall and wide fronds as the river approached the mountain.

Not much time left. Needed to scout out the enemy. Locate them. Call in Schnier and his platoon to a confirmed target.

Steeper white-water. The rapids strained the motor. Freshwater splashed over the rim. River currents battered my boat left and right.

Darkness fell. Time running out. Harder to navigate the narrower and faster river.

Somewhere out there rested my enemy. Likely sitting down to dinner, unaware of my approach.

I worried about the growling of the outboard motor, but surely the nearby green foliage dampened it? Even where it rained 15 inches a day during monsoon season, jungle growth, the thicker and taller trees, followed the river banks.

Pulled out my sat phone. Tapped the button to record. Transmit. Switched on the low-light setting to pick up infrared and what photons remained of those scattered from the stars.

Military shockproof. Watertight. No worries about dropping it. Could find it again by the light from its screen.

Helped me see a little. Guided me up the river's turns. Set it to forward back to base. The images would help Schnier's follow-up team.

Assuming they didn't depart before I had a confirmed location.

Something tangled my boat's propeller. It ground to a halt with a scrape and snarl.

SNAFU.

Phone held in my left hand, I pointed its camera at whatever was caught in the prop. Looked like a wire-core net. Fishermen collecting on the river?

A splash near the tall muddy bank. Two more. Motion through the water, like streaking torpedoes.

Someone had seen me.

Did they think me a Muslim woman, out after dark. Perhaps lost?

Were they coming to rescue me from my predicament?

A young man loomed from the river. Pushed down on the edge of my boat to climb aboard. Water streamed off his scraggly beard and bowl-cut black hair.

Wet hair pressed beneath a jungle camouflage headband. A broad hunting knife clenched between his teeth.

Not a civilian.

With my right hand, I hammered his fingers gripping the edge of the boat. Kicked him in the nose with an unladylike boot.

His head snapped backward. Dropped the knife with a splash. Blood gushed. He sunk back into the water.

Could I get the prop untangled? I flipped off the power so it was safe to work on.

Grabbed a piece of netting. Pulled.

Two more military-age men. One on each side of the boat.

Too many.

I shoved my phone into a cargo pocket. Dove over the stern. Hoped to put the netting between me and them. Slow them down.

Always been fast in the water.

They climbed over the underwater web. Chased after me. They used long, strong, overhand strokes to follow me on the surface of the stream.

I dove down. Might lose them in the muddy depths.

Something touched my heel. A hand?

I kicked out. Made contact with a head.

Sped away. Lost my religious hair covering to the water resistance.

No more disguise.

Reached the bank. Dug my fingers into the muddy soil. Grasped roots. Hauled myself along.

Air ran out. Needed to surface. Pulled myself above the water.

Wipe out.

The open barrel of a Chinese Arsenal 66 stared me in the face. An AK-47 style Type 56 rifle. Short. Open wire-frame folding stock. Long banana magazine. Pistol grip.

Common in southeast Asia.

Deadly.

Feet propped against the river bank, I raised my hands in surrender.

Crazy the details you notice when time slows down. When your focus approaches a peak.

Black shirt. Camo headband.

His eyes widened. Looked across the river. Shouted something like "not a whore."

A split second looking elsewhere is all the distraction I needed.

Didn't wait to see more. Pushed off the bank with my legs. Backward. Downward.

Water rushed into my nose.

Bullets shattered the river around me.

Fast objects striking water hit more like impacting on concrete. After two or three feet, the compressed liquid resistance halts even rifle bullets.

Doubted they had special CAV-X rounds, designed to penetrate water, for this situation.

Not an ideal plight, either way. At some point, I needed air again.

So I turned over. Snorted out water. Kicked. Swam along the river bottom.

Tugged at round stones, smoothed by centuries of tumbling down the mountain, to propel myself forward.

Approached the opposite bank.

Reached under my flowing black robe. Snagged the M17 from the concealed carry holster tucked under my shorts.

Surfaced. Sucked in air.

No one on the bank in front of me.

Shouts behind me. Semi-automatic cracks in the air. Aimed fire impacted the water and the bank.

They could barely see me. No point in giving them a better aim-point by returning fire.

Unlikely to hit with a pistol at this range, anyway. Not while treading water.

Another deep breath. Ducked down. Let the current take me downstream. Along the bank, rather than away from it.

Held my breath as long as I could. Minutes.

Crawled out of the water. No one in sight.

Pistol in right hand, phone in left hand to see with, I slithered through the jungle. Squirmed around tree trunks. Wriggled between vines and branches.

Found a clearing. Nothing human visible. Just dead undergrowth. Tall trees.

A trail. Dangerous visibility.

I raced across. Crouched low. Needed silence.

Tripped. Thwap. Hung in the air.

Lost my pistol. Dangled from a noose around my ankle. A dozen feet above the ground.

M17 in the rotting jungle below. Blood rushed to my head. I scanned around with my phone camera.

Foliage crunched under enemy boots. Dark shapes entered the clearing from three sides.

Drew my multi-tool from a cargo pocket. Opened the blade. Reached for my ankle.

Dislodged my damp robe. It followed gravity. Tumbled down around my waist and chest.

I stabbed at the rope. Caught the edge. Sawed through.

Fell on my head. Dropped my multi-tool. Reached for my pistol in the dirt.

Three men dog-piled me in the dark.

I squeezed my phone. Slashed at someone's throat with it. Choked on an assailant's arm. Poked at their eyes. Kneed another's groin.

Lightheaded. Blood pumped, but no oxygen reached my brain. A tingling warmth passed over my legs.

My chest.

Vision turned gray. Shrunk to a pinpoint.

Vanished.

Pahk aimed the FY-6 man portable antiaircraft missile at the sky above the mountain's peak. "When the Flying Eagle acquires an infrared target, ensure the back-blast area is clear and then pull the trigger. The advanced seeker will do the rest, with a 70% single shot probability for targets maneuvering up to 4g at low or medium altitude."

"*Allahu Akbar!*" one of Omar's men exclaimed. Another dozen men echoed him.

Well, Chinese technology was great, Pahk supposed, so they were half right.

Omar stepped forward to take the long tube from him. He peered at its parts. "How many?"

Pahk smiled. "Two tubes and a dozen reloads for each. Enough to defend this place from an airborne regiment, or shut down an airport indefinitely."

The four-foot-high circle of rough stone crenelations surrounding the jihadists' mountain-top lookout protected its defenders from small arms fire.

With the high ground, defenders would have the advantage over any of the surrounding areas, but they'd be vulnerable from the air.

Used to be vulnerable from the air, that is.

Right now, Omar's senior guerrillas filled the clearing. More looked on from one of the trio of jungle trails which climbed the mountain cliffs.

Everyone wanted to see the destructive toys their new best friend brought on his boat, but rank hath its privileges.

Omar hefted the tube on his shoulder. Uncovered the toggle switch. Flipped it on. Looked through the targeting window. "Built-in night vision?"

"It's a digital infrared seeker. Flares won't fool it. Intelligently tracks the specific heat source you aim it at. No reason not to use the four all-aspect sensors in the seeker to provide an infrared targeting display for the user to acquire a missile lock with."

"Good. The infidels claim they own the night. This will show them differently. The range?"

"Minimum 500 meters. Out to six kilometers. You can reach beyond the coast from atop this mountain."

"Gozar Air Station is only a kilometer away. The Army believes they're safe there. I must consider the best time to disabuse them of that notion."

"Now, let me show you one of the trio of W85 heavy machine guns I brought. They're effective not only on land but also against anything within the Flying Eagle's 500 meter minimum range. Fires ten rounds per second, so I brought thirty cases of belted ammunition."

"*Allahu Akbar!*"

One of Omar's men pushed his way through the crowd, hair plastered to his face, as if he'd been swimming.

He panted to a halt in front of Omar. "We've captured an infidel in disguise on the river approach! An American!"

"*Allahu Akbar!*" This time, their chant echoed from the cliff walls, to be absorbed by the surrounding jungle.

Pahk grinned.

Schnier dropped his ruck on his bed in their headquarters hut. "This is the worst trip I've ever been on."

Sergeant Kilkenny nodded. Kept a straight face. "I want to go home."

"What is it this time?" Schnier expected a negative report. Lately, it was always bad news.

Kilkenny adjusted his load strap. Cleared his throat. "Check your computer, sir. Intel sent a video."

Apparently, his sergeant didn't want to be the one to say. So, terrible news. From Harper's platoon.

"Michelle, you're gonna wanna see whatever this is." He gestured her over from where she sat, staring at her own laptop.

Probably checking on the littoral combat ship 7th fleet was sending over to pickup their gear now that the deadline for finding the tangos had passed.

Schnier pulled up the video as Michelle sauntered over. "It's from Harper. That loco lieutenant took video of his river ingress. His platoon sergeant thought we needed to see the most recent few minutes."

They watched as enemies intercepted Harper. He fought. Got swarmed.

The video ended.

Michelle was the first to react in the stunned silence. "Just like him to screw over my life even more."

Schnier stared at Kilkenny. "What else do the intel weenies have?"

"Not much, sir. A rough location on the side of a mountain. The video cut off there. He'd been sending a live feed to ensure the video wasn't lost if his phone dropped in the river."

"This changes..." Schnier straightened up. "Your deadline doesn't matter now. We're going to Lubang Island."

"D.C. will be pissed."

"Not as much as they will when a bunch of jihadi jabars post a video of Harper's beheading to the world and we go snipe the Filipino politicians supporting them."

"Not saying we shouldn't go. I'll arrange transport."

"We?"

"This entire country is my mission, remember?"

Schnier ignored the issue for now. "How long will it take to get the LCS Johnbee here?"

"Hours, then hours more to load up and make it to Lubang. But they carry two Seahawks. Between them, those'll take up to 31 men, you and your entire platoon, wherever we need to go."

"32." Schnier corrected her. How do you divide an odd number of passengers across two birds?

"31, plus one woman."

Dames! Maybe she'd fall out on the way.

Dead or alive, they weren't gonna leave Harper behind.

Kneeling in the darkness, Larrikowal extended his left arm horizontally at shoulder level. Swung it to the front and side in a sweeping motion.

His team caught the signal and dispersed farther apart. Experienced in rural village combat, they took advantage of concealment as they moved.

Once they'd reached the range he wanted, close enough for mutual support, far apart to completely observe this half of the complex, he swung his extended arm up and down to the side until everyone took cover.

His senior sergeant, Maria, slowly settled into a low spot behind a cinnamon tree. Aimed her night vision at the wall surrounding the nipa hut resort.

Andre, that FNG, rustled the branches of a wide leafy shrub as he nestled his way in. His disturbance released a musky fragrance from its tiny white flowers into the night air.

Hopefully, no one heard him, or if they did, they dismissed it as an animal of some kind.

He settled himself prone, where he could see Maria and Andre as well as the complex wall. He flipped up his NODs and pulled a small screen from his pack.

Oriented the screen away from the resort wall. Propped his carbine within easy reach against a round stone.

Their support detachment guarded their vehicles out of sight. They'd launch a small observation drone and feed him the overhead video.

Time to wait. See what they observed.

Might take all night and the next day to learn enough about the inhabitants to plan an assault.

To set up a raid in the early morning hours of the next night.

A rumbling in the distance. The distinctive thwapping of helicopter blades echoed across the water on the other side of the resort.

Had someone else approved a mission to assault the resort, and they were going in hot?

This made no sense.

His team's drone feed went live on his screen. Low light images. Thirty or so heavily armed silhouettes on the beach. They stood in a line. Faced away from the huts.

Away from his soldiers, toward the water.

The rotor noise grew. Two helicopters landed in formation on the beach. The enemy shielded their faces from flung sand. Ran in a line to climb their sides.

Boarded as efficiently as if they performed combat drops every week.

Who were these guys? If private mercenaries, they held to higher standards than he remembered ever seeing before.

Right now, just contrast on a screen. No clear markings visible in low light nor infrared.

Should he order his men to attack? They'd just settled in. Didn't know who was still in the resort's huts.

Too risky.

No, no time to stop them, but had they been tipped off? If that was their entire force, if they were rushing off right after his team arrived, the timing was too much of a coincidence.

But what could he do about it?

He signaled for his long-range radio operator. Maybe someone could scramble aircraft to intercept them. At least track them on radar.

He'd call the closest air base and find out. The Philippine Air Force (PAF) might even send their lone AWACS up to monitor.

Their rotor noise vanished as the helicopters disappeared back out to sea.

PART TWO
LUBANG LOCKUP

Chapter Twelve: Captive Audiences

Someone rubbed a damp cloth across my forehead. I maintained my breathing pattern. Listened.

A rustle of clothing. Light footsteps. Scrape of a sandal on stone.

Cracked open my eyelids.

A woman with dark brown hair poking out from beneath a headscarf. Her side to me, she dipped a rag into a pitcher.

No immediate threat. I blinked. Groaned. Turned my head to see what restrained me.

Steel shackles attached to lengths of chain bound my wrists and ankles to posts embedded in the rough marble floor. Some kind of cave.

She turned to face me. "I've cleaned your wounds." Not Filipino. Too tall. Twangy English accent.

An older version of the photo of the college-age woman Schnier carried around with him. Showed people. Hunted for.

His ex-girlfriend who fled her family in Texas and he hadn't heard from since.

Raven.

What do I do with that information?

More to the point, how do I get out of here? Would she help?

"Thanks. Very nice of you. You're American?"

"Used to be Texan, but that was a whole 'nother life."

I smiled. "Am I going to live, doc?"

She frowned. "That's up to my husband."

"Is it, though? I only see you here." I tugged on a chain. Solid.

She responded to my overture, but a shuffle of feet in the cave corridor outside interrupted our discussion.

Omar pushed aside the curtain dividing this space from the outside. He lifted his ankle-length loose white robe over the threshold and ducked his head to clear the shorter cave entrance.

Not from around here, either. Too tall.

"So, our guest awakes."

"I have cleaned his wounds. Nothing serious, mostly scrapes and bruises."

"Good, we want him looking good for television."

The chains were barely loose enough for me to lean up on an elbow. "I'm right here. No need to talk about me as if I can't hear you."

Omar looked me over with a critical eye, as if he didn't trust Raven's assessment.

"Don't worry, we'll have you signing confessions and admitting on camera to your many atrocities in short order. But for now, you're worth your weight in gold for moral and recruitment purposes. Must take care of you."

Positively jolly at my capture. If I were to ever consider suicide, this seemed like the situation. Still, with inside information on Raven, maybe I could work this out.

Besides, Schnier would come for me. Just had to ride this wave until then. He never left anyone behind and wouldn't let someone like me ruin his record nor stain his honor as a Texan.

Omar chivied Raven out of the room in front of him.

"Don't worry. I'll be back soon with my tools."

Which, of course, he meant to cause me to worry. Can't say it didn't work.

Michelle stood behind four of Sam's rangers. The rangers sat in a row at a table in their make-shift intelligence center hut.

A tangle of cables ran across the table from monitors to computers and out to power outlets, antennas, and other sensors.

Shouldn't a military unit be neater than that? Bunch of computer nerds, anyway. More green-framed glasses than rigged rifles, despite their ranger scrolls.

She liked it. Always used her brain to get ahead. Well, that plus a few other assets.

The closest monitor displayed a map of Lubang Island overlaid with infrared dots. Expert systems took the drone feed and updated it with real-time analysis of heat signatures. Tagged individuals, vehicles, structures.

Built up a tactical picture over time as more data poured in.

The drone from the LCS Johnbee had only recently arrived on station, but besides the civilian areas marked on the map, dozens of tangos on and around the mountain showed.

A few scattered handfuls guarded three trails and the river flowing from the mountain. A permanent structure built from stone protected the entrance of a lake. They only noticed the occupants when one took a moment to water the jungle outside.

Men. Couldn't ever keep it in their pants. Not even on duty.

Worked to her advantage at times, though.

No path led from Gozar Air Station to the presumed jihadi base location, but it was the closest place to set a helicopter down.

Schnier and his men could fast rope just about anywhere into the jungle, but they'd need more space than that to exfil the area, unless they intended to walk out.

He'd used that to convince her to stay behind. That because she couldn't fast rope, she'd never be able to keep up with them, anyway.

That she'd help Sam the most by doing her own intelligence job instead.

Her main point of hope and concern was a hot spot of activity near the mountain's peak. It both showed their main camp must be nearby, but also gave them a commanding height to cover all approaches from a distance.

Climbing a mountain while under enemy fire wasn't something anyone in their right mind did.

Perhaps a drone missile could take the place out? Would she get approval to launch against a location with unknown occupants?

Probably not. She'd already been studiously ignoring her

email now that her boss would be back in the office. He'd figure out soon enough they weren't evacuating quite yet.

"Crap... excuse me, Ma'am."

The ranger across the table from the ones she'd been watching interrupted her chain of thought.

"Don't worry, I've heard much worse, growing up in the barrio, not to mention hanging around the army lately."

"Umm... we just intercepted a series of messages between the PAF and SAF."

"PAF?"

"Philippine Air Force, Ma'am."

"Of course." She stepped around the table to see what he was talking about.

"The SAF requested they track a pair of helicopters taking off from the west coast. Included start coordinates. I mapped them."

He gestured at his screen, where a dot showed on a map of the Philippines. Right at the location of their resort.

"Crap."

"Yes, Ma'am. They must know we're here. Probably on their way now, both to here and to wherever the birds land, if they manage to find them."

"If they're not already outside. They spotted Schnier's pickup somehow. Must have a drone overhead. Can you jam it?"

"Unless I can find the frequencies it's using, not without cutting off our own communications with a broad spectrum of noise."

"Wait until we're ready to leave, then do it."

"Leave?"

She looked around the room. At the remaining ruins of her mission.

No time for hesitation. She raised her voice.

"Okay everybody. Listen up. We've been compromised. In a short time the SAF will come through the resort gates. So shut everything down. Set thermite charges on anything you can't hump out of here.

Most started moving, used to following orders. The analyst who'd found the message traffic paused. "What about Captain

Schnier's mission?"

"They'll have to abort for now. Meet us on the LCS. We can't support him. You get busy getting us out of here. I'll call him. Give him the bad news."

How was her boss in D.C. going to react once he found out the SAF located them?

And even if they slipped away from the SAF, what would happen to Sam?

Larrikowal's team were slowly rotating on and off active surveillance duty. With a wall around the complex, their drone had a better view, anyway.

He sat back in one of their vehicles, tucked behind brush in a clearing off the road. A monitor in his command truck displayed the unchanging drone view of the complex.

He'd relieve his senior sergeant in the field once he'd completed his own paperwork. While half his force rested, he listened to his boss on the radio.

"Your warning to Lubang got a response, but too late to capture anyone."

"Oh?"

"A local customs officer spotted a stowaway on the ferry. Gave chase, but lost him among the housing along the shore."

"Might not be related. Could be a local hitching a ride."

"Described as a tall, blonde, foreigner. Ring any bells?"

"One of the counter-snipers. A mercenary killer for hire."

"Exactly. So what's he doing on Lubang instead of the resort you're at, or on one of those helicopters you've got the air force chasing down?"

"Good question."

"I know."

None of this made sense. High-level contractors or military forces protecting the Speaker. Why would they be on Lubang with the assassins?

He took a shot in the dark. "Maybe they're all after the other snipers. They shot at 'em in Manila. Disrupted their attack. Wouldn't be a stretch to think they'll continue going after 'em. Maybe the helicopters are meeting him there. Sort of an advance scout."

"Perhaps."

A squelch of static burst out of the truck's speakers. If she said anything else, he lost it in the noise.

The drone feed went dark. Shot down? Something wrong with their electronics on the truck? A busted antenna?

He rewound the video feed to just before it went dark. A stream of individuals leaving all the huts simultaneously, just a few seconds before they lost contact.

Enemy action for sure. How did they know they were here? Must've spotted the drone, as unlikely as that seemed.

But they'd jammed everything in the area, and not for no reason.

He powered off the radio. No use now.

Turned to the corporal in charge of the command truck. "Wake everyone up. We're moving in."

Chapter Thirteen: Captive Flights

Raven carried a clear plastic pitcher of water and a matching cup with her as an excuse to visit the American prisoner.

He lay, dressed as a tourist, in seeming meditation on the cold cave floor.

She still wasn't sure what to make of the fact that her old college boyfriend, Schnier, was in the Philippines. According to Pahk, a soldier. Somehow involved in Omar and Pahk's business.

Had he been the one to fire at them in the parking garage? Or was that this man here?

She needed answers, but quietly. She placed her lips near his ear.

"Wake up."

He opened his eyes. Glanced around, as if assessing the situation for threats.

Suspicious, although as a prisoner, he had cause to be. His eyes settled on her face.

"Raven?"

Her eyes widened. He knew her name? "So Schnier... Schnier knows I'm here?"

"Doesn't know. Suspected he might have seen you. Dismissed it as a mirage, but he's been searching for you in his spare time, ever since we arrived here."

"You are soldiers together? I've lost track of my old life."

"Rangers. Special Operations. Here to protect the Philippine people from China and terrorists like Omar."

So he knew Omar's name as well. "Yet you come in secret?"

He tried to shrug, but the chains turned it into a half-movement. "Sometimes a sheepdog has to help where the wolves are. Can't always just hang out with the flock."

"Sorry about the chains. Omar's idea." She looked away from him. At the floor. "He uses them for new girls. Ones not properly broken in to the life here. Says it's too dangerous to just let them run free. Unsupervised. Might give away the camp."

"Do you have any tools? Something to open these?"

They'd attached his shackles to the chains with a nut and bolt, reinforced by washers and a spot weld. No key. Lack of tools and time limited escape.

"It's no use. There's a guard outside, at the end of the corridor. Unless you can bore through solid rock, no one leaves this section of the caves without passing him."

"If we can figure out a way, are you willing to help me escape?"

Was she? "I... I'm not sure. I can't risk harm to the others."

"Others?"

"The other girls. Omar trusts me now. I could've left months ago, except I know he'd punish the others. As long as he's happy, we're safe."

"What if we could get everyone out?"

"I've thought about it, but haven't found a way. We all live under guard. They're supposed to keep people out, like a harem, but they're just as much to keep us all in. Omar's favorites, at least."

"Are they all willing to leave?"

She thought so. Probably. If this was her chance, she couldn't show doubt. "Why wouldn't they be? Omar mistreats them all. They'd leave, if they could."

He smiled. "Call me Sam. Find the tools to get me out of these chains. Or at least something we can use as a wrench. Some kind of metal tube. I'll take care of any guards. That's the first two steps covered. Let's talk about the rest."

Could he really, or was this a false hope, destined to doom them all, rather than save them? Could she trust his confident bravado?

Fortunately, she didn't need to decide right away. She'd find out more about him, instead.

She answered his questions by describing the layout of the base. The cavern structure. Where various equipment was located. Where they stored spares. Their food and water supply.

The multiple paths in and out. Routes up and down the mountain. The waterfall, lake, and river. Plus the fortified lookout post on top of the mountain.

Sam leaned forward and his eyes narrowed as she described their weapons and traps.

After she'd given him the lay of the land, he tugged on his chains.

"Do you have a source for acid? Maybe a tile cleaner? Rust remover? Mold remover? Bar Keeper's friend? Citrus juice?"

"Omar's armorer uses diluted hydrochloric acid to clean their weapons. We have to buy it for him special."

"Even better. Can you get the undiluted container?"

"I'll put the container in the pitcher. The guard doesn't check inside."

"Awesome!"

Could this work? Might she get out with the other women?

Michelle followed the shadowy outlines of Sam's ranger platoon in the dark.

They jogged in a loose line. Down the firm part of the beach, the sand recently watered by the sea. Used night vision to remain on course.

Michelle held diplomatic immunity, so in theory, she could just turn herself into the local police and show her passport. Nothing they could do except kick her out of the country.

Embarrass her. Maybe even get her fired for causing the State Department to lose face, but not actually hold her.

But she wasn't about to finish tanking her career without a fight, and that didn't apply to the rangers running with her.

Behind them, the flames of burning nipa huts filled the sky. She, or rather the agency holding company she'd used to rent the place, would eventually have to pay for the damage to the resort.

But that was better than leaving top secret equipment and information on their mission behind. Once they began burning it all at high temperatures, there'd been no way to stop the thermite from devouring the wooden flooring and spreading to the roof and wall thatching.

Normally, they'd at least pile the equipment in the sand, but there'd been no time.

Schnier and Sam's platoons originally arrived in the dark via rubber boats with outboards. They'd stashed them in a grove of palm trees, covered with foliage, to get them out of sight.

Besides being slow, there was no reason the remnants couldn't depart the same way. Would take them time to reach the LCS, though. Hours.

Assuming their remaining fuel held out that long.

A loud crack, and then a boom as something exploded behind them. She instinctively ducked. Glanced back.

No immediate danger from burning debris, but the flames silhouetted figures with weapons.

Had they left in time?

Larrikowal really missed his jammed drone feed. The drone would auto-return to its launch point once it lost communications, but meanwhile, his force moved in blindly.

They overlapped in pairs to reach the wall surrounding the resort complex.

With an enemy this disciplined, they couldn't risk an ambush. Besides, where could they really go? No one in the area was going to accept a bunch of strangers with guns in the middle of the night.

Not without calling the police, anyway.

Maria reached the wall ahead of him. Gestured to Andre to give her a leg up. Peered over the top. Dropped back down. Reported as he arrived at her side.

"Flames in the windows. Targets have fled to the beach."

"They're torching the place?"

"Appears so."

"Get someone to call in the... never mind, they've jammed

everything. No fire department. Well, hopefully a neighbor will notice and call it in on a land line." He considered the problem. "Actually, Andre, go find a land line and call in what's happened so far. Get them to send the fire department. We'll relay further updates to you."

Nothing like sounding decisive in the field to boost the troops' confidence in their captain.

Andre glanced at Maria, as if expecting her to maybe countermand his orders, then took off running when she glared at him.

Maria turned back to Larrikowal. "Looks like they've abandoned the gates. Undefended. Permission to go blow one in rather than make everyone climb this wall?"

As usual, she understood the overall situation. Came from more than a decade as an NCO. "Go ahead." The flames reached the roofs, showing above the wall, even from a close angle. "This whole place will be a loss, anyway."

She jogged around the wall. Collected select SAF members as she went. The ones certified in demo, who habitually carried explosives.

He followed behind her. Ensured everyone else kept sufficient distance to both not be caught bunched up by surprise, but also not be caught by the impending big boom.

Maria's ad hoc team set directional charges on the connection points of the resort's gates. Tall wrought-iron barricades, out of place against the stone and wood surroundings.

Guess they could charge guests more for a fancier looking entrance in their brochures.

Fiery scene through the front now. Flames devoured each individual building, but they hadn't spread to the foliage yet.

Just a matter of time, once it dried out.

Maria stepped back. Got everyone near the gates into cover. Shouted "Fire in the hole." three times.

Tugged on the detonator.

Four explosions cracked as one. A boom as the remains of the gate fell over on its side.

The team on point rushed in. Spread out. Scanned the area for threats.

Larrikowal and Maria followed more casually. Masters of all they surveyed.

Which was a group of giant bonfires near the beach, surrounded by a wall. No enemy in sight.

"Send out the scout teams up and down the beach. Get someone going in our vehicles to search the nearby roads. Send a runner to Andre, have him request piloted air support with infrared, although these fires are going to make that tough in the immediate area. Hell, he can call the navy. Maybe they have a boat nearby which can check the water and the shore."

Maria nodded. "Roger that."

"We need to hunt them down. Figure out who they are."

Even if they weren't truly the enemy, even if the Speaker had hired them as extra protection, they would pay for not only the damages to this resort, but for the risk to his force because they didn't share information.

And if they *were* enemy troops, here for some nefarious purpose of their own, he'd ensure they paid double.

Chapter Fourteen: Captive Collisions

Schnier didn't want to abort. They were so close. Loaded for tangos. Shooters ready to go. Just offshore Lubang Island. Flying only feet above the wave tops.

He gestured to the pilot, then remembered his headset. "Hold here. We have a go/no go decision to make."

The pilot put the Seahawk helicopter into a slow bank. Their second copter followed.

His men's harnesses kept them in place. The ones seated closest to the doors on the lower side of the tilted deck got a great view of the water.

The resort was compromised. Sam's MI platoon would be useless as real-time intelligence support, fleeing for their own freedom.

But Sam was out on that mountain somewhere. Locked up, or worse, laying dead.

Schnier wasn't always sure their missions were completely legit by local's standards, even when blessed by the highest military authorities back home, but rescuing a buddy, a fellow ranger, that topped his personal righteous priority list.

But he didn't have only himself to worry about. Independent command hung heavy on his shoulders. He glanced at his fifteen men vibrating inside this bird with him.

All serious. They knew about Michelle's call. Sam's predicament. Waited for his decision.

He'd be taking responsibility for dropping thirty rangers into a firefight with very little support.

Sure, the LCS crew might be able to run a drone for them, try to tag targets, or vector them onto trails, but it wasn't the same as their normal trained hand-in-glove working relationship.

"Sir, we're going to be bingo fuel in five. Running out of time for both a deployment and return to base."

As much as he hated to, it was time to pull the plug. They'd refuel, meet up with Michelle and the rest of the rangers, then return.

At best, a few hours. At worst, until the next night.

"RTB to the LCS. Stay on the deck, but keep an eye out for the outboard boats."

"Aye, aye, sir," the navy pilot responded. He manipulated the collective, stick, and pedals to level out their curve into a straight line back their landing pads on the ship.

He just hoped that if Sam was alive, he'd last that long in the hands of the self-styled Wrath of Allah.

His nose took in the bouquet of fish and salt water from the airflow blasting through the copter's cabin, but it was ruined by the stink of fear for his friend. Worse than ridin' bareback on a bull.

What a colossal screw up as a commander he'd turned out to be.

Lord, please let Sam live long enough for us to rescue him. Preferably, in one piece.

Pahk tossed down another shot of rotgut gin, called "Stainless" by the locals. Omar didn't indulge in front of his followers, but he kept a supply for his benefactors. The Wrath of Allah had no sense of style, though.

Wasn't anything like the soju from his homeland.

Omar made up for his lack of liquor education with his enthusiasm for Chinese weapons. He stood near the top of the fortified mountain lookout post, using missile tube electronics to scan the sky for infrared targets.

They planned to interrogate the American prisoner, but one of Omar's men had interrupted with urgent news of a pair of low-flying helicopter sightings off the north coast.

At least, what they took to be the engine heat signatures of helicopters. Pahk had his doubts about their ability to use the sophisticated weapons.

No sign of them now, but that didn't stop Omar from rushing up to use his new toy, the FY-6 Flying Eagle missile tube.

"Perhaps they were in transit to another island?"

Omar grunted, but continued to scan the sky for the enemy.

"Or a fishing boat. This is all new to your men, they might have mistaken infrared signatures on the water for ones in the air."

"Do the Americans have a stealth helicopter?"

"Yes, but they're quiet and have a low radar return, not immune to giving off heat. Maybe diffuse the signatures a little. Why?"

Omar pointed with the tube almost vertical and leaned back so he could point at the screen. "What's that, then?"

A pair of parallel hot air streams fluctuated in prop wash on the display. Too small for a plane. Circled too fast to be a helicopter.

Nevertheless, Pahk recognized the signature from along the Korean DMZ.

"You've got an MQ-9 up there. American Reaper drone."

"I'll take it out."

Pahk shook his head. "Consider, you'll let them know of your new weapons. Wouldn't it be better to allow them to watch? Destroy them when they attack?"

Omar leaned forward to look back through the targeting reticle.

"I've warned you before not to try to teach me tactics. If the infidels monitor us in the open, they will send missiles and bombs from far outside your toy's range. We'd have to flee, or huddle in the mountain caves to wait for them."

"Not if you have a hostage. Say, an American soldier?"

"Not good enough. They'll experience Allah's wrath and learn their folly."

Pahk took three steps backward. "Careful with the backblast, firing so vertical. Don't want to torch your own feet."

"*Balik-harapis.* Do you never want us to use these tools for fighting the infidel? Allahu Akbar!"

He toggled the firing lever. Flames exploded from the tube's rear with a whoosh. The missile itself leapt from the tube, appeared to stall in the air for a split second, and then took off into the night sky, trailing white smoke and fire in a winding curve.

The three other soldiers in the outpost clearing responded with their own repeated chants of "Allahu Akbar!"

The display lit up with heat far above. A boom, like quick thunder out of a clear sky. When the screen cleared, no more drone heat signature.

Omar handed the launcher to one of his men. "See that it is reloaded and ready to go, then keep further watch."

"Yes, emir."

"Come." Omar turned to Pahk. "I'll show you Onoda's sword."

Pahk poured himself the dregs of the bottle, gulped it down, and then picked his way down the mountain trail after Omar.

The people he'd put up with to give his mother and sister a new home with the Chinese!

He grinned. At least now they could return to interrogate the American. No pain-dulling drinks for him.

Who was the prisoner now? He looked forward to the expression on the American's face when he realized who held him captive.

Could I trust Raven? Certainly more than I could rely on Omar for anything positive.

Besides, what would be the point of her betrayal? Psychological head games? It didn't fit Omar's style.

My back ached from the cold marble floor. Water seeped through the stone from outside, leaving the equivalent of tide marks to turn it more green or blue.

A bruised side kept me awake. Not sure if they'd cracked a rib when they knocked me out, but there was nothing really to do for it besides rest.

My head bugged me. I kept wanting to feel, to rub, to check the scrapes and bruises they'd inflicted, but couldn't reach above my neck with the length of chain the tangos left me.

But how would I escape?

I tugged on the four chains holding me to the floor for the hundredth time.

Still securely embedded into the stone.

Technically, some kind of concrete. It looked like they'd drilled a hole, dropped a steel bolt and maybe a nut or two into it, then stuffed it with cement to hold better.

Strong enough to restrain a person without much leverage.

At least the temperature in the cave was cooler than outside. All that rock mass was good for something.

My favorite captor's wife stopped by again. Their marriage was seriously messed up. At some point, I wouldn't mind having a family like my parents, but not like this.

Raven looked around to be sure she was clear of the corridor outside.

The one I'd never actually seen.

She uncovered the pitcher. Pulled out a plastic bottle of muriatic acid, about the shape of a short water bottle. "This will do?"

The commercial bottle had 31% blazoned across it. Not as concentrated as I'd hoped. I gave her a smile.

"Sure, all we can do is try it." I scraped at where a chain bolt entered the floor. "Pour as much as you can into the the depressions around here. It'll slowly eat through."

She nodded. Uncapped the bottle. Carefully poured, only splashing a little on the floor.

I edged away. Last thing I needed were my own acid burns.

After she finished the four pours, she capped the bottle. Set it on the floor. "How long will it take?"

"Maybe hours?" Truthfully, I had no idea, just that it wasn't fast.

"What if Omar comes before then? Sees what I've done?" She squeezed her headscarf on both sides with her hands, pulling her eyes and brows into a panicked line. "He'll kill us all!"

"I'll lay like this." Rather than cringing away from the acid, I spread out my arms and legs. Set them in front of the bolts, angled above. "He won't notice."

She stared. Took a deep breath. "As long as he doesn't get down low, it's not visible."

"Not likely he's going to come crawling to me on his knees."

She laughed. "No, not Omar."

"Take the acid and return it. Don't want it missed."

"Sorry, I freaked out for a second there." She picked up the bottle. "Anything else?"

"No problem, dude. It's a stressful situation. I don't know how you keep it together. There is one other thing..."

She cocked her head.

I gave her my most convincing smile. The one that always works for me when I'm chained to the floor in a terrorist camp.

"A back-up plan. We need a lever and a fulcrum."

"A what?"

"Something long and tough, like a steel pole. Think crowbar. Plus something strong for it to press on. A small anvil would be ideal, but I'm not sure you could get that past the guards, even if you had one."

She scratched her chin. Considered. "The second part is easy. I have a tall cast-iron pot I could bring without much suspicion. Put some cooked potatoes in it or something. Not sure about the lever. All our poles are wood. Mostly bamboo, at that."

"Maybe a rifle barrel?"

She shuddered. "The armorer is unlikely to miss a bottle of acid for a few hours, and if he did, he'd think he misplaced it. But not a rifle. They lock those up."

"Just a thought. Weapons are generally made pretty tough."

"Onoda's sword. Omar only gets it out to show off to visitors." She smiled. "It's not his actual sword. Even I'm not dumb enough to believe that, but it's a pretty good example of a Japanese officer's sword."

"Tempered steel. Perfect. Stronger than these chains, anyway."

"I'll bring them on my next trip. I can fit the sword inside my robe, where the guard won't feel it."

"Thank you. You know, Schnier has been looking for you ever since we got here. He wanted to find out what happened to you. This is going to blow his mind."

She sighed. "I wish I'd never... well, that was all a long time ago."

As I watched her sway out of the cave, I wished this was all a long time ago as well.

But I needed to stay mentally in the present. My life and that of Omar's female captives depended on it.

Secretary of Defense Dorenza listened as Captain Larrikowal gave his after action report.

Their prized AWACS had paid off, but Dorenza wasn't sure he'd have chosen to know, given the opportunity to do it again.

Larrikowal's voice crackled from the speakerphone on Dorenza's desk. "After tracking the helicopters to the LCS Johnbee, they spotted multiple small craft making a rendezvous with the Americans. The evidence points to the Americans supplying the counter-sniper team and taking over the resort."

"CIA, Special Operations?"

"It's not clear. They left nothing identifiable behind and my casual inquiry to an American green beret captain I've liaised with before on counter-terrorism got me nowhere. Not even the local American military seems to know who they are, so I'd lean toward CIA."

"The President would have a fit if he knew covert American commandos were running around Manila shooting up parking garages."

That was perhaps more than he should've admitted to a junior officer, but the SAF was used to being thrust into politically charged situations.

"Yes, sir. Can't say I'm too happy about it myself. Put my force at risk, not to mention wrecked the resort."

What made sense to do next?

They couldn't send a frigate out to the American LCS to demand to know why they'd been in country. They needed the 7th fleet to help keep China out of the West Philippine Sea, as much as it galled him to admit his own navy wasn't up to the task as a solo mission, even to himself.

Did he tell the President? Withholding the information, if it came out, would give him good cause to finally demand his resignation. If he won the election, beat the Speaker, the President's hand-picked successor, then it wouldn't matter.

Would the President, with his penchant for freezing out the Americans and siding with Chinese cash, betray their national interests before the election if he knew?

He couldn't take the risk to his country.

"Captain, you need to put a lid on this. Figure out who can tie the pieces together and I'll order them to sit on in. For now, it's classified top secret and I'm the only one authorized to approve sharing this intel with anyone new. We can't afford to have an incident with the Americans right now. Understood?"

"What if they leave the ship? Return to land?"

"Have the AWACS keep an eye on them. You may have to go sit in their control center to keep things under wraps. Call it all a capability exercise. Tell them I wanted a demonstration of our abilities versus a difficult target. Notify me immediately of any fresh developments."

"I'll take care of it, sir."

Dorenza's election prospects now rested in the hands of an SAF captain and a bunch of cowboy Americans.

Well, it wouldn't be the first time his career depended on his soldier's abilities.

He'd have to consider whether to reach out to the American ship directly. How would they respond? Outright denial? Or would they slink away, caught?

Chapter Fifteen: Captive Torture

The LCS Johnbee's Commander wasn't super-excited about Michelle's change of plans. He held his cap under his arm in the wardroom, so she could see his forehead turn red and the blood vessels in his neck bulge.

She stepped across the monotonous gray non-slip floor to move closer and set her hand on his arm. "Thank you for all your crew's fine support. I don't know what we would've done without you here to rescue us all. I'll make sure the agency sends some kind of unit-level commendation over to the Navy."

Salt water permeated the ship's air. Probably why these naval officers always seemed wrinkly and well-preserved.

He gave a gruff cough. "My orders were to pick your mission up off the beach and return you to Japan, not steam around the islands and launch air assaults on friendly powers."

"It's all top secret, of course." She smiled. "I'm sure you understand. Probably taken part in lots of counter-terrorism missions lately."

In actuality, Michelle knew this was only his second time away from dock in command of a ship and that as an executive officer, he'd spent more time in the North Atlantic playing hide and seek with the Russians than anywhere near a terrorist.

"Of course, but what shall I tell my HQ?"

"That the agency has requested you spend a couple of more days in the area in order to complete the freedom of navigation cover mission. Make it all look good to our Chinese friends. Wouldn't want them to suspect we weren't telling the truth about why you're here, would you?"

"No, of course not."

"Good. Then it's settled. I'll discuss with Schnier anything else we need to get done, and we'll work out any details with your exec."

She carefully refrained from calling Schnier captain. In her experience, naval officers were a bit touchy about that aboard ship, especially when they were the captain of the ship, but only a commander in rank.

He sighed and then turned to go. Nodded to the entering Schnier as they passed each other.

"Get your men settled in?"

"Tight quarters, but we've seen worse. Once the crew refuels the helicopters, we can get back in the air right away." He waited until the naval officer was out of earshot. "Did you ask the captain about using his command-and-control facilities for our intelligence platoon and running the raid?"

"We didn't discuss it, directly, but I'm sure the exec will be more than accommodating. Captain agreed to stay in the area for another 48 hours."

"Then I'd better get things moving. Bad enough you getting run out of the Philippines forced us to abort. Our job is to be out protecting other people, not running away from the wolves."

Was he really going to blame her for the SAF knocking on their door? They'd been perfectly isolated and undetected until he and Sam had to cowboy off to Manila with his vaunted shooters and then get involved in a sniper fight.

"Our job isn't to get caught, either, like Sam."

"Sure, knock him while he's down. A prisoner. Maybe even dead."

She took a deliberate breath. Now wasn't the time to air out their relationship problems. Smiled. "I'm sorry. I guess the stress is getting to me more than I'd like to think. I forgot, you don't know."

He shrugged. "Know what?"

"We lost the Reaper."

"*Lost?*"

"Okay, probably shot down. It picked up a SAM signature

just before going off the air. Most likely Chinese. Their weapons are everywhere around here."

His mouth gaped open. "You're just now telling me that if we'd gone ahead with the raid as planned, we were facing surface-to-air missiles?"

"Yes, so you can see how that complicates your return. We need to get another drone up, if nothing else."

"Complicates? You mean prevents, don't you? We'll have to go in on boats. They'll have plenty of warning. We'll have no overhead intelligence. They'll be on the defense, with interior lines. We'll be moving blind, which is how Harper got himself caught. But yeah, sure, *complicates* matters."

Okay, maybe she hadn't realized what a big deal that was.

"We'll figure it out. Just need to do some mission planning. Maybe we can take the SAM site out ahead of time."

"Those are unarmed recon and cargo birds out there, not A-10s. They're not setup for going after anti-aircraft installations, or anything like that."

"Maybe the exec will have some ideas. After all, this ship carries lots of missiles, doesn't it?"

"Some. Not a lot. Couple dozen, probably. Mostly anti-ship missiles. A HELIOS directed energy system for anti-missile defense. I wonder what the range on that is? Either way, we're going back in as soon as possible."

"Go check with the experts and create an op plan. I'll see what I can do to figure out how to obtain better intelligence over the target. Maybe I can get a satellite. There's a guy who owes me a favor, so I don't have to call my boss in D.C."

Schnier cocked his head. "How's he taking all this, anyway? Give a new deadline now that the old one has passed?"

"What he doesn't know won't hurt him."

"You're playing with fire, there."

"Always." She pointed at the hatch. "Now go."

But could she get herself out of the figurative frying pan any other way?

Pahk caught his foot on the threshold of Omar's combination living, dining, and meeting room. He righted himself before any embarrassment.

A glorified cavern with wall hangings and woven mats to disguise it. To kill the echoes and pretend they weren't inside a mountain.

Oppressive, but hopefully he could depart soon enough and return to the even closer quarters aboard ship.

Omar rooted through a cabinet. "Songbird! Where is my sword?"

Raven appeared in the entranceway. She clutched at her stomach. "Have you checked the chest in your bedroom?"

He growled. "Why would it be in there? I never bring it in there."

"I'll go look, just in case." She shuffled toward the adjoining room.

He strode toward the rough stone opening. "Never mind, I can look myself."

While Omar banged around in his bedroom, Raven minced her way to a stand-up closet. Sort of a tall box made of bamboo. She flipped through the contents, moved papers, squatted to look under some of its contents.

"There's nothing in here, either." Omar called.

Pahk wandered toward the bedroom door.

Behind him, Raven chuckled. "Here it is. Leaning up against the back of the closet."

Omar stormed out of the room. "That's the first place I looked."

She shrugged. "As you often say, sometimes things aren't as easy to see to those who seek them directly, wise master."

He frowned at her, but picked up the sword and toddled over to display it lengthwise to Pahk.

"You know swords?"

Pahk nodded. "We have steel craftsman in my country."

Omar slid it from its bamboo sheath. Medium length, the sword showed the marks of tempered steel, slightly curved with a thin cutting edge and a thicker squared-off side.

"Here, take a look." He presented it hilt first.

Pahk picked up the sword. Light. Balanced. He held up the hilt for a closer look. Almost certainly authentic. At least seventy years old.

"I told you the story of Onoda, who used these caverns before. Lasted for decades to strike his enemies. That was his sword. Bought it from his widow."

Pahk returned the weapon. "I see. Very symbolic."

Omar grunted. Slammed it home in the sheath. "Tough, like us." He leaned it back against the back of the closet. Picked up a wooden rod and a small leather case instead. "Let's go."

Raven seemed to shrink away from the sword and rod, but Omar didn't look at her, so Pahk followed him out to the rocky corridor.

His little buzz from the Stainless roiling in his gut would help him get through this next part.

Captain Larrikowal stood formally at ease in front of Secretary Dorenza's massive desk.

"No further activity from the American ship, but they also haven't moved away from Lubang Island."

"We've long suspected a terror cell in the mountains there. If they conduct a strike on them and the wrong person notices... this is the information age. We can't stop some peasant farmer's video of missiles and gunfire in the night from going viral."

"But how can we stop them?"

"Perhaps we can't, but we can at least make known to them that we know what they're up to. I'm sending you out to the ship. Fly to the coast and then take a cutter from there. Bring some supplies. Fresh fruit. Bananas. Tourist trinkets for the sailors to take to their families back home. Call it a goodwill visit."

"And my true mission? Am I to spy on them?"

"Nothing so awkward. Talk to them. Find out who the ranking officer for those soldiers is. Convince him we are aware of what they've been up to. Maybe he'll offer an explanation. Perhaps you can keep this from blowing up in our faces. Explain you're just there to prop up our rickety alliance."

"Do you think they'll believe me?" Larrikowal bit down on his lip.

"The truth shouldn't be difficult. It doesn't suit my purposes any more than theirs for our government to continue to fall into China's orbit. Make them see reason. Their operation, whatever it was, is blown. Too risky to continue."

"Very well. I'll report on our discussions from the ship." He turned to leave.

"And Larrikowal..."

He paused.

"Get my approval before making any deals, hmm?"

He nodded. "Of course."

He'd do what he could to put Humpty-Dumpty back together again.

I lay half-propped up. Attempted to protect the tiny pools of acid from discovery.

Omar loomed above me. Whipped down a wooden rod on the tendons in my upper right arm. Ouch. That one stung even more than the last dozen.

Pahk huddled by the door, turning green. I'd been shocked to watch him walk in behind Omar. The last time I'd seen him was in Seoul, when we sent him back across the DMZ.

What was he doing here? Fronting for the Chinese, or did Pyongyang take a new geopolitical interest in the region?

Omar smacked my left arm. "What's your unit?"

"Just a tourist. Got lost while hiking. Exploring."

"We already know all the details, but you must confirm them for us."

He jabbed me in the belly. Fortunately, my core is an area which decades of surfing develops. I instinctively tightened it.

The stick bent, but didn't break.

Was like he'd stabbed me with a knife.

"Your unit!" He gestured toward Pahk with his rod, as if it was a campaign stick. "You recognize my companion, here. He recognizes you. It's no use denying it."

"Of course." I gasped. "Good to see you again, Lieutenant Pahk Geon."

Pahk nodded. "It's captain now."

"Congratulations." I groaned.

Omar tapped me softly on the left leg, as if measuring his

next stroke. "You see. Not so difficult. Now, your unit?"

After forty-five minutes of piling on the bruises, I figured I'd had enough to be believable. Besides, no chance Pahk didn't remember who I was with.

"75th Regimental Special Troops Battalion. Military Intelligence Company, third platoon. On loan to the Ranger Reconnaissance Company."

Actually, second platoon, but who's counting?

Omar looked at Pahk. He nodded. I got away with the little lie.

"Very good. You're learning. Now, where is your base? Remember, we already know, so why go through more pain?"

I doubted that. Time to implement the strategy I'd long ago determined to use if ever captured and tortured.

Lie as much as possible in not easily checkable ways until even if they eventually force you to tell the truth, they won't know what to believe.

"Manila. We setup in Manila."

"Good. Where in Manila?"

"I don't remember. You know they don't really use street addresses there? Not like where I'm from. Our driver always just knew where to go."

He whacked my left leg on the kneecap.

Damn. That hurt. Same knee I injured in Korea. I couldn't stop a wince.

"Where precisely?"

I sighed. Had to maintain enough strength to escape later and kick this dude's ass back to Mecca. "Fine! F7 warehouse on Tobias and Gandia streets, but when I didn't return, they may have left. Gone elsewhere."

In truth, we staged some equipment there when we setup the counter-sniper teams, but other than some packaging and trash, nothing remained except a slightly richer landlord.

"Your mission in Manila?"

Half-truths are the easiest. "To protect the government leaders. A secret agreement with the President. He didn't want anyone to know he was relying on American rangers instead of his own Department of National Defense, but he doesn't trust the Secretary to protect his people. They're enemies."

"Liar!" Omar slammed the rod down on my right thigh, missing the kneecap in his excitement, but giving me the worst charley horse ever.

What had I screwed up? Had to think through the pain. Concentrate quickly. "Okay, okay. Enough. I give up."

Of course! If Omar was working with the President...

"Your true mission?"

"We had intelligence someone would shoot the Speaker, so we were to stop it. Prevent it. That part is true. It wasn't with the President, though. He didn't know. Just the SAF. A joint-mission."

Plausible, but not too incriminating for anyone, as long as he thought the locals had invited us.

Omar straightened up. "I have sources in the police who can confirm for me your words. If you lie, this will feel like a thousand soft pillows in your dreams."

He nodded to Pahk. "Let's go. I'll send Raven to clean him up for the next round. Mustn't wear out our guest too soon."

Well, that didn't sound pleasant. I needed to get out of here!

Chapter Sixteen: Captive Meetups

Michelle slumped head down on the metal wardroom table. Her laptop connected to the ship's systems, she'd been using it as a make-shift office, ignoring the trickle of naval officers who passed through to get some coffee, or more likely, a look at the agency chick.

Right now, her eyes preferred temporary closure. She'd been up all night with Schnier, the exec, and their staff planning tonight's rescue attempt.

Supposedly it was daylight outside, so she should go to her assigned rack and get some sleep. Get rest for tonight's mission.

But her body insisted she not move. The slight rocking of the ship begged to differ, but ultimately would put her to sleep right here.

Someone fumbled their way through the hatchway.

Michelle opened her eyes and groaned. Was she imagining things, or was her latest wardroom visitor dressed in an SAF uniform and carrying a black briefcase?

She rubbed her eyes with her fists.

Schnier came in behind the interloper, wearing a rumpled uniform, like he'd been sleeping in it. He stretched his arms wide, until they bumped the low ceiling.

"Michelle, this is our new liaison from the SAF, Captain Larrikowal."

"Liaison?"

"He brought over some goodies for the crew and happened to mention to the Captain that he'd love to speak with the Special

Operations troops he had on board and compare notes."

Schnier held his finger vertically to his lips behind Larrikowal's back.

"Ahh... welcome aboard, then. Make yourself comfortable. I'm a diplomat with the embassy, just here as a liaison myself."

She yawned. Had to stop doing that.

Larrikowal stepped over to her and extended his hand. "Most excellent to meet you. So you are the agency representative in charge of this covert mission?"

Michelle shook his hand and then her head. "What gives you that idea?"

"Cards on the table, as they say. You should know that I'm here because we tracked your movement from the resort compound you left in flames to this ship via helicopter and small watercraft."

This was the last thing she needed. More interference in her work, this time from the locals.

"As a diplomat, I must say that the Ambassador and the State Department would never approve of activities of the nature you describe. That sort of covert operations might cause a diplomatic incident."

"It's okay, I won't tell if you won't. At least... as long as we can come to a mutually beneficial agreement. My Secretary of Defense is keeping this matter close to his chest. I'm here to negotiate on his behalf, but neither of us wishes to alienate your country."

Schnier leaned forward. "Makes sense. We're the biggest kid on the block, after all. Better to keep us on your side."

Michelle gave him a look which she hoped he successfully translated into "shut-up already!"

Larrikowal grinned. "China would disagree, at least in this particular neighborhood, but as it happens, we're on your side. Unlike the President and the Speaker of the house. You may have noticed our impending election?"

Michelle nodded. "Of course." No harm in admitting that she kept up on local politics.

"We're especially curious why an American counter-sniper team would be in Manila to protect the Speaker, who has made no secret of the fact that he favors China in these types of matters."

She shrugged. "No idea. You'd have to ask whoever it was."

After all, he couldn't prove a thing.

He set his briefcase on the wardroom table. Dialed in a combination. Clicked open the locks. Folded it back. Removed a manila envelope. Slid out an 8x5 photo. Handed it to Schnier.

"An excellent likeness, don't you think? The entire area is covered by cameras, there are plenty more, including images tracking you and your other teams to and from the coastal resort in vans."

Schnier's ears actually turned red as he stared at the photo.

Idiots, they hadn't accounted for the cameras in all their gallivanting around town?

She'd have to recover the situation somehow. "So theoretically speaking, let's say intelligence came to the attention of a U.S. military unit about a terrorist attack and they were in a position to help prevent it. It's possible they might in an emergency take some sort of action outside the normally accepted diplomatic channels."

Larrikowal grinned. "Of course, this is all theoretical." He took the photo back from Schnier and tucked it into the envelope. "But in that situation, local law enforcement would likely have appreciated advance notice of such a situation."

"As a diplomat, I have to say that inter-governmental contacts like that can be delicate and slow. For example, my State Department would normally insist such information would need to go through your Department of Foreign Affairs. Would probably need to include the source of the information, which could compromise all sorts of confidential methods and personnel. You see the problem."

He nodded. "Yes, I believe I do. Not to say you would be forgiven, but it may be in everyone's best interests in such a situation to come to an agreement which saves embarrassment all around. I mean, who is to say you weren't working covertly with the SAF the whole time? That is, if you had a liaison you were sharing information with..."

This guy was too smart for his own good. She'd need to roll

the dice on his honesty, because otherwise she'd blown her mission and her career along with it.

Not to mention they'd never get Sam out with the SAF sitting on top of them if they weren't in a cooperative mood.

"You'd better have a seat. As it turns out, my recollection is that you've been our official SAF joint-exercise liaison on this matter for more than a week now. Does that match what you remember?"

Larrikowal's grin grew broader. He pushed his briefcase to the side and sat at the table. "I believe that may match my recollection. Perhaps you can refresh my mind on what we've been doing together?"

Schnier stepped forward. "Now wait a..." He broke off when Michelle held up a hand.

"Captain Schnier, this sounds like a diplomatic problem, don't you think? You're welcome to join us, of course, but I can handle this matter."

She yawned. Assuming she could stay awake long enough.

He nodded. "I'll get us all some coffee. I'm going to need it, even if it is that liquid tar the navy serves." He started across the wardroom towards the coffee maker.

Smart man.

Larrikowal leaned forward across the table. "I believe this may be the beginning of a beautiful friendship."

Michelle smiled, careful to ensure her eyes crinkled to make it believable. She reached out her arm. Placed a hand on his forearm across the table.

Not so smart as he liked to think, if he didn't understand that she'd toss him to the wolves if it saved either Sam or her career.

Hopefully both.

"We might have a problem with a shared opponent, but we may also have a collection of intelligence regarding other mutual foes which would interest you. I think we can come to a beneficial arrangement which your Secretary of Defense will approve."

Pahk leaned against a granite boulder next to a hard-packed dirt trail. A waterfall hid the nearby cave entrance. It bounced its way off rocks and into the pool below.

Enough noise to hide his conversation from any of Omar's men who watched.

He spoke into his radio. Just enough range to reach the Chinese covert torpedo boat hiding in a cove along the north shore.

"I need to arrange a future pick up."

"When?"

"That depends. Relay to the Admiral that one of the targets identified by Comment Crew is being held by my host. Find out if he wants me to negotiate an acquisition or have him terminated. We're currently working to confirm intelligence he's provided, otherwise he's unlikely to last much longer here."

"Roger. Will relay and get back to you with instructions."

"I'll check back in two hours. If it fits with the answer, coordinate the rest, including any proposed payment, from your end and provide a rendezvous time tonight at our most recent drop off point. I'll have more information about the Imperialists at that time."

There, that demonstrated his continued value to Admiral Hu.

"1... 2... 3..." Raven yanked on a chain together with Sam. She grunted with the effort.

It didn't budge.

"Enough." He looked up at her from the floor. "The acid isn't eating through the bolt nor concrete fast enough to make a difference."

She dropped the chain. "Sorry I couldn't get the sword. Omar was showing it to Pahk. The stars just didn't line up."

"Hey, I'm stoked about what you're already willing to do." He rubbed one of his bruises on the arm they'd been working to free. "No need to get caught in a sketchy situation."

"You know, when Schnier told me he was joining the Army, I tried to talk him out of it. Asked him why he would go join a bunch of baby killers. Thought he was dumb for not knowing any history. Broke up with him over it."

"We all make mistakes. I didn't like Schnier either, when I first met him. Total Barney. The dude grows on you, though."

"Now I'm doing manual labor for the Army." She laughed. Flexed her arm. "Fetching, hauling, and pulling."

"You're doing awesome. No way I have the leverage to get free of these chains myself. Not laying on the floor."

"Is he married? Seeing someone? Single? I can't picture him settled down with someone else."

"Schnier? He's... it's complicated."

"So he is." Her heart sank into her flat tone of voice.

He rushed out an explanation. "Been dating an old friend of mine, a co-worker, really, but not in the army, but they haven't been getting along totally fine lately. Doubt it'll last long."

"Well, that was a long time ago, anyway." Technically, she was married, in the eyes of Allah, anyway.

Compared to Omar, Schnier was a prince among men. Or at least, a cowboy of a man.

"Of course, but you never know. I mean, he obviously cares about you. Even a relationship newb like me can figure that much out. He spent more of our time in Manila showing your photo around and asking if anyone has seen you than he did on our actual mission. That kind of dedication isn't just casual interest. Must think he owes you something, still."

"Thanks. Shall we try a different chain?"

Sam looked at each one in turn. Settled on the chain connected to his right ankle.

"My strongest leg right now, and the chain looks just as not eaten away as the others. Last try before we bail."

She took a two-handed grip on the ankle shackle. Bent her legs to get more power. "1... 2... 3..."

They pulled together. She yanked up with all her might.
Nothing.
They stopped. She sighed. "No use."

"All we can do is wait longer for the acid to do its work, then."

Could she risk it? She'd already approached two of the other women. They'd been dubious. Doubted there was really a way to escape.

The longer it took, the more doubts they'd have. The more likely Omar would be to hurt Sam in some new way.

Even execute him on camera.

If she were to have any hope at all, she'd have to.

"Maybe there's still another way. Omar already showed Pahk the sword. He won't look for it again so soon. I'll go get it right now. Bring it back, along with the pot. What did you call them?"

"Lever and fulcrum."

"Right."

He held up a chained arm. "I'll wait here for you."

She laughed. As if he had any choice in the matter.

She'd smiled more honestly today than she ever had the entire time since she'd met Omar. Maybe some of her old inner sunlight could return as well, if she let it.

Chapter Seventeen: Captive Plans

To Larrikowal, sitting in an American wardroom while a ranger captain and the CIA station chief horse-traded with him was more than surreal.

He'd dealt with the Americans before, but there'd always been a feeling of superiority on their side. A reminder that his country only had their independence because the Americans decided to give it to them.

An acknowledgment they were the world's number one military, and he belonged to maybe the top half of the middle.

One U.S. aircraft carrier cost more to build than the entire defense budget of the Philippines for ten years.

But for now, he had them backed into a corner. Caught with their hand in the cookie jar, as the saying went.

But how to best take advantage of that?

"The SAF will supply our own technical experts. Your intelligence team will show them how they intercepted our communications and infiltrated our networks. In return, we'll give you at least short-term access to any specific data you need for your mission."

Michelle nodded. "We can accept that arrangement, but we'll want your cooperation for a live fire exercise on Lubang Island."

That confirmed for Larrikowal that they'd also tracked the sniper team there.

"A live fire exercise? If you mean a mission to eliminate the team who fired at the Speaker, you should be more explicit. You may not be aware, but they shot at me that day and hit my partner. Why shouldn't the SAF take the lead on their capture?"

"You can have the terrorists. Their entire camp, for all we care, but... and this is where things become delicate, but I know we can trust you... they've captured an American soldier."

"I see your interest, now. Still, if the SAF takes the lead, we can free your soldier."

"In normal times, that would be fine, we don't doubt your prowess, but we're currently sitting off the coast with everything needed to effect a rescue and it'll take the SAF at least another day or two to get approval and then plan an effective raid."

"It would be a great embarrassment if the SAF were to be seen to step aside and allow Americans to take care of their internal problems."

Schnier leaned forward from his spot against the nearby wall to interrupt their negotiations.

"My company lost a great ranger to enemy fire recently. That still wakes me up some nights, because there were things I could've done to prevent it. Let me make myself perfectly clear..."

He shifted around Michelle to stare Larrikowal directly in the eye. "I don't care if my platoon must swim to Lubang Island with a knife between our teeth after I lock you into my footlocker; We ride tonight. So make your peace with that fact and let's figure out the most advantageous way for us to work together, instead."

Definitely the serious one. He'd take what he could get from the Americans. Now that he knew Schnier's priorities, it'd actually be easier.

Larrikowal nodded. "I'll come with you. The SAF will be officially running the mission, but I'm happy to defer to you and your men and transportation. Meanwhile, I'll arrange for my own force to get there as quickly as possible to take over the scene and mop up any who escape into the surrounding jungle or villages. In return, we just need those technical details. In addition, once the raid is over, this fine LCS should go put a scare into the Chinese fleet circling the Spratly Islands."

After a glance at Schnier, she nodded in agreement.

He smiled at her. "That's its public mission, after all. Perhaps we can also arrange a future training date based on our obvious affinity for one another."

Michelle chuckled. "Not the first time I've been asked for a date on a navy ship, but your version of seduction has a certain macho appeal."

She was just attempting to throw him off with her flirting, wasn't she? Well, he could give as well as he got.

"In our navy, women and seaman don't mix. Prevents pregnancy."

"I'll bet it does." Her phone buzzed. She picked it up and glanced at the screen. "Sorry, one of my alerts. It's another message for the missing soldier from his girlfriend, but I can't tell her where he's at. I'll deal with it later."

She set her device face down on the table. "So, now that we have an agreement on all the major points, next steps?"

"I'll confirm our deal with the Secretary of Defense, arrange for my force's movement to the island, and send our technical experts to this ship. Then I'll join you to help plan our joint operation on Lubang against the snipers."

"It's a date." Michelle grinned. "But Schnier and I were up all night, so we're going to get some more rest before dusk arrives again."

Time to prepare his force for war.

Schnier followed Michelle down the ship's cramped passageway. Up a ladder. Down another ladder. To their assigned quarters.

"Hey, wait."

Michelle stopped, but stretched. "I'm tired."

"I know this is a navy ship, but we could be tired together."

She sighed. "I've been thinking..."

That's never a good sign. Almost as bad as "We've got to talk."

"Yeah?"

"Maybe we need a break. A bit of a breather. This independent command thing has been full of stress for you. This mission is about to ruin my career. If we keep trying to make things work, they're liable to blow up instead."

She might as well have started this conversation the other way.

Schnier dug into his heart. Was it breaking?

Surprisingly, no. More numb. With a bit of a hole, perhaps; lonely, but not broken.

"Okay. I agree."

She glared at him. "What do you mean, you agree?"

Women. No pleasing 'em.

"We could use a break. Stay friends. Co-workers. Just lay off the romance for a bit. Figure it out after this mission is over and we're back to our normal lives. You and Sam managed that whole friend thing, right?"

"Um... yeah. Friends. That's what I was going to say, anyway. Glad we're on the same page. We can talk more about it later. For now, I'm hitting the sack."

"Good night. We'll have another incursion to plan tonight, assuming your new SAF buddy comes through for us."

"Oh, he will. One way or another. I'm not used to taking no for an answer."

"Good."

He turned toward his compartment and its waiting bunk. One less thing to worry about. To keep him awake once he lay down.

Between his platoon, Sam, and Raven, he had enough of those already.

Not long after dark, Pahk obtained fresh orders from Admiral Hu. He tracked Omar down in his stone quarters.

Raven departed as Pahk arrived. She walked with a tiny sliding limp.

Was Omar back to his usual practices?

Well, none of Pahk's business how he occupied his time and his wives.

Omar set down his cup and looked up from his cross-legged seat on a mat near the table. "Ah, Pahk. I have interesting news for you."

More sponsor, but Pahk wasn't one to quibble. "Oh?"

"My contact in the office of SAF, a trusted brother of the faith, knows nothing about the American's mission. He tells me everyone there is confused about who the counter-sniper team was. Our captive is not telling us the complete truth."

"I'm curious as to your methods. How have you established a relationship inside the counter-terror police force?"

"I was born into a good family, with traditional values, but because of the anti-Muslim policies of the authorities, I found myself committed to one of their prisons for a period of three years."

In reality, Pahk knew from China's background materials that he'd been caught as a motorcycle thief, but he just nodded.

"In prison, I met my true brothers. Found my true calling in the faith, that of jihad. Proved myself to them by removing a menace. We formed a firm society of trust, as only those threatened by destruction by those around them can."

Omar picked up his cup and took a sip. "We were able to exist because some of the guards sympathized with our views. Of course, they also benefited from the outside assistance our senior members arranged. Gifts were given. Items of need smuggled through the walls. It was a fine system."

So, a prison gang, with guards on the take.

"I can see how as a minority religion your member's organizational skills would benefit you."

"Yes. After I completed my time there, I kept in touch. Eventually, that led me to my current position as the emir of the cause, but it also led some of those former guards higher into the hierarchy of the police. I made my own small contribution to one officer's advancement by arranging for him to single-handedly capture a terrorist cell."

He set his cup back down and leaned forward. "Catholic terrorists, of course!"

His rolling laughter echoed from the cave walls. "So now he is my creature. He owes me everything, and I can expose him at any time. There is no better basis for trust than to hold a man's balls in your fist."

Pahk chuckled to keep him in a good mood. "We must find out more from your captive, then. He's another you have a good grip on. But, I too have news which may impact your decision in this matter."

Let Omar believe he decided. Pahk didn't care.

"Please, sit." Omar gestured to a floor mat. "I will send for refreshments if you desire."

Pahk took the indicated place. "I must apologize. I'm operating under a time restriction. My ride off the island will return soon, and I must leave your most excellent hospitality for at least a few days."

"That's unfortunate, I've enjoyed your company, as well as your contributions to our jihad."

"I do have a new proposal for you. A group is keenly interested in your prisoner. Don't worry, they are another of the Imperialists' enemies. This isn't a ransom, but they'll pay highly for him."

Omar leaned back and rested his chin on his hand. He stroked his beard with his thumb.

"Based on our past relationship, I think you already understand the level of enticement this action you request would require."

"Are you familiar with the Uyghur?"

"Yes, the People of the Faith who are oppressed in north-western China, between Mongolia and Pakistan."

"Exactly. What if I could have some of them freed? Delivered to you?"

"We are not a refugee camp. How many are we talking about?"

"Perhaps six nubile Uyghur women? After all, young women are the most vulnerable, are they not?"

Omar stroked his beard again and then smiled. "A dozen. You can have him for a dozen, but no less. Bring them here and he's yours. Who knows, perhaps I'll even find them suitable husbands among my faithful followers."

This would be the difficult part of their negotiations.

"I can't. I must take your captive with me today, so I can trade him elsewhere for them." He checked the time. "We must leave soon if I'm to make my pickup schedule. But I've already demonstrated I'll keep my word by delivering all of the promised weapons and even a bonus from our last agreement, have I not?"

"Your track record is excellent, but like last time, I would appreciate a deposit of good faith. Reputation is important, but one hundred-thousand American dollars in a safe account is also quite useful."

Pahk could've gone as high as a quarter of a million as a good faith deposit, but no need for Omar to know that. Perhaps he could claim Omar had negotiated better and wanted the deposit split between accounts, one of which would help support Pahk's family.

Something to consider.

"A difficult bargain, but we have an agreement."

Now to seal his deal with Omar with a drink, gather his belongings and the American, and then meet his boat.

Just another boring day at the office.

I hated wearing chains. Didn't suit me at all, especially the limited mobility for using the bathroom.

Chamber pots stink. Literally.

Raven staggered into my prison carrying a cast-iron pot. Set it down.

"Good to see you. What's wrong with your leg?"

She grinned. Hiked up her robe to reveal jeans. Slid a sword from underneath the long flowing black material.

"Tough to walk with this thing." She handed it to me, hilt-first. "Left the sheath behind so I only needed to conceal the missing hilt."

Good steel. A working soldier's katana. Single edge. "Perfect. Flip that pot over and slide it next to where the chain attaches to the floor."

For maximum force, we needed the shortest length of steel between chain and pot edge and the longest out where I'd apply pressure.

She moved the pot into place as requested. "What next?"

With the pot in place next to my left wrist, I slotted the sword into the open chain closest to the floor. Pressing the sharp edge against steel chain might dull it, but it'd keep it in place and put more pressure on a smaller surface area.

"Next we see what breaks first."

I leveraged the flat edge on the pot. Not the wide side, too prone to snap, but the thin and flat side opposite the edge.

Put my back on the sword. Bent my legs to lift my lower half. Dump as much weight as possible on the hilt.

The sword flexed, but the chain held.

If we applied enough pressure, either the chain would give, or the bolt would. I refused to consider the sword breaking.

I bounced up and down on the hilt.

Still nothing. Without enough pressure, this wouldn't work.

"Come here." I patted the ground next to my right side.

She picked her way around the edge of the room and stood up against my shoulder.

"Need you to sit on my chest."

"Okay..." She turned and lowered herself down.

I held the hilt under my back, so I couldn't help keep her on. Only a light pressure, though.

"No, put all your weight on me."

Her pressure shifted. Tough to breath for a moment. Had to thrust my chest out.

The chain creaked. I lifted my legs. Gave the sword the tiniest bounce.

With a crack, the chain deformed and parted.

Gravity did the rest. I landed with the sword between me and the stone ground. Ouch.

Raven landed on top of me, having given way unexpectedly. Slid her hip into my chin.

Double-ouch.

I lifted my left wrist and rubbed beneath the shackle with the fingers of my right hand.

Victory! I could scratch again.

The sword now had a tiny flaw in the edge, perfect for lining up another chain. We repeated the maneuver three more times, each easier than the last as I gained the use of more limbs.

To free the last leg, I just jumped on the hilt. She didn't even need to help.

Shackles and a couple feet of chain remained on my limbs, but with the other end free, I clanked around the edge of the room just to stretch out and for the exercise.

"Okay, from your previous description, there's the corridor outside, which leads to the harem on one end and a guard on the other?"

Her cheeks turned red. "Yes, I suppose you could call it a harem. I never thought of it that way, just as the place the wives lived. Omar rarely entertains *male* captives."

"Lead the way."

I followed her into a long and thin natural rock passageway.

She turned left. Strode quickly ahead.

We arrived at an open area. Not large enough to call a cavern, but more the size of a living room, with carpets and rugs covering the walls between smaller openings into individual or group sleeping quarters.

A pot of rice steamed over a two-boiler portable propane stove. A woman in baggy cotton pants and blouse stood slicing carrots into it.

Her stew smelled pleasant, like the aroma of home around Thanksgiving, but when she noticed me, she sucked in a deep breath in preparation to scream.

Raven stepped forward. "Quiet!"

That cut her off with only a brief strangled shout. Hopefully, not enough to cause a guard to do more than wonder what that noise was.

Four other young Filipino women sat cross-legged on the floor playing a game with hands full of brightly colored cards containing weird symbols.

At the noise, five others peeked their heads out of their sleeping spaces. One of them said, "Oh!", but the rest followed Raven's admonition.

Only the cook appeared older than Raven, and she's in her late twenties, like me and Schnier.

I stood just inside the entrance, bruised, dangling two chains, dragging two others, and carrying a naked sword.

Probably not the most reassuring sight.

Raven took charge. "Gather around, everyone. It's time to leave. Don't be afraid, this is Sam. He's going to get us out of here. You know where his chains are from. He's an American army officer. A ranger."

The cook at the stove pointed her knife at me and thrust it into the air as she spoke. "He shouldn't be here. How do we know he doesn't plan to rape us all and abandon us in the jungle?"

A titter flew around the room.

With a frown, Raven moved toward her. "Now don't be silly. I grew up with another officer he works with who is nearby. Omar captured him, he's not here of his own free will on some sort of raiding expedition."

Another of the girls slid from her room into the common area and stood up. "Well, I heard he was an imperialist who came to kill us all."

"I can assure you ladies, I wouldn't harm a hair on your head."

Another girl turned sideways and stroked her arm. "Then what's the sword for? Your own not deadly enough?"

Raven let out a long sigh. "You know what it's like here. We were each assigned a man. Only they got a choice. Some of us to the same man. We're here to please them, feed them, and clean their quarters. Nothing else."

The cook now turned her knife toward Raven. "But you're the special one, aren't you? Get to take trips off the island. Serve Omar's guests, while we only service them. Why should we trust you on this? We can survive here."

"Don't. The only reason I haven't already left was to find a way to get all y'all out when I could. I have the way. Here he is. You can stay if you want, but we're leaving as soon as whoever wants to go is ready."

The room exploded into chatter as each girl discussed her options with the others. Two began crying softly and one outright bawling, as they stepped on each other's feelings of hope and relief.

At least we had walls of sound-absorbing cloth over solid stone.

Raven ignored them. She went to the largest side chamber and picked up a green duffel bag and a large black robe. Carried them out next to me. Handed me the robe.

"Put this on. You'll blend in better." She hefted the duffel. "This is everything I need. All that remains of my life."

I pulled the robe over my head. Tangled my chains in an armpit. Turned in circles while I got everything where it needed to go.

"Your life isn't in there, it's in the choices you make. Now they have to make theirs."

It took a few minutes to sort out, and I got to answer some pointed questions about the future, to which I couldn't give great answers, but in the end, all ten gathered their belongings to leave.

No desire to tie any up and leave them behind, anyway.

"Any of you have weapons?"

The cook had her knife. She also came up with a way of tying my ankle chains up my calves with a ribbon so they didn't scrape across the ground.

"Okay, Raven will go first. The guards are most used to her coming and going. I'll follow with the sword. We'll keep you and your knife at the back, where you can fend off any surprise attackers."

Raven took one last look at the open area. "Let's go."

We filtered down the corridor, single-file.

I kept my head down, headscarf flopped forward. Contemplating to conceal my face.

Two guards, presumably to keep each other honest, rather than viewing the harem women as a serious threat, stood on either side of where the thin rock corridor met a larger cavern.

Each carried an AK-variant with a banana magazine slung over his shoulder.

I whispered to Raven. "You go first. Once a few feet past, get their attention. I'll take care of the rest." I hoped.

The rest of us paused slightly behind a curve as she stepped out as if without a care in the world. Strode toward the tangos.

The guards stared at her. "Omar didn't send for you."

She didn't break stride. Lifted her duffel. "He told me earlier to bring him these trinkets from my former life as a punishment." Stepped between them.

They naturally turned to track her as she walked away. I crept forward.

She stopped. Turned back. Held up the duffel. "Do you want to see?"

With their attention fixed, I rushed forward. Okay, lugged chains forward as quickly as I could sprint with ten pound ankle weights.

The guard on the left heard something. He half-turned back.

I ran the sword into his side, under the ribs.

He groaned.

We must escape.

The other lifted his rifle to level it from vertical to horizontal. Turned toward me.

The sword hung up in the first guard. He collapsed to the stone floor. I released the hilt.

Swung the chain connected to my right wrist at the second guard. Whacked him in the face with the end.

Knocked off balance, he turned too far.

I swung my left chain.

He fended it off with the end of his rifle.

Mistake.

My chain curled around the barrel. I yanked backward. It slid toward me, and then the chain caught on the iron sights.

I pulled the barrel to the left. Used my right wrist steel cord to smash him in the neck.

The chains gave me a significant reach advantage, if a slower one.

Raven hit him in the back of the head with her duffel. Surprised us both.

He hunched forward.

I kicked him in the balls. Sometimes the classics are best.

He grunted. Folded farther forward, halfway to the floor. Released his rifle, but the strap hung up on his arm.

Now we were both tangled up with it. No ability to separate, so I kneed his rapidly descending nose.

It exploded into blood. Got all over my gown.

Raven kicked him between the shoulder blades.

It wasn't fair, but she may've had a special grudge for this dude. I kicked him in the face to put him out for good.

Raven took the dead guard's rifle. Butt-stroked the other on the ear.

I held up a hand. Gasped in a breath. "I think he's out. Thought I told you to let me handle it?"

"This one liked to take advantage of his position guarding the women. Omar should've castrated him." She pounded him again in the throat.

Not sure he'd survive that hit. "Okay. Enough. Get the others." If he ever came to, he'd find breathing difficult.

While lying around on stone floors, I'd had some spare time to think recently about when it was okay to use force. What made me and the rangers different from Omar. I concluded that what made the violence of my job moral was that people need protection against aggressors and evildoers. A sheepdog against the wolves.

So I couldn't quibble too hard when a victim punished the guilty herself. In another place and time, I'd cry for her obvious pain, but here, I needed to get through our escape first.

If she didn't have that right, then how did I on her behalf?

While she moved back down the corridor, I untangled myself from the second guard's rifle. Checked the bolt. One magazine, no extras.

Looked like it would fire, but no quiet way to know for sure, so I retrieved the sword.

The cave in front of us spread out into a wide, zigzag cavern from left to right. Cables ran to an oversized light fixture at the apex of the cave. Looked too large to just be illumination, but no signs of any cameras and maybe the tangos were just poor electricians.

Shoddy work.

From what Raven had told me, left, uphill, led to Omar's living area and the other men's barracks. Right, downhill, to a guarded waterfall entrance.

Raven guided the women up behind me.

Distant voices echoed from the direction of the men's area. Gradually grew louder.

Caught between two enemy forces with a bunch of civilians.

No real place to hide. Now what?

Chapter Eighteen: Captive Clashes

Michelle squirmed on her seat in the LCS Johnbee's combat control center. Just couldn't seem to get comfortable in the spartan naval accommodations.

The new Reaper drone she'd sent ahead of Schnier's helicopter force reached the edge of the island and began sending back signatures of structures, individuals, and vehicles to overlay on the command screen map.

The ship's commander had told her he wanted this one back when she finished with it, but in her mind, better to risk a drone than a helicopter full of rangers.

Ideally, Schnier's teams would drop either near the mountain peak and fight their way down. If that area was too hot for even a fast rope exit, tiny Gozar Air station, closed down at night and on the far side of the mountain, would at least provide a known clear location to let the rangers and SAF representative land.

Gozar also served as the primary pickup location for the mission.

If they couldn't get good intelligence on the tango's mountain hideaway, and thus not risk flying close to the mountain top, their alternate drop zone was the beach. That should provide the longest range if the mountain-top SAM site remained an active threat.

The ship's commander had refused to consider bombing the SAM site from his ship. Something about bombarding another country out where everyone could see being considered an act of war, which it'd be difficult to cover-up, even for the Agency.

Navy pukes! Always sitting on uncomfortable chairs.

Nothing for her to do now but wait.

Her electronic mail diverted her attention. Another missive from Hyo-jin to Sam. She'd have to set that girl straight sometime.

Why not now?

She started a new email. Let's see. Goals for this operation: Make her believe I'm her friend. Convince her Sam is too busy for their long-distance relationship, which is why he hasn't replied. Point out he has a dangerous job, and she'd just putting him at risk with her demands.

That if she really loved him, she'd stay far away from him.

Yeah, that should do it. She wrote the email.

A masterpiece of disinformation.

All for Sam's ultimate benefit, right?

He'd thank her later, if she ever let him know about it.

The drone reached the air above the mountain. Circled to remain on station. Fed back great information. Red dots everywhere.

She zoomed in on where the previous missile had come from. What were the odds they'd acquired more than one?

One-hundred percent, she decided, as a thermal bloom announced another missile launch.

Prepared this time, the drone operator attempted to dodge.

Too close. Not fast enough.

The drone tracked the missile as it approached and then its feed went down.

The ship's commander was gonna be pissed at more lost hardware. Reapers were what, about $16 million each?

She'd better call Schnier, halfway to the island by now, and give him the bad news. Looked like the beach landing and long hike would be the only realistic way to fight their way in.

He deserved to walk, anyway, after their last conversation.

In the meantime, she'd see what she could get about the target using only the ship's sensors. Maybe they'd let her have one more drone, if she promised to keep it out of missile range of that SAM site.

The tangos would have a perimeter set. They'd be expecting

someone, after two nights of drone hits.

Waiting in defensive positions.

Hitting a target blind in the middle of the night was like drawing to an inside straight. Not something you typically wanted to do on purpose, but occasionally the only option you had remaining.

Pahk admired the footwork of one of Omar's men. He skidded around the corner to interrupt their final drink together.

"*Allahu Akbar*! We've taken down another infidel drone."

Omar frowned at the interruption, but then grinned at the news. "Your weapons are getting great use."

Pahk nodded. "It seems you haven't discouraged them enough yet."

Omar shrugged. "Who knows how long they've been monitoring us from the skies. At least now, we can fight back. Make things expensive for them. The exchange ratio severely favors us."

"Their resources are closer to limitless, if they decide to bring them all to bear." Pahk held up his cup of Stainless. "But I congratulate you on your victories over the imperialists!"

Omar stood. "Let's go congratulate our watchmen in person."

"What if this is a prelude for an assault? Might they not be coming to rescue our prisoner? They clearly at least suspect he may be here."

"If not, the practice will help defend against a future genuine attack." Omar turned to his soldier. "Gather the off-duty men. Arm them from the armory and meet us at the entrance to the men's quarters. We'll celebrate on top of the mountain."

Pahk nodded and smiled, but he was more worried about how an assault would impact his departure with the captive and making sure his ride didn't leave without him, rather than about how to celebrate Omar's minor victory over what was in the end, just a machine.

It didn't matter if the jihadists made it through alive, as long as Pahk brought his captive to Admiral Hu.

Raven turned her head like her namesake to isolate the voices in the distance.

They came up the zigzag cavern from the men's quarters. Macho talk from Soldiers of Islam gathering outside the entrance there.

She and Sam looked at each other.

Sam pointed down toward the waterfall exit. "Let's go. Now!"

She led the way through the maze of rock openings and corridors. Followed the path she'd taken with Omar in the past.

Sam stayed right on her heels, peering ahead into the gloom.

The other ten women tracked behind them.

She winced every time one of them stomped too hard, or bumped into another. Way too much noise.

Just before the last curve, Raven held up her hand to stop them all. "The steel door, barred from the inside, is here. Normally at least one guard to let people in. There's an opening where he can see and hear outside."

In fact, she could hear the splash of the waterfall outside.

Sam glanced around the corner. Ducked back. "Too far away for the quiet approach. Much too likely to hear us coming. How plausible is it that you'd be sent outside by yourself?"

By herself? He was kidding, right? "Never."

Shouts from behind them. Near the women's quarters. They'd obviously found the bodies.

Omar's men would surely be here in moments.

"Well, that tears it. Come on."

Sam put his rifle to his shoulder. Turned the corner. Fired twice.

Raven followed, looking for a target. She hadn't grown up in Texas for nothin'. A guard slumped to the ground.

Sam swung his barrel to the left and fired twice more.

The other guard, in the middle of turning around, crumpled to the ground.

"Get the women outside. Up the mountain, not down. Find some place to hide." He took up a position at the corner, where the others could pass him, but he could guard the cave corridor.

"But shouldn't we..."

"Quick! No time to argue."

She led the others out. Unbarred and pushed open the steel door. Slipped out from behind the waterfall. Onto the trail around the pool.

Ten women followed, cowed into compliance by suddenness of the gunfire.

"This will be difficult, but you can do it. Help the woman behind you over the rough spots."

Rather than taking the path around the pool, or the continuance past the waterfall and up the mountain, Raven chose a bare patch of rock to climb on this side of the falls.

She rested at each ledge and helped the woman behind her to climb up. Repeated the action a dozen times to reach thirty feet or so up the mountain.

By the time the oldest woman was halfway up, Sam appeared. Clambered quickly after them. Pushed her the rest of the way.

Above the top of the waterfall, the land evened out. A slight slope, but one where the stream feeding the falls could flow normally.

The frequently used trail to the top of the mountain, easier going, ran along the other side of the stream. They weren't visible from below, but they'd need to remain quiet.

Raven shushed them with a finger to her lips and then motioned them all away from the stream. Pressed into the brush and jungle trees. Thorny, but out of sight from the trail.

Sam lay under a bush next to the cliff. Kept watch.

Raven crawled out to him. Whispered, "Now what?"

He shushed her. Pointed down below.

Pahk and Omar, with about twenty armed men, gathered in a semi-circle on the trail around the waterfall.

Omar pointed back inside the cave system. "You three investigate the women's quarters. See if they're safe; clear the area and then post guards at their entrance and here."

Pahk interjected. "This must be the work of the prisoner, but if they can confirm he's gone..."

Omar nodded. "Send word of what you find."

The three men closest to the waterfall entrance vanished beneath the water.

Raven mimed a hand-pistol to Sam. Mouthed "bang bang" and pointed at Omar.

Sam shook his head. Pointed at his partially empty magazine, and then at her rifle. Held up his ten fingers and then silently counted them down rapidly.

His message was clear. Not enough powder propelled projectiles to get them all. He wasn't suicidal.

"You." Down below, Omar split out two-thirds of the remaining group. "Spread out. Search for whoever did this on your way, but then reinforce the perimeter ambushes. This can't distract us from the possibility of an attack. Those drones didn't send themselves."

"*Allahu Akbar!*" they shouted in unison and then departed at a jog along the trail system.

An attack? I knew Schnier would come for me eventually, but what if they were on their way right now?

Even if Schnier's rangers had to face Omar's mountain fortress without me, right now I had to lead these women to safety.

"The rest follow me." Omar led his jihadists along the trail past the waterfall.

His group hiked up the mountain trail toward the peak, with Pahk, the only one without a rifle, in the rear.

Raven turned back to the group of women, who watched her closely. Once again, she held an upright finger to her lips, and then pointed at the trail across the stream.

As long as they didn't splash across and investigate, they should be safe.

If they made too much noise, Raven and Sam would find out how many remained once they ran out of ammo.

Chapter Nineteen: Captive Battles

Pahk stumbled up the mountain trail after Omar and his men. There was no need for him to be here. He just wanted to take the captive ranger and go.

At this rate, he might miss his boat. How long would that crazy bitch of a boat driver wait for him, anyway?

They were trying to stay covert, not end up in the middle of a firefight.

If this went on much longer, he'd just quietly cut out. He could explain to Omar later. Who was to say he didn't just get lost?

With the stream on their left, the path was steep, but easy to follow. Only a few switchbacks, it'd been designed for mountain goats rather than men.

At least they didn't need to carve their way out of the jungle.

At the top, within the chest-high walls of stone surrounding their redoubt, Pahk slid over to a dark corner near the reloads to nurse the remains of his drink.

He'd brought the bottle and sucked down the liquid courage straight from the lip.

This beat leading conscripts with no rations except a tiny portion of rice back in Korea, but he missed Soju.

Omar scanned the skies with one of the missile tube's passive infrared sensors. He swept the low horizon.

"What's that, Pahk?" Omar turned around to scan for his supplier. "Come here and take a look."

Pahk gingerly stepped across the rocky ground. Checked out

the display as Omar pointed it down the mountain, past the shore.

"Helicopter exhausts. Two different birds, but at extreme range."

Omar handed him the weapon. "Keep it tracking the first one."

Pahk could do this. He did his best work with a little bit of a buzz on. Not the first time he'd been to the range loaded.

One of the men handed Omar the second SAM tube. He stepped to the side. Started it off in the same direction as Pahk aimed his. "Tracking the second one."

Pahk peered at the rangefinder. Eight kilometers. "Just barely out of range. But closing fast."

Omar's teeth shone in the dark. "Now these are targets worthy of my Flying Eagles. Prepare to fire on my command."

Schnier rumbled through the air in the rear of the lead MH-60 Seahawk. Strapped into a harness which gave him limited, but secure, movement around the heated cabin.

He leaned against left-side cabin pillar and watched the water rush past 100 feet below. Ran through their mission keys and time-line in his head.

Visualized flying back with Sam.

Dude would probably insist on surfing back to the ship instead of flying.

Mission review drove Michelle and Raven out of his head.

The shore loomed a couple of klicks ahead.

A klaxon blared from the cockpit. Missile alert!

Larrikowal, seated next to Schnier for easy consultation, clenched his straps.

The pilot threw the helicopter to the side.

Too low for dumping flares to do any good, nevertheless the chunk of regular eviction from the flare launcher showed he followed all the right procedures.

A stream of lights popped and then fizzled into the water.

Schnier spotted two lights rapidly approaching from ahead, each one spewing smoke.

The other chopper was off to their left somewhere. On its

own. Left to fend for itself.

As the missile approached, the pilot flipped directions and dove even closer to the water to pick up speed.

The SAM blew past above them. Tried to dive and turn back. Slammed into the water with a flash and splash.

Schnier looked for the other bird. With the other half of his platoon. No explosion. A good sign?

Larrikowal coughed twice, but kept whatever it was down. He croaked out, "So, we head for the beach landing as soon as possible?"

Schnier ignored him. Called to the pilot. "Any word from the second bird?"

"They're safe. Got their wheels a little damp, but dodged as well. Must've been extreme range. Saw them coming from a long ways away."

"Good. Get us down on the beach before they launch more."

People pay good money for rides like this. Like riding a bull in the arena.

Schnier just kept telling himself that. Maybe it'd be more convincing with repetition.

Once Omar and his men were well past us on their way up the mountain, I stood up and motioned for the women to gather next to the stream.

"It'll be easier to cross here and take the trail back down the mountain than attempt to climb directly down."

The women looked dubiously at the fast-flowing water only a few feet above the waterfall.

Raven tried to reassure them. "I'll go first. If you slip, you'll only end up in the pool below. It's perfectly safe."

I stepped over to the top of the waterfall. Tried to sound confident. "I'll catch you, if I can."

Raven splashed through the water and then took up a position on the trail with her rifle. She knelt behind a boulder and faced the direction the tangos had gone.

Following her example, the rest of the women minced across and gathered on the mountain trail.

The final one across, the cook, still holding her knife, had her feet slip out from underneath her. Flailing, she couldn't catch herself with her hands full and refused to leave either her possessions or her weapon.

I grabbed her robe as she floated past. The fabric yanked at my hand and rode up her back, but to my relief, stayed on her.

All I needed was to have to face an angry disrobed Muslim matron!

I crossed the stream myself. Chose carefully where to place my feet. Picked rough and flat surfaces if possible.

Dragged her along sputtering until we reached dry land and she could wring out her clothing.

I motioned Raven over.

"You know these trails much better than I do, so lead the way. Avoid any guards. We can take to the jungle to bypass a fight if we need to. They'll focus on the perimeter outward, not watch for enemies from behind. I'll take the rear. Anyone who catches us, or Omar's roving patrols, will hit us there."

She stood up. Nodded. Looked at the women. "Don't bunch up. Let's go!" She marched down the trail; back toward the waterfall and pool.

Gotta admire that kind of decisive efficiency.

I watched up the mountain until the cook brought up the rear of the formation and then followed her in turn.

We tracked past the waterfall. Around the pool. Deep into the jungle. All downhill.

Limited noises. The women ahead tried to stay quiet, but they weren't so good at it that the creatures of the broad tall trees and thick palmy bushes didn't notice them.

I didn't mind the smell of rotting plant material, disintegrating over time into the jungle floor. Marching outside gave me a welcome contrast to the sterile dampness of my prison cell.

Not sure I want to go back into a cave anytime soon. Prefer at least a light breeze, if I can't have the surf.

Raven stopped ahead, interrupting my reverie of newfound freedom.

The other women stopped as well, so I passed them to quietly consult with the head of our feminine column. "What's up?"

"The trail splits here. To the left is a boat dock on the river. Might have a watercraft available. To the right the guards will have set up a checkpoint on the trail. It's the farthest Omar controls on this side of the island."

"Forget the river. You don't know if a boat is available. There may be guards at the docks or even father downriver. As I found out on my way in here, it's too constrained. Too predicable."

She nodded and turned to face the other way. "We *know* there will be too many guards on the trail, though."

"Better that than the unknown. Once you're past that checkpoint, you're home free. Or at least, should be able to make the coastal villages. Find a phone. I'll give you a number. Call it. Ask for Michelle. Explain who you are. Where you met me. She'll move heaven and earth to get you out and find out how to get me."

"Aren't you coming with us?"

"Nothing I'd like better than to continue to travel with you ladies, but I suspect a bunch of my friends are about to arrive soon and having me inside the wire will be a big advantage to them. Potentially save some lives. Maybe even your friend Schnier's. So I can't go farther, now that I know you'll be safe. Just continue an easy hike downhill and you must eventually reach the sea."

Raven smiled at him. "Thank you for leading us out. I'm not sure we'd have had the courage otherwise."

"It was all you. After all, you released my chains. Now swap magazines with me. I can use replacements for the shots I fired earlier, and if you need more than those I have left, even more are unlikely to help."

She ejected her mag like a pro and handed it to me in exchange for mine. "Let's go, ladies. Through the jungle now, but in this kind of canopy and walking downhill it won't be long before we're beyond recapture."

"Good luck," I muttered to their backs. "I'm sure going to need a rabbit's foot here."

Turning, I hiked back up the trail we'd descended. Each step combined the torment of aching bruises and the weight of dangling chains.

This was all so much easier when I was heading downhill and away from the fight.

Stealth seemed out of the question, so I moved fast and counted on my observation and reaction times to save me in the event of a fatal encounter.

After all, we'd just passed this way, and no one saw us, so there'd be no ambush, just a chance meeting engagement.

My first move would be to dive off to the side of the trail. Hide in the depths of the jungle.

But no need. I retraced our steps to the pool.

A point of danger. Open area. Close to the waterfall, beneath which I knew guards had likely returned to take up their post.

So now I snuck along the edge of the trail, as one does when hauling ten pound chains on each limb.

Slowly.

I reached the far side of the falls. Crept up the mountain trail.

Two missiles lit up the mountain with their fiery exhaust. Shot away toward the coast. Trailed white exhaust to reflect the moonlight.

Angled downward from the peak.

Must be a target on the other end of that. Friendly planes or helicopters.

No obvious explosions, but their trails stretched below the jungle canopy from here.

I kept off the trail when I could. Edged up the mountain. Used the miniature stairs cut out of rock. Cut the switchbacks to save time. Panted.

Climbing, even on two legs, sucks energy out.

Carrying a rifle was like catching an early morning wave off Point Loma to me, but my chains together weighed as much as a packed ruck.

Much rather be surfing.

Noises above. At the end of the trail. Chants of "*Allahu Akbar!*"

I found a ridgeline. Felt my way along it, perpendicular to the trail. Shuffled sideways. Kept my face toward their voices.

Once I'd reached far enough away to hide, I climbed upward. More difficult without the trail, but the slope was easy enough.

Almost to the true peak, I found a spot overlooking the bad guys.

A rough circle of stone surrounding a clearing where the trail ended. A dozen men focused down and outward. A fistful near two with missile tubes.

Omar and Pahk. They leaned over the edge. Aimed down the mountain. Toward the sea.

At targets carrying friends of mine, no doubt.

I found a flattish rock. Laid down. Focused through the rifle's scope. Mentally adjusted for the distance. Maybe fifty yards.

Tough to miss, but downhill can be tricky.

Made sure once I fired, I could quickly scoot back and have rock once again between us. Too many of them to do otherwise.

Watched their body language. Pahk and Omar argued about something. Omar cursed him out for inaccuracy.

Pahk slurred his words. Handed his tube to another man, who took up position between me and Omar. Pahk sat next to the reloads, his back to the stone wall.

Should I shoot now, or wait to fire until I could get Omar or Pahk in my sights?

The stone blocked most of Pahk. The other man occluded Omar.

They decided for me. Seemed to get a lock. Prepared to fire again.

Couldn't let that happen.

I targeted the closer man. Below the missile tube. Center mass. No mistakes. Limited ammo.

One shot, one kill.

Exhaled. Paused. Pressed the trigger.

Chapter Twenty: Captive Reset

Larrikowal enjoyed a firefight. Had no problems with cover and move, shifting his aim despite adrenaline pounding in his ears, even focusing while under fire.

But helpless in a helicopter? Bounced back and forth as the pilot dodged missiles?

No control at all?

He squeezed his straps and prayed to Saint Lorenzo Ruiz, patron of the Filipino people, that they wouldn't break and cast him into the sea.

His stomach rumbled, but he kept the unfamiliar American food he'd eaten on the ship down.

Schnier sat there unmoved. Stared down at the white-topped waves blurring past.

The Americans flew helicopters much more than the SAF. Couldn't afford the repair bills.

Land rushed forward. A thin strip of beach met towering palms at the edge of the jungle.

Uninhabited. Undeveloped. Unlikely to be directly defended.

Schnier opened the side door. The door gunner opposite took his cue and did the same.

Before they'd even landed!

Two more missiles tore down from the mountain top, seeking their engines.

Saint Lorenzo, save us all!

This time, their pilot didn't dodge. Was he worried about the open doors?

The first missile, the closest, headed straight for them. Fire roared behind it.

Larrikowal listened for the chunk of flares ejecting. Nothing. Just the thump of the four-bladed main rotor.

Were they out of countermeasures?

Seconds from impact.

Larrikowal crossed himself.

The pilot pushed forward on the stick. Cut the power. The chopper dove toward the sand. He flattened into ground effect.

Touched down.

The missile stayed on target. Its aim remained true.

But in the sky, there are no obstacles.

A big broad palm tree exploded. Rained burnt coconuts.

Fiery fronds fell.

Larrikowal exhaled. The jungle was green. The fire would quench itself.

The second helicopter landed next to theirs. Schnier and his men leapt down to the beach.

The final missile passed overhead. Too high to impact anything.

Between the explosion and the jungle canopy blocking its view, lost its lock. Eventually reached the end of its range without re-acquiring anything.

Plunged into the sea.

He unhooked his harness. Followed the Americans down to the sand. Relaxed. Stepped over to Schnier.

"Easy enough, but I'll stay here. Wait for my force to arrive. The pair of patrol boats shouldn't be too long behind us."

Schnier nodded to acknowledge him. Carried on a quick chat with their command center back on the LCS.

"They can't have many more missiles. Already fired half a dozen. Convince him to authorize one more drone. Bad enough we have to climb through the jungle to attack without doing it completely blind."

The other rangers spread out with their weapons. Found positions of cover to watch the jungle and the sea.

Larrikowal tracked the exhaust trails of the missiles back to the mountain peak. They slowly drifted down, but would take a while to completely break up.

Until then, the missile tracks pointed the way to their primary enemy, so he tried to memorize exactly where they touched the mountain.

Revenge would be nice.

Schnier didn't sound happy. "Okay, if that's all he'll do, having one high up and just out of missile range on this side will at least cover our approach to the mountain. Better than nothing. We'll wait for it to get into position. Give more time for the SAF boats to catch up, anyway."

At the end of the trails through the sky, at the place Larrikowal stared, an explosion lit up the mountain.

He tapped Schnier on the shoulder and pointed. "That's exactly where the SAM site is. Where they launched the missiles from."

Schnier grinned. "Change of plans. We just watched the missile site blow up. Send that drone overhead. Assuming they don't shoot it down, we're taking the helicopters."

He cocked his head to listen to Michelle before replying.

"No, if he won't send it overhead, we're taking the helicopters in, anyway. So ask him if he'd rather lose a pair of thirty million dollar machines and their pilots, or a sixteen million dollar drone."

Larrikowal decided he'd continue to stay here and wait for his SAF boats.

Schnier made a circling up motion above his head. "That's what I thought. Relay when it's in position."

The rangers gathered back to the helicopters from where they'd dispersed to provide security.

"Good luck." Larrikowal shook Schnier's hand. "I'll go watch the jungle until my people arrive."

Schnier climbed back into the helicopter and strapped in. He waved.

Better him than me.

Burning coconuts are pretty, though.

My appropriated AK fired as my trigger press interrupted my concentration.

Loud and painful. No ear protection.

The tango with the missile launcher collapsed. Good hit to center mass.

I shifted aim to Omar's beard.

Two of the others reflexively fired full auto into the darkness. Omar dropped out of sight behind a stone wall.

Dratz.

They knew I was out there somewhere, but not where. One shot when they weren't paying attention to my upward location wasn't enough to find me.

No need to relocate yet.

I hunted for Pahk in my scope. Too close. Glanced over the top to take in the entire scene.

The enemy hunkered down. Peered over stone battlements. Watched the dark jungle mountain-side.

Who next? At least they wouldn't be firing at my friends any time soon. So I waited.

Patience is a sniper's best quality.

I counted my heartbeats against the flat rock under me. Calmed them.

Two hundred beats later, a tango ran past the one I'd shot. Left him there. Grabbed the missile tube. Ducked down by the rock wall.

In plain sight from here. He'd chosen the wrong side of the redoubt. The far side was totally exposed.

Locked my cross-hairs on his head. Exhaled.

Paused. Pressed the trigger.

Head exploded.

My eardrums rang with the shockwave.

The rest shifted. Turned their heads to find the source.

I didn't wait. Slid back on my belly until out of sight. Hustled a dozen meters around a rock formation. Used it as a partial shield. Leaned forward to examine the flat, cleared area surrounded by rock wall.

One trail in and out. Omar left the clearing. Hustled down that trail. Carried a missile launcher.

Pahk followed after him. Held a missile reload over his shoulder.

I shifted my aim to catch them.

They jogged away. Turned a corner.

Vanished.

Too late.

I sighed. Shifted back to the redoubt. Found a new target.

Another tango took advantage of my movement to grab the remaining missile launcher. He moved across, hidden by the rock wall closer to me.

Next to the stack of reloads for the weapon. Stood up next to them. Aimed at something in the sky.

Got a lock.

My cross hairs floated past his body.

I fired one shot. Short on ammo.

The bullet tagged him in the shoulder. He pulled the firing lever. Fell to the side.

His missile launched horizontally into the sky. Away from their previous shots. Other side of the mountain.

The exhaust lit his foot on fire.

And the boxes containing the remaining reloads.

I ducked back. Behind rock.

The clearing exploded. I got just the reflection. Plus the sound.

Multiple detonations.

The full force hit the jihadists.

Don't use your fighting position as a magazine for storing explosive devices, no matter how convenient it may be.

I moved because paranoid is better than dead. Turned around the other side of the rock. Watched them burn.

The tangos closest to the explosions were gone. Vaporized into ash, no doubt. At least painted the rock walls.

Those farther away ran screaming. On fire.

The smartest one stopped. Dropped to the ground. Rolled to put out the fire.

I shot him.

The rest ran in terror until they collapsed.

Put them out of their misery?

Short on ammo, but the fire was short on fuel. Not much remained to burn in the dirt and rock clearing.

I slung my rifle. Bounded down the hill like flowing down a wavefront. Drew the katana.

They didn't even see me. It was like slaughtering pigs.

I finished them all, the stench of burnt flesh and voided bowels in my nose.

Where did Pahk and Omar go? Chasing Raven?

The adrenalin of the fight wore off. Dude, my legs were sore.

The rumble of helicopters filled the distance from down the mountain.

Must be friends or allies. Right?

Once Raven saw the other women were past the perimeter jungle guards, she instructed them to just keep going downhill until they reached the sea.

Sent them ahead without her to find rescue. Gave them the name and phone number Sam provided to reach help. Told them she'd catch up later.

She owed Sam that much. He shouldn't have to face the enemy alone, and she carried the other rifle. Knew how to use it.

Wouldn't mind using it on that fascist Omar.

Besides, she'd be careful.

So she snuck back through the jungle. Uphill. Exhausting, despite her fitness.

Didn't get lost. Avoided the guards in the darkness. Found the trail again.

High on adrenaline.

She snuck up the trail. Stayed by the edge. Flitted between the shadows of the trees.

Reached the edge of the pool. Heard the splash of the waterfall. Watched the current it created in the water.

Footsteps on the path ahead. Low male voices. Then two large shapes. Men, carrying some kind of long tubes?

She raised her weapon. Couldn't miss from here, but didn't want to kill someone she couldn't be sure was an enemy.

So she waited for them to get closer. They'd have to step out from the shadows as they approached, clear of the trees.

The top of the mountain exploded. Briefly blinded her.

Illuminated her for them.

She threw up her hands instinctively. Blocked out the light.

Blinked her eyes to clear them.

Omar reached her first. Clubbed her rifle away with the metal tube he carried.

Pahk arrived next. Dropped his load. Grabbed her arms.

Omar ripped her rifle away. "So, I've found you again, my Songbird. What are you doing out here? Where are the others?"

Pahk slapped her. "Did you release my prisoner? Is that him on top of the mountain?"

Raven cringed away from them. Sat down. Refused to cry.

No tears. Not for Omar.

What an idiot she'd been to return! At least the other women would escape.

Omar glared at Pahk. "Don't dare to strike my woman. *I* will discipline her."

Pahk puffed out his chest. Slurred his words. "See that you do. She's almost cost us everything!"

One of Omar's men stepped onto the trail from the jungle. Pointed at the sky. "Look!"

A rhythmic thrumming filled the jungle. New ripples in unfamiliar shapes spread from one side of the pool to the other.

Two helicopters flashed overhead, a machine gunner in each door.

Omar hefted his missile tube. "Restrain her while I destroy our enemies."

Pahk grabbed her arms. Shook her.

The copters flew past too quickly for Omar to track them. They vanished behind the mountain.

What would they find up there?

Pahk had a suggestion for Omar. "The missiles seek heat sources. It's expensive, but you can use them against ground targets with an infrared signature to track. Like up on the mountain top."

Omar nodded grimly. "I understand. Perhaps we can redeem the situation after all."

Chapter Twenty-One: Captive Revenge

Schnier flew with the doors open. He secured the thick braided rope next to him with his heat-resistant gloves, ready to fast-rope from the helicopter.

The *Rangers Lead the Way* philosophy meant he'd be the first to jump out.

Michelle spoke in his ear, "Cowboy, flames on the IR, but not many signs of life near the top. Best bet is to land as planned, clear the area, and then assault from the high ground."

"Roger that, BB."

His tactical computer, strapped to his side, where he could flip it up at a glance, showed a view from the drone circling high above the battlefield. It confirmed her words, but also marked individuals at the dark pool below as well as groups set in ambush around the perimeter of their claimed area.

Too bad Schnier's platoon was about to bypass all those defensive formations and drop into their midst.

Their bird cleared the curve of the mountain. Approached their burning LZ, surrounded by rock walls. Tilted upward to a forty-five degree angle in order to rapidly kill forward momentum.

Leveled out. Descended to five meters.

Schnier and the ranger next to him tossed the bundle of rope out the open door. It attached inside the roof.

He gripped the rope.

"Go!" from the crew chief.

Schnier jumped. Clamped on, just hard enough to slow for safety, but fell fast enough for friction to fry the surface of his gloves.

Bent his legs near the end. They absorbed the ground impact.

He dodged to the side, one of his men controlled-falling right above and behind him. He ran to face outward and set security.

More followed his example as Schnier checked out their unresisting target and unstrapped his sniper rifle. "On-target."

Dead enemies. Burnt.

As the last man hit the ground and cleared the bottom of the rope, the helicopter crew chief pushed bundles of supplies out the side. Food and water, sure, but also cases of ammo, Carl Gustaf anti-tank rounds, mortar shells, and the heaviest of them all, a Modular Advanced Armed Robotic System (MAARS).

Padded for protection, the MAARS would require a little setup work, which the heavy weapons guys could take care of later, but having their own M240B machine gun and quad-barrel M203 grenade launcher armed ground robot might be the difference between life and death in tight quarters on the assault.

Closest thing to a portable unmanned tank available.

The crew chief detached the rope and let it tumble to the ground. Their bird tilted forward to speed away.

It would secure their primary exfil point, nearby Gozar Air Station, while the second Seahawk dropped the rest of his rangers here.

One man carrying a scoped AK at the ready stepped from the shadow of a rock wall.

Schnier instinctively raised his rifle and then lowered it as recognition dawned.

"Like a cockroach, aren't-cha?"

Sam stuck out his hand. "Glad to see you too, dude."

Schnier shook his hand, but also grabbed him in a manly hug for the length of three pats on the back, squishing their weapons to the side.

"No reason to worry, then."

"Naw. Everything's under control. Still, could use a ride out of here."

"This your work?"

"They asked me for a light. Wouldn't have been polite to decline. Plenty more out there for you, though. I'm not greedy."

Schnier flipped up his tactical screen. They'd drawn notice from the perimeter players, who'd sent at least some of their numbers back toward the mountain center. "I see that."

Sam pointed at where a path down the mountain led to a pool. "That's the heart of the operation. Cave complex behind the waterfall."

Schnier nodded. Tapped his transmit button. "Ball-buster, initial target secure, but we found some surfer here who is pretty destruction prone. Condition green. You want to claim him?"

Michelle exhaled into her mic. "Roger that, Cowboy. Marking objective ocean complete. Give him a kiss for me."

"Negative on that last." Schnier shrugged and released the button. "She's excited to hear."

Sam held up his wrists. Showed Schnier his chains. "More on my ankles. One of your dudes got the platoon's breaching bolt cutters handy?"

What'd he been through? Had to be a story there, but it'd need to wait. "Sure, our pleasure to help you get dressed this fine morning."

Schnier gave the necessary orders for his men to get Sam's chains clipped and then showed him his tactical screen.

Sam studied the screen, all business now. "Let's set an over-watch on the pool area and send a few of your dudes down to secure the area. That's where everything else meets together. From the pool we can keep the tangos split-up and from here we can protect their flanks."

"I'll defer to your local knowledge."

"Good, because I'm not sure I can hike this mountain again just now."

"You MI weenies always were out of shape."

Schnier gave his platoon their orders and tagged Sam to spot for him while he set his Stoner's bipod up on top of the rock wall next to the trail down the mountain.

Two pairs of his rangers remained behind to snipe other areas down below from the other two points of their triangle. Could cover almost the entire area of the mountain's sides this way.

A fifth man, his usual spotter, handed his scope to Sam and got to work stamping out the remaining fires before they spread.

Great location for a fort. Probably why the tangos chose it.

His, now.

Time for battle. Standing to get the correct angle for his Stoner down the mountain, he seated the butt into his shoulder. "Set."

"Three, no make that four, targets visible on the far side of the pond." Sam checked his viewfinder. "Approximately 625 meters, downhill. Target is standing in front. The others are together behind and to the left of him." He adjusted his spotter scope to zoom in.

"Contact." Schnier found the target Sam described. Ignored his men pounding down the trail. Needed to clear the objective of enemies before they arrived there in a couple of minutes.

"Go to glass."

Checking through his scope, he saw a narrow, but detailed view. "Target carrying a launcher. Just above the water. At 10 o'clock, two more."

"That's your target. Omar! Check parallax and mil."

Schnier adjusted the knob on his scope for maximum clarity. Paused his breathing to steady the man in his cross-hairs. "Ready."

"Check level. Hold over, five point four."

He shifted aim slightly higher to adjust for the distance. "Ready."

Sam paused as he double-checked his ballistics computer. "Wind left point four."

Omar shifted the point of his aim. The gaping maw of the missile launcher faced directly at their position.

Would the lingering heat from the explosions and fire provide an infrared lock?

Schnier shut it out of his mind. Focused on Sam's tiny adjustment for the wind.

Pressed his trigger.

Crack. The bullet immediately went supersonic. Flew down

the mountain.

Omar's side exploded. He dropped the launcher. Collapsed.

"Good hit. New target, 10 o'clock, three meters."

Schnier shifted his view. Adjusted for clarity again in his optics.

Raven! Held by a short Korean?

"Raven? What the hell, Sam?"

Sam took a deep breath. "And Pahk. Guess I should've mentioned that part already." He looked through his better optics. "They're staring at Omar. Pahk's restraining her. Not going for the missile yet."

"I'm not shooting her."

"Good, because she's on our side. That's how I escaped. No idea why she's back. Should've been at the beach by now."

"Must've caught her. He'll kill her when my men arrive. Or they will."

Schnier got back on the radio. "Three tangos, one down, with female hostage across the pool near the trail. Repeat. American female hostage. Do not risk her."

"Roger that." Crackled through.

Michelle jumped in. "Perimeter groups are moving in toward the pond area to re-group. We need to hold it for this to work. Just take the shot, Cowboy."

"Negative. High value hostage." At least to him. "Let's see if we can't force a surrender. I'll be right down."

He picked up his Stoner. Flipped it over his shoulder. "You've been down this trail before. Lead the way."

Sam groaned, "Don't remind me!", but he grabbed the spotter scope and his AK and descended the beaten mountain path with a sort of bound-hop-slide combination which moved him faster than a rodeo clown dodging a bull's horns.

Schnier followed more like a herd of turtles, with short steps and slides. "What, are you surfing mountains now?"

Sam increased the distance between them with continued reckless abandon. "Falling with style!"

They cut down switchbacks, ran across rocks, slid over carved steps. Anything to reach the bottom sooner.

The trail turned into a straightaway. A stream flowed next to it.

Schnier's men completed their earlier, more cautious deployment where the trail passed by a waterfall.

Sam hit his full stride as he reached the turn in the trail where it departed from the stream.

No way he'd stop in time at that speed.

Instead, he dropped his equipment at the edge of the trail. Unlike him, *it* skidded to a halt.

Sam lengthened his stride. Turned his chin sideways. "Set up here. Listen for my voice." He faced forward just in time to dive into the end of the stream.

That momentum combined with the current to wash him over the waterfall hands and face-first.

Screwball surfer!

Chapter Twenty-Two: Escape Trick

I meant to rescue Raven from Pahk. Diving over the waterfall seemed like a good idea at the time.

Splashed into the pool of water below, off-kilter from the force of the descending stream. The sound of the normal rapid pounding should disguise my entry.

Reached the rock bottom. Pushed off. Stayed under as long as possible. Swam blindly across.

Pictured their location from the memory of my spotting scope.

Tangled my arms in long green stalks. Traced them upward. Giant lilies. Hadn't noticed them in the dark.

Lifted my head above the water to peek.

No Pahk. No Raven.

Just Omar's launcher, abandoned in a splash of blood-stained earth on the trail next to the far side of the pool.

Too late.

I treaded water to the edge of the pool, my previous effort wasted.

Cupped my hands in front of my mouth to form a makeshift funnel. "Schnier, bring your men down. They're gone."

Climbed out of the water. Panted on the rocky trail and my need for oxygen caught up.

What would happen to Raven?

Could she survive?

Raven jerked her head up at the shot from above. Where did

that come from? Sam?

Omar collapsed to the dirt trail. His launcher slipped out of his now-relaxed grip.

Pahk grabbed her left wrist. Twisted it behind her in some sort of karate grip.

Pain flooded her arm. She stood on her toes to reduce it.

Omar's other soldier rushed to help him. Checked his pulse at his thumb. Took off his shirt. Bundled it up. Pressed it into his side to slow the bleeding.

She tried to turn.

Pahk prevented her from moving around with minimal effort.

She was bigger than Pahk. Taller. Why couldn't she fight him?

All she needed to do was delay them until whoever took that shot arrived.

Pahk grunted to the soldier, "Carry him with us to the river."

Raven's arm pivoted, turning her body as if it had a mind of its own. She marched down the trail, away from the pool of water, away from safety, following the river at Pahk's unspoken command.

The other soldier hefted Omar over his shoulder. Staggered down the trail after them.

With no way to escape, no way to even relieve the pain at her wrist, Raven trudged forward.

Pahk leaned closer to her ear. "Don't worry, I know the Americans, they won't put you in danger. Too weak to do what is necessary."

She tried to stumble. To bow forward and force Pahk to release her arm.

He merely bent forward as well and then grabbed her hair from behind to lift her body. "None of that!"

She sighed. Complied. Tears ran down her face.

So close to freedom! What an idiot. Again.

They reached a short river dock. A camouflaged Chinese missile boat, at least twice the width of a normal speedboat, sat silently at the ready.

Pahk shoved her aboard. Into the arms of a uniformed sailor.

She kicked. Screamed.

He dodged. Hit her in the face.

Her nose gushed.

Pahk wasn't amused. "Control her, you idiot. Tie her up or something. Don't you sailors know knots?"

Two more of the crew dog-piled her. Restrained her arms and legs in order to tie them to loops built into the boat.

Pahk carried Omar aboard. Lay him out on the deck, partially protected from the weather. "Get this man a medic."

A female sailor approached them. Held her head high. Must be in charge. "You said one passenger, an American male, not these two."

Pahk looked down his nose at her. "They're both coming. Both important. Admiral Hu will want them both."

She hesitated, as if this change of plans didn't compute in her military mind. "Very well. Your responsibility."

"Of course."

The boat pilot turned to her sailors. "Cast off."

One flipped the final cable from the pier.

Raven wished she knew what Pahk was getting her into.

Disconnected from the dock, the pilot fired up the engines. Pressed her dual throttles forward. Twisted the wheel with the knob built into it for that purpose.

Sped them down the river, the current aiding their progress.

Shouts from behind. American soldiers at the dock. Was that Sam with them?

Too far to tell for sure before they vanished behind a river bend.

I pounded down the trail into the jungle. Gasped for breath.

Schnier led the way, despite my greater familiarity.

Guess Omar's torture and the trips up and down the mountain took more out of me than I thought.

Five of his men followed, weapons out, packs dropped with the rest of their platoon back at the pool, not used to their captain taking point.

I recognized a few, had worked with them before, Spec 4 Watkins, a great cross-country runner, among them. He blew right past me. I tried to give encouragement and directions from behind. "Stay on the trail. Not much farther!"

Three others passed me when I slowed. I became the second to last man running.

Sergeant Madsen, the last guy, felt he needed to guard our rear. At least, he kept looking back and around at the jungle, as if a jihadi terrorist could pop out at any moment.

To be fair, they could, but Schnier and I didn't care just now.

Madsen carried a light machine gun over one hefty shoulder and a case of ammo in his other hand, but I insisted to myself that I wasn't so beat up by Omar that I wouldn't have stayed ahead of him even without all that.

After all, we'd made it through Ranger Selection together and I'd been much faster back then.

The path split ahead. One route tracked along the flowing water. The other trailed deeper into the forest, toward the beach.

My side ached. Chest burned. "Follow the river!"

Schnier went left. Pointed the three men after Watkins to divert right. "Recon only. Report any contact."

He could've at least had the decency to gasp a little.

I followed the river-bound pair.

After another minute of jogging, just the two of us remained. Madsen and me.

Schnier and Watkins outpaced us. Faded into the jungle ahead.

"Need me to carry that?" Madsen pointed at my AK.

"Shut up and run. Did you know ranger is another word for dung-hole in Tagalog?"

He smiled.

We caught up to Schnier where the trail dead-ended at a four-foot floating river pier.

A PLAN Houbei class missile boat spat water out its twin rear engines. Curved around a bend in the river.

Too big for us to engage, anyway.

Schnier looked at me. Pointed as it vanished. "She was on there. They all were."

I held my side. Gasped. "Air... support?"

He tagged the boat on his tactical map. Requested drone

coverage from the LCS.

Called some Filipino dude on the radio. "Still on the beach with your men? Good. Call your boats back. Sending you an intercept course. Head for the mouth of this river. Got a Chinese missile boat coming out."

Who the hell was he talking to? This was supposed to be a covert deployment. Under the radar. Non-attributable. No local contact. Nothing official, upon pain of international incident.

Whoever was on the far end confirmed his readiness to interdict the unofficial Chinese invasion of his country.

"American hostage aboard, so don't just blow them up. Intercept and detain."

"They got away with your captured soldier?"

"No, a civilian woman. Very important we protect her."

"On our way."

Once Schnier hung up with the locals, Michelle jumped on the circuit. "Cowboy, who's this high-value hostage you're been chasing?"

Uh-oh. Not sure how Michelle was going to react to Schnier chasing his ex-girlfriend around with her resources. She'd made it clear enough after their arrival in the Philippines when he started asking around about Raven that her whereabouts weren't a CIA priority.

Schnier paused before answering. "Sam discovered that the spotter in Manila is an American female. Probably brainwashed or something. Married to and abused by Omar. Anyway, she's why Sam escapes. Turns out her name is Raven."

"Your ex? That Raven?"

"Small world, huh? Now we know why she vanished. Married into a jihadi terrorist organization. Been trying to get away and then Sam showed up."

This time, Michelle paused. "We'll talk about this more later. Gather up your little posse and head back to that central pool. Whole bunch of jihadis on their way to take your scalps."

He looked at his tactical display. Showed it to me. "Roger that, ball-buster."

The mass of red dots swarming toward our sprinkling of blue positions in the middle looked like a school of angry piranha at feeding time.

I nodded to Schnier. "We'd better walk back. Save our strength for when they arrive. Got any spare mags for an AK?"

Already knew he didn't.

Chapter Twenty-Three: Escape Scrape

Pahk hoped the boat driver bitch was as good as she thought she was.

They'd crossed under the bridge over the river near the coast and then fled the river mouth for the open sea when she'd pointed for his attention to the surface radar screen.

Two short lines moved fast; angled toward them from the east.

"What's that?"

The 40 knot headwind carried his words away, but she read his lips enough to reply. "Patrol craft. Judging by their speed, Shaldag Mark Fives. The latest thing in the Filipino coastal fleet from Israel."

"Can we outrun them?"

She turned the wheel to point west, now that they'd cleared the northern tip of Lubang. Aimed their twin-bows toward the Spratly Islands.

"We'll stay ahead of them. But without rougher seas, which work to our advantage, we won't escape them. They'll track us to the fleet."

Pahk looked back. Couldn't spot their opponent. If they were back there, they were too small for his eyes.

"Thought this was supposed to be a stealth model. If we're just a radar blip to them, can we discourage them with a missile?"

"It is, but that applies mostly to sound. The quiet jet propulsion instead of screws. Not modern radar. I'll pretend you didn't suggest that last. We're not authorized to start a war."

"Admiral Hu won't be excited that you're leading them right to his fleet."

"This is your mission, I'm just driving the boat. Perhaps you should contact him with an update? Get new orders before we run out of sea room or fuel."

Raven sat against the back of the boat's cabin, exposed to the elements, but protected from the headwind. She gripped the ropes locking her in place against the boat's bounces and skips with white knuckles.

Would Admiral Hu actually want her? If not, then at least she'd be easy to dispose of at sea.

Perhaps he could keep her in his cabin for his personal use.

A PLAN medic stabilized Omar inside the cabin. He was becoming more of a liability as well, despite his jihadi army and contacts.

Still, they were the only bargaining chips Pahk possessed. He too, might be considered a liability.

Had to consider the lives of his sister and mother back in Dalian. They lived at the PLAN port only under Hu's continued sufferance.

Based on Pahk's continued usefulness to the CCP.

He stared at the radar display. Tried to make sense of it. Tapped the screen. "What's this larger surface contact?"

"The Americans. Not moving yet, but they're just as fast as either of us, despite their size. Wouldn't worry unless they launch more air assets or move to intercept."

The three forces formed a triangle, with their fleeing ship farthest west.

"I'd better call the Admiral."

"Yes, you'd better."

Just had to figure out how to spin these events to him first.

Larrikowal much preferred the way their new Shaldag Mark V fast patrol craft cut through the sea over the American's bouncing helicopters.

It helped that the waves were mere ripples on the water.

He wished they could go faster, though. Schnier sounded desperate when he'd called for help.

Larrikowal sent his force cautiously inland to support the Americans and round up any jihadi stragglers under the control of his senior sergeant, but at Schnier's urging, taken command of the sea pursuit himself.

By the time he'd recalled the pair of ships which had dropped them off and returned their landing boat to load it up on the back, the Chinese naval vessel turned the corner on the northern tip of the island.

Now, all they could do was chase and track them.

He radioed the spy lady aboard the American LCS. "We're not gaining on them."

Frustration in Michelle's voice. "There's an American citizen being held captive on that boat. Captured on Filipino soil. Isn't there anything you can do?"

"They won't escape, but we can't stop them without launching a missile. There's no way we can create that sort of international incident. Would give China too much of an excuse if we started something. Besides, the hostage wouldn't survive blowing them up. What about your drone?"

"It carries a pair of missiles, but same problem. Not like we can target everyone except the hostage, and the optics of Americans sinking a PLAN warship aren't great."

"Our remote control fifty cal mounted on the front is stabilized for accuracy. We could fire a warning shot, then shoot to disable their engines, but we'd need to be a lot closer for that. Any way to delay them? Cut them off?"

"Even if I could get the captain of this hunk of junk on the move, he won't start a war either, and we're even more out of position than you are."

The boat under him skipped up from an especially large wave. Still better than a helicopter.

"I don't know what to tell you. We can follow and track them via surface radar, but they're ten meters longer and carry more fuel than we do. Eventually, we'll refuel and lose them, unless they go straight back to their fleet."

"Might as well track them from the air, then. It's not like the

Chinese fleet cruising the Spratly Islands is a mystery. We already know they're out there. This missile boat will go running home."

Larrikowal frowned. "I'm going to break off pursuit, then. Return to Lubang. Remember our deal about sharing information. Securing our systems."

"I remember. I also know Schnier is in the middle of a firefight with an army of jihadists surrounding that mountain."

"So does that mean you'll tell him the bad news?"

"Yeah, I'll break it to him."

Good. Larrikowal respected the American captain and didn't want to be the one to tell him of their failure.

Schnier ran back to the central pool and waterfall. Took one man with him. Always travel in pairs. Left Sam and the others to set an ambush on the river trail behind them.

According to his tactical computer, courtesy of Michelle's drone and the MI platoon's support and analysis, that'd interdict one of the approaching enemy formations.

Only left two more groups for the rest of his platoon to deal with. At least they'd already taken out the central defenses on the top of the mountain.

The ability of his snipers to reach out and touch each group of attackers as they approached, before even in sight of his defenses, provided his rangers with a tremendous tactical advantage.

Now they just needed to ambush and execute.

And remember that the tactical plot wasn't foolproof. Not like their intelligence element couldn't miss someone here or there under the jungle canopy.

Still, Sam's platoon was on the ball in providing tactical intelligence, despite his absence.

Schnier chuckled. Or maybe because he'd left them behind. Have to save that one and tell it to him later.

Assuming they all survived this.

His radio earpiece filled with Michelle's voice. "Cowboy?"

"Go ahead."

"The PLAN boat is just as fast as our pursuit boats. We could destroy it before it got out of range, but that won't get your friend back. I'm sorry."

Raven was lost to him? But he'd just found her! Even if their only contact was through a sniper scope.

He'd known something was missing. That his life in the rangers, his relationships, were lacking something. Some higher purpose.

At first, he thought it only related to their role as protectors. As companions in arms, rather than alpha bulls.

He didn't realize before seeing her again, before losing her, that the hole dug into his heart was Raven-shaped.

Schnier couldn't lose her again. Wouldn't lose her again. He refused.

"What about air assets?"

"They can't stop them, just destroy them. Nothing we can do short of starting a war with China."

War with China? Not a bad idea, in his present mood. He took a deep breath. Triggered his mic again.

"Track them from the air, at least. Once I get out of here, back to the LCS, I'll expect Sam and his platoon to figure out a way for us to retrieve her. For now, we have a battle to win."

"Roger that. Go get 'em."

"Rangers lead the way. Cowboy out."

As much as he wanted to chase after Raven, his mind needed to be here. The Ranger Creed required that "Never shall I fail my comrades."

He tallied his assets. He'd left three sniper teams up in the mountain fort, plus one ranger to provide local security and coordinate.

Sam led four on the river trail.

He'd arrange five more to block each of the approaching groups. With advanced knowledge of their approaches from the drone overhead, they could bushwhack them in coordination with the sniper teams.

That left a ten ranger command and reaction element, including Schnier. They'd stay central. Respond to either join a firefight and sweep the enemy away, or else provide a tactical reserve if anything didn't go to plan.

Once the bullets flew, something always refused to follow the plan.

Chapter Twenty-Four: Escape Ambush

I hoped the tangos had never heard of Major Rogers.

One of his standing orders issued to his Rangers in 1759 was to never march home the same way. Instead, take a different route to avoid ambush.

Time for an ambush.

I found a section of the river trail where it followed a curve in the river bank. Water on one side, dense jungle brush on the other, the trail itself only wide enough for two men next to each other.

Only five of us, so limited firepower.

I'd traded my AK to the ranger who returned with Schnier for a trusty M4A1 carbine and a trio of 30-round magazines of 5.56mm cartridges.

Not enough remaining ammo, otherwise.

According to Michelle's drone data, we could expect a dozen tangos to come traipsing down the trail, with a lead element of one twenty yards ahead of the rest.

No way we'd catch them all, but we just might stop them from reuniting with their buddies near the pool and waterfall.

I had one M240 gunner, Madsen. He and his assistant carried two cases of belted ammo between them.

Plenty for a single ambush with a medium machine gun. We'd make do.

I had Madsen setup just past the turn in the trail. In the bush, but where he could target right down the trail itself.

He'd form the lower limb of our L-shaped ambush.

Sent his assistant off with his carbine to provide security twenty yards farther up the trail behind him.

The enemy point-man would need to walk past our machine-gunner if we were to catch enough of the rest in our designated kill zone.

His assistant could warn us against unknown forces from farther up the trail, but really I counted on him to take out the point man before he could flank our machine gunner once he opened up on the main body.

Two more men with M4s and grenades. Light from packing into a helicopter for this mission, doubly light from haring off on our running adventure to catch Pahk and Raven. We'd left the rest of the heavy weapons dudes back with the central HQ group, along with the snipers.

I sent Watkins twenty yards the other way down the trail. Led him before. Knew him. Trusted him.

Smart.

He'd pull security in the jungle where we expected our enemy to arrive from.

Barely within sight of the trail, we just needed a radio click when they arrived to warn us, and then he could take out any stragglers.

He'd also be the first overrun if they got smart and sent scouts through the brush rather than following the trail.

Couldn't be helped. War has its own little risks, after all. Even if they shot him first, that'd provide its own warning that our ambush was blown.

The last gentleman of the gun and I spread out to catch the long L portion of our kill zone in a crossfire converging on the machine gunner's arc of fire.

Madsen could take the entire straight portion of the trail under fire, and swivel to take out anyone using the river as cover.

All three of our fire zones overlapped from different angles to form the kill zone. We needed as many tangos there as possible when this kicked off.

We settled into place to wait.

I found a nice boulder, half-embedded in the jungle soil, to rest my rifle on. It'd give me a little bit of cover from return fire.

Otherwise, I lay in six inches of dirt brown foliage, partially concealed by stems carrying long thin green leaves, but able to spot down the clearer trail.

As we became one with the forest, the normal wildlife started up again. Birds trilled to each other. Insects buzzed, looking to party.

Something rattled off to my side. Unlike the hills of San Diego, this place didn't host deadly rattlesnakes. No, probably just an insect rubbing its carapace. Innocuous. Non-deadly.

Not like us.

Pahk kept his voice low into the boat's microphone so neither the pilot bitch, nor his prisoner, could hear him well.

"Admiral, Omar's American wife freed the ranger prisoner. A company of special operators hit the mountain camp right afterward. She probably communicated with them this whole time. I took the initiative of securing her as a prisoner for interrogation. Omar's men will melt into the brush after killing as many imperialists as they can and then regroup later. I've also brought Omar out with me, as he's wounded."

"Speak up, Pahk. I can barely hear you. Why not simply leave Omar to his fate? What are we going to do with an American Muslim woman? Are you out of your mind?"

This wasn't going even as well as Pahk envisioned as the worst-case scenario. Time for damage control.

He tapped the microphone to create an excuse and then pressed it closer to his lips.

"We can still use Omar. He is now firmly on our side, as his hatred for the Americans grows. A deniable and now more reliable weapon for you to influence events locally over time. His soldiers will return. His influence will grow within the country. He has contacts at the highest levels of their government."

"*We* have contacts at the highest levels of their government. None higher, in fact. However, I'll think on it. At worst, we can drop him in the sea. What about the woman?"

The boat chose that moment to skip off a wave instead of plowing through it. Pahk glared at the boat bitch, who ignored him to smile toward the horizon.

"She's both Omar's wife, and thus important to control him, but the Americans may also trust her. Surely it's worth finding out her exact dealings and relationships with them before we hastily waste her as a resource?"

"Send her photo and vital details to Comment Crew. Maybe they can come up with something we can use."

"It shall be done as you order, Admiral."

The sun would rise behind them soon. Maybe he could get sleep before facing the Admiral in person in a few hours.

At least the surface radar showed that the enemy boats had broken off their pursuit.

He'd gotten away clean. If only he had a bit of soju to drink closer than his ship locker. Might clear up this headache.

Schnier needed to get back onto a horse. He sat on a rock near the top of the waterfall, but the ache in his rear-end reminded him he spent more of his time ruck marching or jogging, not sitting.

His ad hoc ten man quick response force lay scattered along the cliff, weapons ready. From here, they could defend the more central pool area, but also rapidly join any of the ambush teams who needed assistance.

Not sure his three-man mortar section would see much use, but he'd had them pre-register their M224 60mm mortar to cover the trails into the pool area, anyway.

Never hurt to have too much firepower covering for you.

Meanwhile, he waited for the rodeo to begin. Passed the time. Stared at his tactical computer.

Ruined his night vision.

Couldn't help it. His job was to step back from any firefight enough to direct the entire battle.

Prevent surprise in their ranks. Inflict it on the enemy.

The three sets of outlying blue dots on his screen settled into familiar ambush shapes. The same maneuver practiced in one form or another by rangers for hundreds of years.

Three strings of red dots, tracked by drones hovering high in the early morning air, trailed toward them.

They wouldn't all reach at the same time; the first ambush may trigger more caution in the others, but his rangers would prevail.

If not, the ten of them, including the mortar, plus the sniper teams up-mountain, would intervene.

But what had he missed?

As if to answer his question, one of the red strings vanished from his display. The single file group which had been following the trail leading to the other side of the waterfall disappeared one by one.

Where'd they go? Some sort of advanced camouflage to hide their heat signature? But why just then? Why there?

They hadn't reached the planned ambush yet. Not even close.

He tripped his radio. "You see that?"

Michelle's voice filled his Invisio X5 noise-canceling and amplifying ear pieces. "Wait one. MI guys are analyzing."

Great. Just great.

They'd lost track of at least a dozen killers.

Chapter Twenty-Five: Escape Denied

One click in my ear from our security element, Watkins.

Instinct told me to hold my breath so the enemy point man didn't hear it.

But I needed oxygen for the fight ahead, so I kept it slow and steady. Besides, he crept along the trail at least ten yards away, visible only through thin fronds and dark green leaves.

I tried to project my thoughts at him, without actually staring, so his subconscious didn't magically pick up my gaze.

This is the thousandth stretch of jungle you've looked at tonight. No different from the other nine-hundred and ninety-nine.

Just trees and bushes. Nothing to worry about.

The night birds fell silent at his approach, but the buzzing insects ignored him.

A trickle and splash as the river beside the trail ran over rocks and slowly carved into its bank.

He stepped lightly. Avoided any piles of leaves, fallen sticks, or out-jutting branches. Anything which might give him away, if we weren't already watching for him.

Reached the bend in the trail. Where the river curved and Madsen lay silently with his machine gun back in the bush.

Proceeded out of sight past the turn without so much as a glance at him.

The next ten trudged loudly in comparison. Shuffled their feet, heads down. Glanced only at a murmured word from their companions, otherwise watched the trail.

Didn't want to get caught in the brush, or slide off into the river.

The front of the single-file group almost reached the curve by the time the last one entered our kill zone.

I tracked the fourth man in my M4's scope, big as a wave off the north shore.

The ranger to my right whispered, "frag out!" into our radio headsets as he tossed a grenade. That was the signal for all hell to break loose.

Madsen opened up on the lead terrorist. Walked his fire down the line to his second target.

The immediate confusion in their eyes turned to terror as comprehension dawned.

My companion's grenade detonated at the end of the line. Caught two of them close enough to fill both with high-speed metal fragments.

The fourth man in line dropped to the trail. Unslung his rifle.

I shot him twice in the head.

An M4 double-tap echoed from farther up the trail. Madsen's assistant.

That'd be the last of their point man.

The other five dove for the river bank. The closest cover not closer to the source of their death.

Madsen's lance of fire from his M240 nailed the closest as he rolled over the top. He didn't stop before hitting the river.

Their last man, pulling rear security, and thus out of our kill zone, stepped behind a v-shaped tree. Opened up on the bushes and trees at the turn of the trail. Sought out Madsen from long range; used his muzzle blast to track him.

Watkins, farthest from us, who'd given the initial warning, shot him from his flank and behind.

One of the four hiding along the river bank tossed a grenade.

Boom! It peppered the trees between me and Madsen with metal.

He shifted his fire to enfilade the bank.

They couldn't hug it close enough. Another screamed and died.

"Surrender! Toss your weapons to the trail."

The remaining three did as commanded, their AKs arcing into sight to thud into the dirt.

I toggled my radio. "Cease fire. Cease Fire. They've surrendered."

Three splashes in the river, like a cannonball into a swimming pool.

I stalked forward to their rifles, M4 ready to hit anything suspicious.

Three tangos swimming with the current. No weapons visible.

I raised my rifle to get a better look through its scope, but wasn't about to shoot unarmed fleeing men.

"They're gone. Let's pack it all up and move out. Back to Schnier."

The SAF would need to interdict those three. Shouldn't be difficult, not with them missing their long-range weapons.

I'd call it in.

Larrikowal listened as Lieutenant Harper described the men fleeing his ambush.

"Roger. We'll take care of them."

He and his small SAF force floated up the river in a pair of rigid rubber rafts.

Normally stored ready to launch on the back of their deep drafting fast patrol craft, they provided a way not only to board ships interdicted at sea, but also an option for shallow inland-waters like this river.

He knelt in the front of the lead raft, rifle at the ready. Maria led the other raft behind them.

They began drifting toward the bank.

"Andre! Straighten us out. Keep us pointed up the middle of the river."

That guy was useless, even for just steering. Wasn't even wearing his helmet.

"Roger that, captain."

They slid back toward the middle current. Overshot. Edged toward the other bank.

Larrikowal gritted his teeth. If he said anything else, he was liable to shoot the man, or at least relieve him of duty.

A buzzing sound, like a hornet, flew past. Pops in the distance to their left. Splashes around the boat.

Their course shifted. Headed directly at the left river bank.

Fifty meters beyond the bank, muzzle flashes exploded from the firing ports of a concrete bunker covered in earth and brush.

Larrikowal ducked. Got as flat as possible without entering the water. "Contact left!"

No infrared signatures. No warning from above of their river fort.

He'd have to re-evaluate their night assault procedures in the future to not rely quite so much on drone night vision scouting.

At least Andre was taking them to the bank, which would provide cover while they disembarked. Had to give him credit for that.

The boat didn't slow. Just rammed up on to the bank.

Good thing it was designed for rough landings!

Larrikowal used its slowing momentum to jump from the bow. Collapse on the bank, head in the enemy's direction.

With no enemies immediately visible or threatening, he looked for better cover to move to. Something with a field of fire overlooking where the shots came from.

"Fire and maneuver!" he ordered.

Maria's boat arrived twenty yards downstream from his boat. Came to a gentle stop on the bank.

They had the more experienced driver.

The rest of his force followed his example, although some of them needed to drop over the raft's rigid sides into the water and then wade ashore.

Except Andre. Andre sat with one hand on the outboard motor, a bullet hole leaking blood in his forehead, the back of his skull missing.

That FNG! How dare he?

Schnier raised Sam and Michelle on the radio. Sam breathed loud and fast, hustling down the trail after his successful ambush.

The other ambush went almost as well. Those ten rangers

weren't moving quite as fast in their return to the central waterfall area where Schnier waited for them. They had one wounded, a stray AK-round in the lower leg.

He'd survive, but needed to be carried.

His final ten rangers, designated to ambush the tangos who vanished from his tactical display, held in place as a blocking force until further instructions.

Schnier needed to figure out where the enemy had gotten to and how to counter-act them.

Fast.

"Surfer, why do you think those tangos are missing?"

Sam spoke between breaths as he ate up the distance at a jog.

"Not enough light for anything but infrared, so they're inside or behind something. The jungle canopy isn't thick enough to hide someone for long. Must be underwater, a cave, or some other type of underground structure."

Michelle piped in. "The SAF mop-up force is getting hit hard on the river from a perimeter bunker. Neither their drone nor ours spotted the occupants before they began firing."

So maybe a bunker of some kind. But why there? Partway between their established perimeter to the north and this central pool?

"Where they went to ground, does it overlook that side of the mountain? What's the strategic or tactical advantage of siting a bunker there? Of a defensive position so far from their perimeter guards?"

"Crap!" Sam must've come to a conclusion. "It's not a bunker. It's an entrance to the cavern complex inside the mountain. Nothing else makes sense. They didn't take the trail back because it's quicker and easier to cut through the middle, instead of going around the outside."

Michelle interrupted. "But they took the trail on their way to reinforce their northern perimeter."

"You only spotted them going out that way because they started on top of the mountain. Didn't make sense to go back to the caves and then through when they could just hike down the north face directly. But they're not coming back up the mountain, they're coming through the caves. Could be right underneath you, Cowboy."

Last thing he needed was a surprise assault from inside the mountain. Even if they just stayed put, how were they going to flush them out without more casualties?

Why had he wanted his own independent command again?

"Surfer, best speed up your return, unless you can guarantee me their only way to exit those caves on this side is the door under the waterfall you showed me."

"Just warn the sniper teams. Only Raven would know how many alternate exits exist and she's not exactly available."

Sam's subtle reminder jabbed a spike through Schnier's heart.

Before he could respond, Michelle broke in again. "We have the other women she sent us secure on the beach. I'll task someone to get details on the cave complex."

"The rest made it out?" Sam sounded hopeful, even if Schnier wasn't just now.

"Called me from the village to announce their escape. SAF sent the local police to take care of them."

"Tell them to ask the older woman. The cook. She's been around the longest."

Schnier needed to focus on the here and now. "Get your team back here, Surfer. Going to need to consolidate and redistribute the platoon to guard from all directions while we wait for more info. SAF won't be here anytime soon, either."

"Roger that, Cowboy. Running towards the next fight as fast as I can."

Chapter Twenty-Six: Escape Caves

Keeping to a reasonable jog-walk pace, I returned to the pool with my ambush team simultaneously with Schnier's other rifle squad carrying their wounded ranger.

Besides the ten-man blocking element Schnier left in place to deal with the vanished tangos, the whole band was back together again.

Schnier met his wounded on the trail just past the waterfall. Checked on his leg.

I joined in. Officers visits were always good moral support for the troops. Not only showed them we cared, but reminded them they could take us out any time we got too annoying.

He'd live. Even keep the limb, so not too bad. One more purple heart in the platoon.

Schnier motioned me, his platoon sergeant, and the rifle squad leader for my ambush team, off to the side.

Handed me his tactical display. Leaned on a boulder. Took off his helmet. Ran his fingers through his ginger hair.

Michelle had marked the cave entrances on the electronic map of the mountain as best she could from the intelligence provided by the former cook. No non-combatants believed inside.

They'd all fled together with Raven.

Still not sure why she'd been caught and the others hadn't. Did she try to return, thinking she could help me somehow?

Schnier replaced his brain bucket. "We need to go in there after them. Can't just leave 'em hanging around, ready to spoil our party. Normally, we'd have multiple robots to take the lead, the squad behind ballistic shields, oxygen and chemical sensors. Fast-roping onto the mountain leaves us a little light on extra toys. Just one MAARS. Ideas?"

The squad leader scratched his cheek. "CQB, just like a shoot house. Clear the caves room by room."

His platoon sergeant shook his head. "Pretty linear environment. You'd think it wouldn't be tougher to clear than a house in Fallujah, but doctrine is to avoid clearing subterranean environments for good reasons. Too many opportunities for traps and ambush. Maybe we just contain them until SAF takes over?"

"Not many doors, just the steel one under that waterfall." I pointed. "I've been inside. It's pure stone in there, marble and granite. So no over-penetration, but also lots of ricochets and no easy way to flank rooms rather than use a single entrance. Very predictable approach. Fatal funnel after fatal funnel."

Schnier took the tactical display back. "Note the additional cave entrances here and here. We must either push them out and ambush them after they leave, or else catch them between us. SAF is still dealing with their own issues, so this is up to us for now."

His platoon leader rattled an M18 smoke grenade dangling from his harness. "Smoke 'em out?"

I shook my head. "We'd have to either advance through the smoke, or else wait for it to clear. Either way, worse for us than them. Might work to hit the other exits with smoke, though. Keep those dudes bottled up."

Schnier nodded. "Dual grenade entrance. Frag and concussion. All combatants, so no risk of collateral damage. Waste of ordnance, but there's more in our ship lockers. Guess we can spare some."

He paused. Looked around. "Don't break the MAARS. Those little tanks are expensive. And you can't use its four grenade launchers indoors. Too much risk of bounce-back."

His attitude had certainly changed now that he needed to account to the bureaucracy for everything expended in combat or training.

I knew the feeling. Korea had been expensive. "Better costs than casualty reports."

"Ain't that the truth!" Schnier stared over at the ranger with the hurt leg and then stuck his finger in the face of the squad leader. "No more casualties. I mean it!"

The squad leader fought down a smile. "Roger that, sir."

I pitched in one more piece of bad news. "Lots of short rooms and corridors. Invariably exposed to the next room. Better if we push the MAARS ahead and just keep going until we reach a securable position. That's assuming we intend to clear the cave complex rather than just contain the tangos inside."

Schnier frowned. "What do you mean 'we', surfer-boy? This is for the professionals. You can follow behind and collect any intelligence which survives our operations."

I grinned. "I'm the only one who's actually been inside there before, remember? You need me to explain the layout and answer questions, unless you want to rely on third-hand notes from a civilian."

His platoon sergeant pitched in. "He's got a point, sir. I already know you're going to leave me out of the fun and make me run things on the surface while you go play cave clearing Casanova. Might as well drag the MI guy along. That way when his intel is wrong, he'll be right there to take the consequences."

Schnier muttered something under his breath about glory hounds and how Michelle would kill him if he let her pet surfer get hurt again, but didn't contradict his senior NCO's analysis of the tactical situation.

Guess I got to go risk my life with the rest of these dudes, after all.

Larrikowal kept his head down. The defenders in the bunker had them pinned behind the river bank with periodic potshots over their head and into the water.

"Maria! Stay here. Lay smoke. Provide a base of fire. Make them nervous that your squad is coming in the front door. We'll go for their flank."

His senior sergeant nodded to acknowledge her orders. "Roger." She shuffled a little closer to the top of the bank and began collecting smoke grenades from the rest of her squad.

Larrikowal decided their right flank, the one inside their perimeter, would be the least defended and most accessible. He organized his remaining half of their force, four men, and led them into the water.

Couldn't be helped if they were to remain undetected until it was too late.

They waded next to the river bank. Kept their weapons high and dry. Short steps, only shifting their weight once their forward foot was secure on the edge of the river bottom.

He led the way into the slow current, one foot at a time. Round rocks. Sucking mud. Tangled weeds.

Slow progress, but enough.

As they departed, Maria began arming and tossing her squad's smoke canisters upwind from the enemy bunker's face.

White filled the air between them. The enemy's fire expanded, as if they could keep them at bay by filling the obscured air with bullets.

Larrikowal edged into wire netting, attached to a post embedded in the river bank and set just under the water level.

Good thing they didn't hit that at speed in the boats!

No easy way underneath, so he crawled out of the water and lay on the bank. Inched his way forward, past the netting, and then slid his legs back into the water.

Pointed it out to the man behind him, so he could do the same. "Pass it on."

Turned upriver to continue. Moved faster now. He'd have to risk his footing.

The smoke would eventually dissipate. The enemy would lose interest. Get nervous that Maria's force hadn't assaulted them yet.

Wonder what else might be going on. Couldn't have that!

He reached a slight bend where the water cut into the bank's curve. A broad-leafed tree jutted almost over the river, its thick roots exposed by the water eating away soil.

This would have to do. He held his rifle in one hand and crossed himself with the other. Looked back at the string of soldiers behind him in the water.

Pointed at the roots, and then at the top of the bank.

They nodded silently.

He slung his rifle over his shoulder. Needed both hands for this.

Grasped a pair of exposed roots. Dug his soaked boots into the bank.

Climbed.

Boots on roots. Hands dug into the topsoil.

Lifted. Grabbed a branch. Pulled.

Used the thick tree trunk for cover.

Smoke ahead and to the left marked the front of the bunker, where it faced Maria's squad. A string of trees and brush led from his position to its upstream flank.

This might actually work!

Flashes from the bunker's firing ports marked their attempts to suppress her.

He helped the next man up behind him. Made sure the rest were moving. Pointed at the side of the bunker.

Ran along the tree-line. Dodged bushes. Partial cover and concealment. Safe as long as they didn't notice him.

Maria's smoke in the air helped conceal him from the enemy.

He stopped opposite the bunker's side. Twenty meters away. A low door, thick plywood, set into the ground at the bottom of dirt steps.

Caught his breath.

His four men arrived behind him. They stacked up behind a tree, ready for an assault.

Larrikowal tossed his own smoke grenade. Landed it just past the corner, in front of the bunker.

The signal.

Maria's squad opened up with everything they had. Poured fire into the bunker's front.

Distracted the occupants.

He sprinted forward. Four men on his heels.

No defensive fire.

Adrenaline pounded in his ears. He calmed his breathing.

They reached the side of the bunker. One man placed a breaching charge vertically on the door. Another reached around the corner and tossed a grenade into the opening. "Frag out!"

The rest of them ducked behind the concrete block backside.

Two explosions, almost in unison, one inside, the other penetrating where the door's hinges used to be.

Larrikowal spun back to the door. Pounded it down with a slosh of his boot heel.

Shot the first man he spotted moving inside.

The next enemy moved in slow motion. Raised his rifle. Aimed it directly at Larrikowal. The barrel gaped open.

Pakshet!

Schnier stood with his back against the rock cliff. Flipped his NVG down in front of his eyes. Activated the IR illuminator to see better in the dark.

The waterfall overhead poured down, obliterating sounds. Sprayed mountain spring water into the air. Not enough to soak, but refreshing, like from a spray bottle in the rodeo stands.

He held up three fingers. Showed them to the lucky squad leader who'd been in on their planning, and then to Sam, opposite him next to the vision opening for the corridor behind the waterfall's hidden steel door.

The squad's Alpha and Bravo Teams, four rangers in each, waited just out of the blast zone.

Sam pulled the pin on a round M67 grenade. Held the spoon tight against his palm.

The squad leader similarly readied a Mk3 concussion grenade. Even deadlier within solid enclosed spaces.

His demo guy removed the dust cover from his two ignition system switches, each separately wired to electric blasting caps; long, thin metal pencils embedded in the C4 cutting charge on the door.

Alpha Team stacked up behind Schnier, ready to push forward once they blasted the way clear.

He silently counted them down by closing each finger in turn. Three... Two... One... "Execute!"

"Frag out!"

"Fire in the hole!"

The demo guy clacked off his electric triggers; the cutting charge detonation drowned out all other sound.

Boom! The charge cut out a man-sized hole in the center of the door, which dropped inward.

Excellent precision.

Two more loud pops as the flash bang and frag grenade exploded.

Thank Uncle Sam for active ear protection!

A rattle of metal fragments ricocheted off the stone walls inside.

Watkins, the first ranger through the hole in the door, flowed right, his back to the stone wall. He scanned for targets to eliminate any threats.

Schnier exercised his privilege of rank and entered just behind him. Checked past the two tangos crumpled to the floor just inside the door. Flowed left along the wall with the opening they'd thrown grenades through.

No live targets. "Clear!"

This space near the door was barely a large closet with a couple of stools. The rock corridor led on, uphill into the dark, with a curve ahead.

The squad's next two rangers entered in turn. Moved deeper into the room. Their M4's IR targeting beams stretched out ahead of 'em.

No sparkle in the beams to indicate tripwires.

Both IR beams stopped and focused on two man-sized shapes on the floor.

Sam appeared from behind in the cut-open steel doorway. "Those two dudes ahead are dead. Shot 'em earlier on the way out."

The closest ranger to the body, Watkins, kicked at one. No movement. "Clear!"

Madsen, the Alpha Team lead, who Schnier had temporarily displaced in their stack, pushed past Sam in order to take up a protective position forward.

He'd traded in his trademark machine gun for a lighter M4 carbine in order to stay light for this one.

They'd secured this entranceway, but based on their intel, the next climb would contain a series of zigzag corridors.

Rangers don't like to walk into fatal funnels, the path from entry to defenders where the assaulter is most vulnerable, prefer to create 'em for others to walk into.

"Foothold established." Schnier pointed at his demo guy. "Bring up Robbie. Harper, make yourself useful and help him out."

It would be all uphill from here. Literally.

The demolitions tech scrambled around the waterfall to where they'd left the single available MAARS.

Sam followed behind him. "Sure, make the engineer do the grunt work and play with the robot..."

Schnier would take mustangs and bulls over fancy electronics, any day.

Sam was unlikely to agree on that one.

Chapter Twenty-Seven: Escape Complete

Time stopped. Larrikowal dropped prone. Gravity took forever.

His enemy inside the bunker tugged at his trigger. Fire and burnt powder exploded out the barrel.

Over Larrikowal's head.

His next SAF soldier pushed through the now open doorway. Shifted to the right side, fired. Double-tapped. Knocked the closest enemy down.

Then the next soldier, in and to the opposite side. Made sure of the one remaining standing target, who'd survived the fire and grenades by being farthest from the bunker door.

Their enemy sprawled across the river gravel floor. Blood soaked into the crevices between tiny round rocks.

No more life.

Larrikowal hoisted himself up on his squishing feet. Turned back toward the riverbank. Cupped his hands. "Clear. Cease fire!"

Maria peeked her head over the top of the bank. Motioned her squad up to safety.

They climbed up on top of the bank.

He slowed his breathing. Lowered his rifle. Walked back toward Maria, through of the dissipating smoke.

Now they just needed to lift their boats up over that wire barrier and proceed inland.

Reinforce the American rangers. Mop up whoever remained

in this jungle.

But perhaps he'd alternate a couple of soldiers jogging ahead on foot to scout each river bank while the rest relaxed in the boats.

Just in case their drones missed someone.

The first light of true dawn cracked the horizon through the jungle foliage and reflected from the river.

Now they'd *all* be easier to see.

Michelle disliked the ship's combat information center. No privacy. Nobody she really wanted to talk to.

Officially morning. She'd been up all night sitting at this table.

With lousy navy coffee designed to blacken her insides rather than please her sophisticated palate.

The XO and his boss avoided her. Schnier was off rescuing Sam. Sure, they'd broken up, but even the Filipinos had abandoned her to hit the beaches.

Just a few sailors and Sam's ranger intelligence analysts in here.

She was pretty sure they didn't like her. Maybe even blamed her for losing Sam. As if she had any control over his actions lately!

Definitely blamed her for this mission. For needing to pack up in the middle of the night, torch their precious equipment, leave behind half their belongings to burn along with their comfortable beds.

In exchange for what? A crowded berth with resentful sailors who already lived in too little space.

It's not as if they'd like her more if she tried to explain it was all their lieutenant's and captain's faults, not hers.

She forced herself to smile at the room. Tilted her head up. Stared at the combat information board which covered the far wall.

A Filipino AWACS cruising in a racetrack pattern above the western islands shared data. Tracked the People's Liberation Army Navy missile boat racing away from Lubang Island.

Maybe it'd lead them back to the PLAN fleet. Make that connection as official as a secret finding could be.

Could even get Schnier's ex-girlfriend back.

Michelle wasn't sure about that one. She'd apparently helped Sam get out, but also been the jihadi's spotter in Manila. Not to mention landed Michelle with a bunch of work resettling female Muslim refugees.

Knowing Sam, that was probably also his fault.

This Raven chick might pull Schnier away from her permanently. As much as Michelle hated to let anyone go once she'd wound them around her finger, it was for the best.

Had she ever seen herself with Schnier long term?

No, it was more of a fling. Thrown together by work, destined to end in a crash and burn.

Her lifelong friendship with Sam was the deeper connection. If that Korean giraffe backed off, as she'd advised.

She shook her head. Whipped her hair around at high speed. That chick had nothing on an agency pro!

Back to work.

The big board showed the SAF unit moving cautiously up the jungle river. Most of the way to the dock at the end, where they'd unload in order to reinforce the rangers.

An outrigger ferry carried more Filipino soldiers across the sea. They'd arrive on Lubang Island in a couple of hours to help mop up the tangos and secure the area.

Larrikowal's boss backed *him* up.

If only her deputy director back in D.C. did! At this point, she was lucky if he even talked to her, let alone tolerated her.

She'd need to figure that one out before this was over.

For now, with American lives at risk, he'd backed off, or at least hadn't completely pulled their naval support.

Best to stand and stretch. Go get breakfast.

Nothing important could happen for a while, right?

She caught the eye of the Duty Chief. "Send for me if something new pops."

"Aye, aye, Ma'am."

The sky lighting up outside did little for us inside the cave. Strictly artificial illumination deep underground.

I unfolded the hard-case built to control Robbie. It's pop-up lid contained a display to relay video from his camera. The case itself contained the electronics for an array of knobs and other controls.

Turned a key in the middle of the console to fire up the electronics.

One joystick in the case controlled the movement of Robbie's two tank-like tracked wheels. Another aimed his weapons.

Red covers protected a pair of toggle switches in the center of the case from accidental activation. I'd leave those down unless I needed to fire his weapons.

Might use the machine gun, but Schnier had disallowed firing grenades from the little guy. Too much range in too small of a space.

The EOD tech finished rigging Robbie up. He fed a case of belted 7.62 into the M240B machine gun and locked it in place. Turned it on and made sure the dummy-lights indicated a secure connection to my console.

Gave me a thumbs up. "Ready to go, sir."

I glanced back at Schnier, where he ran our incursion from the entryway. "Ready?"

"Execute."

I drove Robbie down the rough stone corridor and around the curve. Forward-facing cameras on top in the center, machine gun barrel mounted on the left, four-barrel grenade launcher on the right, his treads clung to the floor's irregularities like a champ.

Needed to consider his five-hour battery time. No spare MAARS nor battery for them, so if he ran down, we were done until I could get him a charge.

Four members of the squad's Alpha Team followed about fifteen meters behind Robbie. Led by Watkins and Madsen, they stacked up with their M4s and stalked down the cave's center to avoid any wall-following ricochets.

The screen showed the same corridor on the other side of the curve, and then the uphill zigzag maze I'd traversed on the way out in the distance.

Schnier wandered over to watch our recon. I kept the weapon switches covered. Flipped on Robbie's audio feed.

The zigzag is where our approach got nasty. A narrower path, nowhere to hide, ninety-degree turn after ninety-degree turn.

Robbie's attached air sensors reported good quality, so no danger there.

"Keep going." Schnier couldn't help a little bit of micro-managing.

"Relax, Captain. We got this."

I focused on the screen. Moved Robbie around the first sharp turn. Scanned the area with his cameras.

Nothing.

Two more corners, the same. No sign of the enemy.

Watkins followed; Alpha Team right behind. They stayed a corner behind Robbie.

When they were far enough forward, their squad leader trailed them behind the next corner, ready for support or to call them back.

The four Bravo Team rangers trailed behind him in a similar stack. Kept their distance to minimize exposure.

Two more turns to the junction cavern above us. The one where paths diverged between the women's former quarters on the same level and the men's living and working area up above.

There'd be more light there from the tango's clumsy-looking electrical work on the ceiling.

I pressed the joystick forward. To the side. Turned the next corner.

Robbie took immediate fire. Muzzle flash on the screen. The camera's view shook with bullet impacts on his body. Echoes of an AK snapping and rattling trickled out to us.

Schnier leaned forward over my shoulder. "Weapons free."

I already had the cover for the machine gun lever lifted forward. Out of the way.

Centered the targeting pip on the screen over the enemy muzzle flash. Pressed the now exposed toggle switch forward in short bursts.

Brrpt. Brrpt. Like a chain gun.

The muzzle flashes and accompanying echoes ended. When the cameras refocused, one tango was down. He'd fallen to the cave floor partway behind and in front of the corner.

This really wasn't fair, but then, war wasn't meant to be.

Watkins, the farthest ranger forward, called out an anti-climactic, "Contact forward!"

"Keep pressing."

I glanced up at Schnier. "Dude, speed kills. Go too fast and we might miss something. They'll be there."

He didn't like that *at all*. "Lieutenant, *I'm* not worried about the robot. It's just a hunk of junk as far as I'm concerned. But if you give them a chance to set their defenses, we may be in for a long fight and need to expend real ranger bodies in my platoon to dig them out of there. So move!"

"Roger that."

His command, his orders.

I pushed Robbie up to and around the dead tango.

The ranger squad crept behind. Kept their spacing by the book.

After the turn, I took the next corridor at full speed. Didn't wait for anyone to take Robbie under fire.

The cavern opened up on the screen. One guard knelt behind a tipped-over table in front of the tunnel to the women's quarters.

Near where I'd been chained like a slave. An animal. Tortured by Omar.

Suddenly, my soft tissues ached again.

From the direction up in the men's tunnel, someone fired what sounded like a fifty-cal.

Work the problem. One at a time. I lay the pip over the guard behind the table. Toggled the firing switch.

Brrpt. Tore through the table and the guard.

A warning light flashed on the console. Robbie's grenade launcher was immobile. Damage to the motor.

I spun him right. Charged him forward at high speed. Fired on the run at the machine gunner to keep his head down.

Brrpt. Brrpt. Brrpt.

A sparkle in the infrared display just ahead.

Tripwire!

Boom! A long roar. Explosion in the ceiling.

Debris rained down. Rocks and electrical parts. Flowed downhill toward Robbie and Alpha Team.

They'd placed a bomb at the central apex of the cavern!

Robbie's camera feed cut out. Black. No signal.

The rumble of the explosion and collapse trickled down to us. Wipe out.

Schnier gasped. "Where's Alpha Team?"

I stood up from the now useless console. "Hopefully, far enough back."

We sprinted forward. Up the corridor. Through the maze.

Caught up with Bravo Team, choking on the rock dust.

Coughed, myself. Air filled with flying particulates. I pulled my shirt over my lower face.

Hadn't exactly come into this with my full equipment load. Last night, I was a prisoner here.

Missed my issue mask, though.

Everyone else put theirs on.

Squad leader took charge of Bravo Team. Got them shifting rock.

They pulled boulders down to clear the corridor just around the next corner. Almost to the cavern where Robbie presumably lay crushed.

The blocked passage before that. Where Alpha Team would've been, waiting to follow the robot.

Out of the direct blast, but within the rock slide after the ceiling collapsed. All four of them, including Watkins and Madsen, stacked together for mutual support.

Schnier turned back to me, his normally ruddy face ashen. "Get help. Medic. Tools. Whatever you can."

I nodded. Turned to depart as fast as we'd arrived.

He bent his back. Grabbed a boulder two-handed. Pitched in to help clear a path.

We'd been raked over by this one.

I ran.

184 | Thomas Sewell

Chapter Twenty-Eight: Escape Rocks

Who could he trust with this info?

Secretary Dorenza lifted a Fighting Cock cigar out of the walnut humidor on his desk. Smelled it.

Good scent. Not too firm. Not too tightly packed.

Excellent.

He pulled a baby guillotine out of his desk drawer. Slid the end cap of the cigar between the blades, right up to where the wrapper began.

Thwack. Clipped the end off with one solid motion.

He'd like to do that to the President's neck, but his oath of office to their constitution restrained him.

As a gesture of good faith in their agreement, or more likely to convince him to approve Captain Larrikowal's initial request for the SAF to assault Lubang Island along with them, their American intelligence contact sent over an encrypted package of data they'd already sorted and collected.

Not the methods they'd used, although those would come soon, but the culled and refined intelligence they'd produced before the SAF forced them out of their resort.

Dorenza had read Larrikowal's report with his veins throbbing at their arrogance.

He scraped a long wooden match alight. Rotated the foot of his cigar to warm the tobacco. Put it in his mouth. Sucked air through it. Lit the foot.

He needed this ritual of relaxation. Concentration.

The Americans delivered. He'd only glanced at the internal

government documents in their package, but he'd read enough to know their explosive potential.

For a politician running for President against the now officially almost martyred Speaker of the House, about as explosive as if China nuked Manila.

He couldn't process it all alone, but who could he trust with it?

Perhaps no one inside the government. The President's party surely had their spies in his defense department. Maybe not as many in the military, but at least parts of the police force. People whose bread was buttered by his political opposition.

Should he turn to his political staff? Those running his campaign?

No, some were really consultants, not patriots, and the others weren't legally cleared for this sort of information.

He took a long, slow drag of the cigar. Made sure not to inhale, before blowing the smoke across his office in a perfect ring.

What comes around, goes around, but who could he trust with proof of the President's corruption?

If any Alpha Team rangers remained alive, Schnier had limited time to get air to them.

Come hell or high water, he wasn't fixin' to let today be the first time he lost soldiers under his command. Not at the hands of those damn terrorists.

He'd work 'em all git-out, dig up this pile of rocks, until he found them all.

He hefted another stone boulder. Hauled it back and to the side. Dropped it on the downhill pile he and Bravo Team built from the rubble in the cavern ahead.

Schnier and two others formed a human excavation chain. Rotated to get a grip on the next stone puzzle piece, and then out of the way to haul it off.

Their squad leader squatted next to the rubble. Dug smaller debris out of their way. Shoveled it two-handed through his legs. Another of his men tossed it to the side, light enough to throw rather than carry.

The cave remained cool, its temperature regulated by the underground stone masses, but he perspired freely. Worked as fast as possible.

Sam returned with a pair of combat medics. The demo guy. Four more rangers from his HQ squad.

Schnier dropped another boulder. Stepped to the side. Let a couple of the non-tired rangers replace him.

Panted. "No explosives. Too risky."

The demo guy held up a shovel. "Just came to dig."

He replaced the squad leader's manual efforts. Lifted shovel-fulls of detritus and tossed them across the cave.

Waiting with Sam and the squad leader was like rolling around in cacti, but the new men weren't as gassed. More effective to allow them to work until he recovered a bit more.

Besides, after leading Alpha Team into this mess, he didn't deserve the relief of manual labor.

Sam fired up a powerful flashlight. Turned the gloomy cave into day. Cast the remaining shadows to the side. Aimed it between the rocks.

The fresh team continued their efforts to uncover their brothers. The pair of medics worked to unroll and get stretchers ready.

They'd surely need 'em.

Their digging revealed the bottom of a boot. Then a calf. The ranger's legs.

Flat on his face.

Schnier pushed forward. Pitched in again. Removed debris from the man's back.

His squad leader arrived. Cleared him off. "Medic!"

He rolled over. Coughed. Doubled-up. Couldn't speak, but he pointed at the next man, whose legs he'd covered. Rested his chest on. His face between.

The two medics piled in. After a quick check, moved him out of the way. Poured him water to clear his throat. Checked his vitals.

Sam and Schnier worked together to clear rubble off the next man's back, who'd also fallen forward.

A moment later, when they reached his head, he pulled it out on his own. "More!" He pointed beneath.

One of the medics escorted him out of the way. He walked easier, his legs protected by the first ranger.

Sam nodded as he passed. "We know. Madsen and Watkins are in there."

No stoppin' there. Schnier handed rocks to Sam. He passed them off to the others. The demo guy, all corn fed two-hundred fifty pounds of muscle, shoveled like his pants were on fire.

They cleared another three feet.

Madsen was almost as big as the demo guy. More rocks on his back. Others slid down as they removed them.

Definitely tough enough to survive this. Right?

Unlike the first two men, his leg rested at an awkward angle. Blood soaked the ground. Bone protruded.

They uncovered Madsen's broken leg. He screamed beneath the rubble.

Schnier gritted his teeth. Kept working. Couldn't leave him there. Especially not with Watkins ahead.

They cleared the scree and fill from off his back. Uncovered his head, tucked into a pocket of stone, and thus protected from the sides and above.

Lucky.

A medic jabbed Madsen with an ampule of morphine. Calmed him down. Strapped a loose tourniquet around his thigh.

Carefully turned him over, stabilized his knee and lower leg in their arms. Lifted him on a stretcher.

Dragged him away while he rested, babbling about Watkins.

More to clear. They worked like robots now. Quick, efficient motions.

One more remained.

Let Watkins be alive. That's all Schnier prayed for in his heart. To find him alive.

Sam uncovered his side. He lay closer to the wall.

Schnier cleared off his legs.

A boulder rested above his head. The demo guy swept everything off of it with his shovel.

Sam and the squad leader combined to pull the boulder back,

away from the wall. Away from Watkins.

He lay there, unmoving.

Schnier looked away. Anywhere but at the broken body of this ranger under his command.

What had he done?

Sam leaned over Watkins' back. Ever optimistic.

"Medic!"

Pahk stood at attention for Admiral Hu. At the Admiral's order, his ride had dropped him off on the PLAN Destroyer which served as his flagship.

The PC Admiral paced across his opulent flag cabin with his arms behind his back.

Pahk waited for his fate to be determined.

Hu stopped. Turned. Gestured to the table he used for staff briefings. "Sit."

Pahk relaxed. Moved to the indicated chair and sat.

He might survive this debacle, after all.

Pushing a buzzer, Hu asked a question Pahk took as a command. "Tea?"

"Of course. Thank you for your hospitality, Admiral."

A steward poked her head through the doorway. "Admiral?"

"Tea for two."

"Right away, sir." She slid back out into the passageway. Rolled a cart through the hatch.

Well prepared.

A red baked clay teapot, the sides covered in subtle thorn bush designs, the lid in rose buds, rested on an oversized square and shallow matching bowl. Two dull red teacups and a pair of similar snifter cups occupied the bowl's corners.

A red cloth with gold-threaded borders covered the top of the cart.

She reached beneath the cloth and removed a jar of tea. Lifted the pot's lid. Used a small wooden spoon to scoop long leaves of Oolong tea into the pot.

A worrisome turn of events. In a navy which ran on face, what had he done to deserve this honor, however abbreviated?

Pahk didn't trust unexpected good fortune.

Hu stepped over to join Pahk. Sat across from him. Smiled. "You've given us the excuse we need to finally rid ourselves of troublesome neighbors."

She removed a glass kettle full of roiling water from the cart's lower shelf. Poured water over the four cups and the pot to properly warm them.

Unsure what he meant, Pahk remained respectfully silent. His chest and cheeks felt the steam's heat.

The steward lifted both the pot's flower-covered lid and the kettle. Holding the kettle at shoulder length, she poured a stream of hot water into the pot until it barely overflowed.

She scooped bubbles and an excess tea leaf from the top of the pot in order to replace the lid securely. Poured more water onto the covered teapot to ensure the internal and external temperature remained the same.

Hu acted as if her performance was an everyday occurrence for him. Perhaps it was.

"You've been out of touch, but Comment Crew connected your female prisoner with one of the imperialist rangers. Based on archived social media posts, they lived together at university in their state of Texas. Both collegiate athletes. Rodeo and football for him. Gymnastics for her."

The steward gracefully flipped over the four cups to expose their mouths.

Hu leaned forward. "Our analysis is that he will want to come for her, even if she weren't an American, even if she hadn't helped the other soldier escape. A valuable hostage indeed."

Pahk nodded. "May I inquire as to your plan for the imperialists, sir?"

She removed a red tea pitcher from beneath the cloth. Smoothly poured clear brown tea from the spout of the pot, filling the pitcher and emptying the pot.

Poured tea from the pitcher into the two snifter cups. Covered the mouths of the snifter cups with those of the full size teacups.

Bent in a bow as she rested the warmed paired cups in front of each officer.

"To destroy them, of course, along with their allies in the Filipino government's forces. They intend to share intelligence.

Unite against us. We can't let that happen."

Pahk and Hu took their pair of cups in both hands. Flipped them over quickly. Tea splashed from their snifter cups into the teacups.

This action brought prosperity and happiness to guests. Pahk could use both, but would take either.

The steward lifted their cups to continue the ceremony. She discarded all the previously made tea as unfit for their consumption. Poured more heated water from the kettle into the teapot.

Re-used the same leaves. Paused this time to allow them to steep inside the enclosed pot.

"I will provide my complete support in whatever way you wish, Admiral. I have a score to settle with these particular imperialists. Your purpose is my opportunity."

"Good. You'll be my new go-between with the Filipino President. Arrange for our terms. His reign soon ends. He'll need a retirement package, but must make good on his promises before he leaves office."

The minute of steeping time had passed, so she gently poured rich, brown tea from the pot's spout into the tea pitcher. Used the pitcher to fill the snifters.

Once again, they transferred the tea from the snifters to their larger teacups.

"As you command, Admiral. I will continue to serve as your weapon against the imperialists."

"I've ordered the female prisoner to the ship's brig and Omar into the infirmary until we decide if he remains useful. Now, drink your tea before it cools."

Pahk took a sip. Heaven in a cup.

He nodded to the steward to show his appreciation for her skill and conclude their tea ceremony.

"Excellent."

A fine day. He'd get his revenge after all.

Chapter Twenty-Nine: Escape Life

I leaned over Watkins, the kid I'd led during Ranger Selection. The one curled up on the cave floor, almost in a ball, right up against the wall.

The ranger I'd gotten trapped under rubble because I moved Robbie too fast and hit that tripwire.

Was too eager to respond to contact. To take out the enemy. To follow Schnier's demands.

The man whose mother and girlfriend would wonder what happened to him if he died here.

His chest lay still. No breath.

I wrapped two fingers around the inside of his wrist. Felt for his pulse. Nothing.

Pressed a little harder. A faint sign of life. Slow, but there.

"Medic!"

The rangers with advanced battlefield medicine training left Madsen's broken leg. Ran over to Watkins.

"He has a weak pulse, but he's not breathing."

One stabilized his neck with a soft collar. The other began pumping air into his lungs with a tan manual resuscitator. Feeding his brain.

They shoved me out of the way. I didn't mind, just stepped back.

How long had he been without oxygen to his brain? His heart could work without conscious direction, despite any brain damage, but his intellect required energy to function.

A few minutes of holding his breath? Unable to move, but

hoping for rescue?

Or had his rock burden immediately compressed his chest. Stopped his breathing. Suffocated him?

Schnier stood next to me. Head bowed. Hands clasped. He mumbled something under his breath.

A prayer.

We could all use one right now, but I wouldn't begrudge his for Watkins specifically.

One of the combat medics slipped a portable pulse-ox monitor on his finger. Pressed a button. Waited for the reading to determine how much oxygen was getting through to his blood.

"Low. Keep ventilating."

His partner pumped away at the bag pushing air into his lungs. Looked over at me. "Can you take this over? Slip your hand in here, then a periodic squeeze."

"Sure." I watched him for a moment to time his rhythm and then replaced him on the manual ventilator.

He organized a stretcher next to Watkins while his partner monitored his vitals.

With a quick count, the two medics and Schnier got Watkins shifted to the stretcher. They strapped him in.

Unconscious, but alive. Critical condition, for sure.

Two rangers from Beta Team hoisted the stretcher. The other two helped Madsen. Their squad leader gave me and Schnier a look of... not quite defeat, but not triumph, either. More of a wearied acceptance that his squad's fight that day was done.

Schnier nodded to him. "Get them to the LZ. Recon doesn't show anything between here and Gozar Air Station, but use scouts anyway."

One of the medics took over breathing for Watkins while the other stabilized his stretcher. The squad of wounded and whole marched downhill through the cave together, determined to reach the helicopters.

The rest of us followed them out. No use here. Unless we wanted to try to blast a series of holes, there'd be no passage up into the rest of the jihadi camp any longer from down by the waterfall.

Morning sunshine filtered through the tall trees to highlight purple flowers in the pool of water in front of the waterfall.

Not exactly the island paradise Michelle had promised us to take this mission, but better than getting locked up in a jihadist torture dungeon.

The wounded squad cut through the jungle to the west, toward the air base. We stood at the waterfall to evaluate our options.

Schnier looked devastated. Like he'd had to put down his favorite horse.

I took him aside. "Snap out of it, dude. You still have two more squads relying on you out here. Not to mention we need to figure out how to get Raven back. You can feel sorry for yourself later."

He glared at me. "Easy for you to say."

I noticed he didn't claim I was wrong.

Behind his back, I caught movement down the trail to the river dock. Filipino-looking soldiers in black and gray digital camo uniforms.

Well armed. With rifles aimed in our general direction.

"Contact!" I drew my carbine to my shoulder. Took aim. Dared I fire before they did?

If I waited, would they kill someone before I could respond?

Schnier pushed my rifle barrel down. "Cease fire! They're friendly."

I let him point my weapon in a safe direction. "Friendly?" We were supposed to be covert, here.

"Yeah, those are our SAF allies. Let's go see if they're ready to relieve us here. I could use a trip home. Might even be able to catch the same flight as the wounded, depending on how slow they end up traveling."

He introduced me to Larrikowal, who apparently recognized me from street surveillance. Already knew all about Omar and Raven. He'd chased them in a boat.

The dude Schnier'd been talking to on the radio earlier.

Schnier explained our casualties to him. That his platoon was down a squad and tired after their middle of the night raid.

"We've routed most of them. The ones outside, that is. Likely still around a dozen in the cave complex, but the uphill route from the waterfall is sealed off, so we'll have to choose another entrance to invade."

Larrikowal cleared his throat. "Glad to hear American rangers aren't invulnerable after all."

The hair on my neck stood up, but Schnier took his comment in stride. "A bad day, but I'll happily turn this place over to you at this point. Our only goal was to free the hostages and help you protect your people from guys like Omar. Now he's all hat and no cattle."

"As you've shown, subterranean assaults are risky. My Defense Secretary may not have the stomach for the potential casualties. We don't have expensive robots to take the lead for us."

I shook my head. "Much good it did us."

His face softened as he considered our casualties. "From what you've described, you already understand the risks. No, I don't think my soldiers will want to enter where rangers fear... I mean, where the enemy has proven to be resolute in their defense. Where's the percentage in that?"

"There isn't one," Schnier growled, "but I guess that means you need us to stick around until more of your men can arrive."

"Let me focus." I took a step away, so they could continue their conversation without me. Stared up at the mountain. Watched the stream cascade into the air. Splash into the pool.

Quite beautiful.

Reminded me of another mountain stream. One I'd ridden into a set of deadly caverns. A similar trap, set by the north Koreans.

Pahk. The cavern collapse would've been his idea, not Omar's. Something to provide enough time for escape if an enemy took over the lower cave.

I stuck my hand into the waterfall. The stream pounded at my palm. Good flow. Pressure.

Turned back to Larrikowal and Schnier. "Got an idea for you. Use the water. The bottom of the cave, the place where it would drain, is plugged now."

I pointed at the stream which fed the waterfall from above.

"Divert that water flow into the highest cave entrance. Won't take long to fill it up, but the water will stay too long for them to hold their breath. Pretty sure they won't have scuba gear and oxygen tanks ready."

Larrikowal laughed. "Brilliant! This solves our dilemma, Captain Schnier. You may retreat with your men so they can rest. My SAF soldier's won't spread rumors, but the more conventional police forces we have on their way to reinforce the perimeter are only an hour behind us. They'd wonder what a bunch of American commandos were doing here. Better if you leave now, for all our sakes."

Schnier nodded. "Sure you can handle it?"

"With no need to enter the caves, I have enough soldiers to both set security against any stragglers in the jungle and cover the exits to kill or capture any who attempt to flee. We'll be fine."

I smiled. "It's decided, then. I can finally go home to our luxury resort and take a hot bath. Soak my bruises. Relax while we consider our next move."

Larrikowal frowned. Looked at Schnier. "You want to tell him?"

More bad news?

Schnier sighed. "We're working out of an LCS. Michelle had to torch the resort to stay ahead of the SAF."

My jaw dropped. "But this dude's on our side, right?"

"*Now* he is. It's a long story. I'll tell you all about what you missed on our hike to the LZ. It's only a couple of klicks. You can explain why Raven is Omar's wife to me in return."

Pretty sure he had the better deal, there.

How much should I share with him of Raven's confidences? Those she shared to convince me to help her? That her need to escape was real? Of Omar's creation of the torture chamber I inhabited?

Of the other women?

He needed to know Raven's situation. Some insignificant detail could help us rescue her.

But he was already devastated. Felt he'd let down the men he commanded. Allowed them to get hurt.

Dared I lay Raven's life after they broke up on him? It'd been her choice, but would he recognize that?

I took a deep breath. Gathered my meager belongings.

"Don't worry dude, we'll get her back."

Time to hike out to the LZ. To tell Schnier of Raven's pain.

With the SAF taking over the Lubang Island clean-up, Michelle allowed Sam's platoon sergeant to take over coordinating their intel with the Filipinos.

In turn, she traversed the hatches, corridors, and ladders out to the flight deck.

The rear-half of the LCS sported a rectangular landing area, the largest in the navy not on an actual aircraft carrier.

The flight deck connected to rolling hanger doors in the center of the ship. Hangers large enough to keep the ship's two Seahawk helicopters and remaining drones out of the weather.

She paced along the outside railing. Watched the water stream by. Looked toward Lubang Island to spot the ship's Seahawks.

Nothing in sight but a freighter the 7th fleet had contracted to drop supplies to the LCS on its way to New Zealand.

Michelle checked her sat phone, tied into the ship's wireless network. The ranger's flights were late.

She sighed. Turned toward the sunrise. A nice enough day on the sea.

While her phone was open, she flipped through her email. The usual bureaucratic junk.

What'd Sam have to look forward to?

She scrolled through his messages. Another letter from Hyo-jin. Should she read it?

Might as well. See if she'd taken Michelle's advice.

Hyo-jin professed her caring for Sam, but that she didn't want to put him at risk nor distract him from his dangerous work.

Good.

Even more interesting, she mentioned not wanting more lonely nights without him. With no communication.

That she'd always have feelings for him, would remain his friend, but that while he was a ranger, they needed to not be in a relationship.

That this wasn't fair to either of them.

Michelle grinned. The desperate athlete had taken the bait. Done what was needed.

Truthfully, Michelle hadn't thought Hyo-jin had the guts to break up with Sam, even if she believed it was the right thing to do.

Must be colder and more logical as a scientist than she'd let on.

Probably helped that Sam hadn't replied to anything she'd sent him before, though.

Hmm... after reading all that mushy stuff, he might try to win her back.

Michelle scrolled through the rest of his email. Re-read Hyo-jin's other messages from when he was out of contact.

Deleted the worst ones. That'd make it clear to Sam how his ex-girlfriend really felt, without muddying the waters with the multiple letters per day she'd been sending.

Too much mush in those, anyway.

A few of the ship's medical staff with rolling stretchers huddled up near the flight deck with a ranger clerk and one of Sam's analysts.

They must be getting closer.

Michelle strode down the deck. Watched the horizon toward the island.

There. A pair of specks grew larger. Turned into helicopters, with the rising sun lighting them up.

Their whomp-whomp rotors provided a baseline for their return.

One circled the ship.

The other lined up in the air with a large circle painted in the middle of the flight deck. Touched down on two spring-loaded front wheels and then a smaller one to support the tail.

The pilot flicked a switch inside the cockpit. The engine roar gradually diminished. Rotors slowed.

She raised her hand to protect her hair from the whipping wind.

The bird's side doors slid to the back. The ship's medical staff pushed three stretchers to its side. A pair of ranger medics lowered a trio of men to them.

The first was unconscious, but the other two rangers complained loud enough to be heard over the dying rotor wash about not being allowed to walk.

While the medics took care of one side, the opposite hatch disgorged more rangers.

No Sam. No Schnier.

As the chopper's blades slowed, they folded in on themselves. Reduced their length.

The infirmary staff departed, rolling their charges away. The flight deck team replaced them and sent the rangers away.

After the helicopter's crew dismounted, the flight deck team rolled it across the deck.

The larger of the hanger doors rolled up. Opened to expose a parking space surrounded by a repair shop.

The team of sailors pushed the Seahawk into place. Locked it down with straps, so it couldn't shift in rough seas. Their chief phoned the ship's control center from a built-in line next to the hanger door.

Efficient, but Michelle just wanted them done so the next one could land.

The phone call must've gotten results. The second Seahawk followed the example of the first to land. No medical staff, but the rangers aboard exited even faster.

Schnier was first out one door. Sam second out the other.

Michelle stood next to the hanger with the ranger clerk and analyst. They'd be meeting them as well and knew where to wait.

She couldn't help but contrast the two junior officers. Schnier in uniform, with bulging muscles and red hair. Passionate in a cowboy kind of way. Obnoxious about women in a Texas kind of way, although he occasionally surprised her.

A real American hero, if that's what you wanted.

Sam ran muscular, but lean. Wore a ripped barong shirt untucked over cargo shorts. Quick-witted to the point of annoyance. Gifted in invention, in understanding physical things, but dumb as a rock in terms of relationships.

Would rather be surfing, but maybe she could train him over time.

Schnier was pre-occupied, but Sam waved as they walked over to their welcoming committee.

The clerk hung back, so the analyst hit up Sam first. "Welcome to the LCS Johnbee, sir."

"Thanks, sergeant." Sam laughed. "Is that really the name?"

"Yes, sir." He narrowed his eyes. Leaned his neck forward. Maybe too inexperienced to get the reference.

"In that case, I wanna go home." Seeing the analyst's confusion, Sam shook his head. "Never mind. I'll explain later. What's the sitch?"

"Everyone made it on-board. Our," He glanced over at Michelle, "agency contact required us to evacuate and destroy the largest pieces of equipment, but we've been able to procure spares from ship's stores."

"Good. Write it up and send me an email with a summary. According to the medics, I'm supposed to go straight to the infirmary for them to analyze my bruising, so I'll check back in with the platoon when the bloodsuckers let me out. Thank them for me in the meantime for taking care of business while I was away."

"Roger that, sir." The analyst departed.

This left the clerk. Schnier glared at him. "You didn't come out here to meet me in order to give me good news, so what is it now? All these requisitions from the Navy driven us over budget again?"

"No, sir. I mean, yes, sir, they have, but that's not why I'm here." He winced.

"Out with it."

"Remember that clerical error at the resort? Well, in the confusion of having to clear out and destroy our records and then reconstitute everything here aboard ship, our limpet mine order may not have been canceled."

Schnier's already ruddy complexion turned beet red. Any moment, he was going to pop a vein. "*Our* order?"

"You signed off on it, sir."

"*May* not have been canceled?"

The clerk pointed at the freighter steaming alongside. Its deck crew worked to package crates with netting and lift harnesses. Got them ready to send over to the LCS.

"They brought a mail-call from 7th fleet, along with a re-supply run. The manifest has limpet mines on it for us."

The Seahawk they'd arrived on was simultaneously refueling and getting rigged with a cargo hook to pick up the freighter's pre-packaged loads.

"What? Already? It takes us a month to get a case of ammo, but they've already sent us a dozen limpet mines?"

The clerk was practically at attention, his back was so stiff. "Yes, sir. Each about the size of a beach ball, sir."

"Soldier, you better give your heart to Jesus, 'cause your butt is gonna belong to the platoon sergeant after I tell him about this." Schnier pointed. "Go. Just go. Get out of my sight."

"Yes, sir. Uh... one more thing, sir."

Schnier sighed.

"The Major called for you. Wants you to call him back just as soon as you step on the ship, sir."

"I'll bet he does. Now git!"

The clerk saluted and then ran.

Schnier turned to Michelle and Sam. Shook his head. "That clerk is so dumb he couldn't pour piss out of a boot with the instructions branded on the heel."

Now that the other soldiers had left, Michelle gave him a hug. Grabbed Sam as well and pulled him into her embrace.

"At least you two came back to me. Had me worried there!"

Schnier softened a little against her. "Oh, you know this is what we do. Just another day at the office."

Sam chuckled. Poked Schnier in the side. "Dude. Didn't know you cared."

Schnier growled under his breath. "I need to go call the major. Find out if I'm totally done for, or if there is some way to get off this bronc."

Michelle released them.

"Good luck. You can tell him the agency said it was all necessary to the mission, although I may have to call in some favors to help pay for everything."

"I'll try it, thanks, but I haven't even reported our casualties to him. I'm burnt gravy on a charred biscuit once he finds that out on top of me blowing our budget."

Schnier slumped his shoulders. Turned to leave.

Michelle looked at Sam. "Let me call Larrikowal and arrange to get our tech teams together back at the resort's beach in order to share methods, and then I'll come find you in the infirmary."

Sam smiled. "Good. That'll give me time to check in on Watkins and Madsen before I allow the leach-monsters to stuff me into one of their beds."

With her and Schnier done, really over, that made her choice easy. And she *was* the one doing all the choosing, as always.

PART THREE
SPRATLY STRUGGLE

Chapter Thirty: Good and Bad News

Larrikowal spoke with the Defense Secretary over an encrypted line, patched into the cabin the Americans temporarily assigned him.

"We flooded them out, sir. The American captive's suggestion, actually. Once we had the stream diverted into the highest cave entrance we could find, it was simple. They tried to break out several times, and we filled a couple of holes to keep the water in, but my force covered all the exits."

Dorenza's spoke with a gravelly voice, even over the radio-telephone line. "Excellent work. Anything of interest?"

"We need to wait for the cave to fully drain before we know for sure, but anything on paper or in electronic form was likely soaked, I'm afraid. Better than getting good soldiers killed, though. That's a win for our side."

"That's too bad, but be sure I'm copied on your report of whatever is found."

"Of course, sir. I will also send you video of our captures. Of wet, bedraggled terrorists climbing out of holes with their hands up. I think you'll enjoy it. Might be something the department can publicize to show our efforts against the jihadis who shot at the Speaker."

Dorenza laughed. "Yes, I can see how that will be effective. Good idea. I'll get the public affairs department working on it once I've seen the videos myself. You know what the reward for outstanding work is, don't you major?"

Major? A slip of the tongue, or did this mean a promotion?

"Yes, sir. More work."

"Exactly. I'm putting you in charge of the team of technical and intelligence analysts who will review all the new data we've gotten from the Americans, plus what we'll develop from the techniques they share with us."

"Me, sir? I'm more of a front-line leader, sir."

"Don't argue. After this, I trust you to do the right thing. That's rarer than you think. Besides, you already know the details, no need to bring someone else in. Unfortunately, a post of this importance requires someone of higher rank, so once I push the paperwork through, you're going to have to get someone to pin your new insignia on."

Larrikowal wasn't sure about babysitting a bunch of intelligence analysts and technical types, nor about the politics of a promotion, but Sheila would be over the moon with excitement. Probably expect him to marry her.

Sheesh... he could afford to marry her now.

"Sir, yes, sir."

"If I had someone besides Harper there to take over, I'd relieve you right now for incompetence!"

Schnier winced and shifted his ear away from the secure radio tied into the ship's antenna systems.

Major Williams could make a rodeo clown cry.

"Sir, no excuses, sir." Schnier sat on his bunk. No point in standing when his CO couldn't see him.

"As I understand it, you have that screw-up Harper back. All that's left is to hand over top secret technical methods to the Filipinos, and then you can drag that sorry excuse for a bankrupt independent command back here?"

"Yes, sir. The CIA Station Chief requested the technology transfer to our allies. There's one more matter, sir. An American citizen held captive by Omar and his Korean supplier. They fled with her in a PLAN missile boat. We plan to recover her."

He couldn't let Raven down, but his CO was quickly reducing his options.

"The intelligence Harper's platoon deigned to share with this headquarters indicated that woman was Omar's wife. Was the spotter for his assassination team. Hardly clean hands. Certainly not someone this command is prepared to start a war with China over. That would require Presidential authorization. Want to know the odds of me running that request up the flagpole for you, captain?"

"You've made your position clear, sir." Just don't actually forbid me from going after Raven while we're still here. "We'll work to complete the CIA's requested mission here and then plan our return to Seoul."

"And figure out how to return those limpet mines for a refund. Can't believe 7th fleet even had those in stores in Japan. Some navy clerk probably jumped on the opportunity to unload them on the army."

And was unlikely to want to take them back without a hefty delivery fee charged to their account.

"Roger that, sir. I'll get my clerk right on it."

"See to it personally. I want no more excuses."

"Sir, yes, sir."

"This isn't over. I doubt you still have a career with the rangers, but depending on how you handle the rest of your command there, I might let you complete your current two-year rotation."

"Working on it, sir."

The major disconnected the line.

Schnier wouldn't receive any assistance from the other platoons in his company in retrieving Raven, but maybe Sam or Michelle would have some ideas.

One thing's for sure, he wasn't about to leave her in Pahk's hands, even if he had to swim over to the PLAN fleet, scale the hull, and free her himself.

He had responsibilities to his command, but Sam couldn't always have *all* the fun.

After checking on Watkins and Madsen, I let the local leeches jab me with their diagnostic tools. Rated my pain for them each time they pushed on a different bruise.

Laying on a gray infirmary bed with an IV dripping into me was almost as bad as being Omar's guest of honor.

Almost.

More annoying than painful. They claimed they'd release me once they got an IV of fluids along with some drugs into me.

Never did like corpsmen when they were treating me. Much preferred they paid attention to other dudes.

They left as Michelle arrived. "Maybe you can talk some sense into him," the last one to leave remarked.

She just laughed. "Been trying for over a decade. Not likely to succeed now."

I ignored their little jabs. "Madsen is fine. He'll get a boot and crutches, but only have to be off his leg for a few months."

"Watkins?"

That killed the mood as fast as a rainstorm at a bonfire.

"Wouldn't let me see him, they're still working, but the corpsman said he's stable, although in critical condition. I guess they'll get his physical injuries fixed up alright, as long as he's not paralyzed long-term, but until he regains consciousness, we won't know about any brain damage from oxygen deprivation."

She laid her hand on my arm. "You did everything you could. Got him out of there as fast as possible."

"Got him into there, you mean." I slumped over. "If I hadn't pushed Robbie so fast, I might've noticed the tripwire before it was too late."

"Twenty-twenty hindsight is the worst kind." She gave me a hug. "If we all knew now what we didn't know then, this world would be a much different place. You and I might've even ended up together again."

I sighed. "Now you're really reaching. No, I told Schnier I needed to take it slower, but I didn't have the courage of my convictions to disobey his orders. My responsibility."

"He'd see it as his responsibility, not yours, if they were his orders."

"Doesn't mean he's right. I pushed the lever forward for full speed. Tripped the wire. Had the last opportunity to avoid it all."

"Have you checked your email?"

"No, Omar's men took my phone. Why? Let me guess, more bureaucratic spam? Do I have a new assignment to the arctic wildlife refuge?"

Michelle logged into my email on her phone. Handed it to me. Sat down in the visitor's chair.

She had access to everyone's data in order to both vet the mission's communications for leaks and protect our cover stories while in the field.

"Just read it. I'll be here for you when you're done."

The tenderness in her voice scared me. Michelle was never gentle. Not to anyone.

Not unless they were an intelligence target. A Mark. Not without wanting something.

But she hadn't asked me for anything. What was going on?

I scrolled through my recent email. Nothing out of the ordinary. No new military orders.

Just a message from Hyo-jin.

I read through it. Her words hit me with a wallop. Then pissed me off. Then another jolt. Racked me across the breaks like a pummeling wave.

Yet another wipe out.

Michelle sat with her hands folded in her lap. Quietly waited for me to finish reading.

Would she understand? She must, if she was acting this way.

"What am I doing here, anyway? Getting locked up in caves and beaten? For what? So my girlfriend feels neglected and leaves me?"

"Your parents? Remember? You've always said someone needed to be the sheepdog protecting the flock. Protecting people like them."

"Sure, someone has to do this kind of thing. Someone needs to protect everyone else." And I believed I was good at it, so always thought it might as well be me, "But does it *really* have to be me? Why not someone else?"

"Lots of people need your protection. People like me, Raven, the other rangers. Someone must stop the bad guys."

"They need protection, but why must I sacrifice not just my life, but my heart and mind as well to be the one to protect them? Someone else can do it. Schnier, for one. There's plenty more who want to be heroes like him. They can take the next best guy at the next Ranger Selection."

"Second best?"

"Second best would be almost as effective. Someone else could've engineered an electronic surfboard besides me, but I might've kept doing that kind of work in an office somewhere. I had a normal life until you talked me into this at WARCOM."

I didn't *really* blame her for getting me into this, but I was lashing out now. Probably not the best time to talk to me. I took a deep breath, but didn't yet feel like coming down off my rage.

She ignored the direct attack to focus on the substance of my argument. "You think you care about Hyo-jin, but without you going to Seoul, she'd be dead along with millions of others. No one else would've talked to the North Koreans. They couldn't stop that dead man's switch from going off. At best, Schnier would've shot Kwon Chol and killed everyone. Is that what you'd prefer?"

I hate it when she has a point. Especially when I'm mad about something.

"So what's the solution? Wait until I'm out of the army to care about anyone? To have someone care about me?"

"Hyo-jin wasn't good enough for you, that's all. Didn't deserve you. You aren't the only one who has to sacrifice. She just doesn't have the level of dedication loving a soldier takes. She's not the only one, but that doesn't mean no one else does."

I wasn't ready to concede that one. "Maybe." She'd sure seemed good enough for me at the time.

Smart. Cute. Tall. Clever. Athletic. Loving.

"Give it some time. Pretend she doesn't exist. It's tough right now, but with time and distance, you'll heal." She smiled. "I mean, I've almost gotten over our break-up, and it's been less than a decade."

This is why I've always liked Michelle. She could talk at least some sense into me.

I took another deep breath. I could put on a brave face. Lock this hurt away for a while. Get on with my job.

Someone needed to do it. Might as well be me, if I was the only one with the skills to do it in my own unique way.

I handed Michelle's phone back to her. Gave her a weak

smile. "We can revisit that later. What's the next job? How do we get Raven back?"

"We're working on that. Right now, we have a joint project with the SAF to show them how we hijacked their communications and processed it so effectively."

"I wondered what you gave them in order to keep our mission here quiet. To get help for Schnier. That makes more sense now."

She slugged me in the arm.

Ouch.

"To get help for you, you mean. You aren't the only one who protects other people. Sometimes you get yourself into scrapes where we have to get you out again."

The old Michelle was back. Good. I could use a dose of bracing reality again.

"Okay. Once they let me out of here, I'll gather up the troops and we'll take your SAF friend to the cable on the beach by the resort. Want to see what you did to the place, anyway."

That'd keep me too busy to dwell on Hyo-jin. To reply to her break-up message.

What would be the use, anyway?

At least Michelle was here for me.

Chapter Thirty-One:
Information Problems

I stood and stared at the sea from the torched resort's beach. Maybe I should go surfing.

Michelle salvaged my eSurfboard prototypes and brought them to the LCS, mostly because I'd stored them next to the rafts she and my platoon used to escape.

With Schnier's platoon having helicoptered ahead and my platoon's destruction of most of their equipment, the rafts had plenty of spare room.

The offshore breeze rushing across the beach did far more to heal my wounds, internal and external, than an overnight in the ship's infirmary hooked up to an IV had accomplished.

I watched as my technical and intelligence analysts explained what we'd done with the Philippines' undersea communications cable to the locals.

Per Michelle's agreement with Larrikowal, a group of six analysts from each country talked through the setup we'd used. They stood on the beach next to the wide rubberized cable, right where it protruded from the sand, but before it entered the water.

My team only had to dig up a few feet of sand to expose the Filipino's communications for manipulation.

We'd all ridden the same Seahawk to meet the local tech types. My dudes, Michelle, Schnier, and Larrikowal.

This time, we got official permission to land.

My tech analysts showed the SAF folks how to hook up and

use an oversized fiber optic tap to intercept their communications.

Schnier watched them chat for a moment, but then turned back to me and Michelle, standing around like government supervisors on a road project.

"No offense, but all that nerd talk is boring. Let's go check out what's left of the resort."

She shrugged. "The SAF already went through it looking for intelligence, but if you think we may've left something unmelted, then let's go."

She walked down the beach, leaving us to catch up.

I strode after her toward the water-side gate into the resort. "Curious what you did with the place, anyway. Not like you to carry a torch for anyone."

"Funny," she said, "I'm not the fiery redhead here."

Schnier frowned. His shoulders slumped as we walked. Didn't seem in the mood for our usual banter.

"What's the deal?" I stepped up next to Schnier. "You're usually happy to look at some bombed out wreck the rangers left behind. Or is it just that you didn't get to do the burning? Jealous?"

He shook his head. Said nothing until we followed Michelle through the gate.

A series of cinder piles and dirt greeted us. The little rock paths they'd built between the nipa huts remained, but the huts themselves had turned the gravel and the interior of the resort compound's external walls into streaks of black, gray, and white.

Schnier finally laughed, but it wasn't a joyful expression. "Wow, I thought you said Sam was usually the destructive one? All he did was collapse a cave, wreck a robot, and put my men in the infirmary. You've literally reduced this place to ashes."

Ignoring his cave comment as born of pain, I pointed at one of the taller piles. "I guess that's what's left of our personal items."

Michelle nodded. "Your platoon did an excellent job ensuring nothing remained for the SAF to identify us from. Sorry."

Schnier grabbed one each of our arms. Tugged us around to face him. "Forget all this. I need you two to help me get Raven away from Pahk and the Chinese Navy. Whatever they're doing to her, it's not pleasant."

Michelle pulled her arm away. "We can ask the State Department to intervene. She's an American citizen. They'll get her back. Can't start a war with China over her."

"I don't care about all that. Pahk is our problem, not hers. If we hadn't let him back across the DMZ, she wouldn't be in this fix."

"You can't save everyone. I know she's your ex, but we're talking about possibly getting involved in a war with a major power. It's not like playing shoot-'em-up in Manila to protect an ally where they'd just kick us out of the country. Millions could end up dead, just to get back one person. Let the diplomats handle it."

They both looked at me.

"Without her assistance, I'd still be chained up inside that cave, and Schnier's platoon would likely be dead in a shot-down helicopter. Besides, she's an American. I say we help her."

Michelle wasn't about to concede. "Maybe, but she's also a terrorist. Don't forget that she was there in that parking garage, spotting for Omar, creating a cover identity for him as a couple."

"Coercion." I could ride that wave if she wanted to toss it at me. "The women were effectively prisoners. Abused slaves. She participated just to get out of the cave in order to find opportunities to help them escape. That's bravery and sacrifice in a high-stress situation, not the act of a terrorist."

Schnier piled on. "What if it were you held captive? Wouldn't you expect us to come after you, no matter what?"

"That's different."

"How?"

Michelle glared at him. "Lots of top secret stuff in my head you couldn't let the enemy have. What can Raven tell them? All about Omar's camp? So what? They already know that. We can afford to wait for a diplomatic effort to get her back. I'll call in a few favors at the embassy. Maybe we can trade China someone they want back for her."

"Look," Schnier wasn't ready to raise the white flag, "when I was a kid, I didn't amount to much. Didn't do pop-warner, too small, wasn't the smartest in the class, didn't really stand out in any way. If anyone noticed me, it was to pick on me."

Schnier? Despite his charms once we became friends, he seemed more like the type to be the bully than the bullied, but I didn't interrupt.

"Then I got into rodeo. All I had to do was balance and hang on long enough. Ride with the bumps and jolts. *That* I could do. Better than anyone in town my age. Suddenly, people noticed me. I won awards. Got my picture in the paper with a big belt buckle. Pappy was proud. Rodeo skill was a big deal on the ranches."

Michelle didn't appear impressed. "So?"

"So I guess rodeo isn't such a thing at Berkeley. But in Texas? My coach explained it to me. People are like bulls. They fight each other for domination. Not to kill each other, but to make 'em submit. Establish a hierarchy. Decide who will be king. Well, in rodeo, I became the king."

"What's this got to do with Raven?"

"Everything. I had that attitude in college. King of rodeo. King of the football team. A linebacker smashing the other team's offense. Establishing domination."

He sighed. "Pretty sure that's ultimately why I lost Raven, that attitude, but once she left, I didn't change. Rationalized that we weren't long term compatible anyway, not with her changing political views and my leading the ROTC hierarchy. Put me in the Army after college. Found bigger men to smash. Thought that's what it was all about, keeping America the biggest bull in the world."

Michelle just glared at him. "I'd have broken up with you too."

"Yeah, well, I've learned a little more since then. Wised up a bit. My coach was wrong, mostly because men aren't bulls, or dogs, or whatever. We don't have to dominate to compete. We can cooperate instead. Bishop and Sam taught me that. As dense as I was, it finally got through."

"Sheepdogs." I held up my hand. "Bear with me. I've been thinking about this a lot recently as well. We're the sheepdogs.

Omar and Pahk are the bulls, or wolves, or whatever. They see people to dominate. Use. Make into their victims. But we're here to protect them. Scare off the wolves. Fight the bulls, but on our terms, to protect the regular folks, people like my parents, so they don't have to be fighting all the time. We do it for them."

"Right," Schnier said, "Sheepdogs. That's what gives us the moral authority to come here and fight the Omars of the world. We're not here to dominate them, but to protect people from them. People like Raven. And that's why I need to go get her. It's my job and she needs me. Needs all of us, really, if you'll help me."

Losing Hyo-jin, I knew how Schnier must've felt losing Raven. Knew this was more personal to him than just his job, but I left him some dignity in his outward denial.

Maybe Michelle could be my Raven. We'd crossed in the night often enough. Could this time be different?

"I'm in, of course. She saved me. You came for me. No way I'm not returning the favor, but I like to think I would anyway, dude. Unless, of course, it was your big fat ugly ginger mug in Pahk's hands. Might let him keep you. Would serve him right."

He refused to take offense. "Thanks. Any ideas? Could really use some ideas how to get her back."

Michelle could see the writing on the wall. "I'll do it, but not if you're going to just go start a war by attacking the Chinese navy in what they claim are their waters, or even international waters. You'll have to find some way to negotiate with them, or get them to attack the Philippines. Then we can spin it as just defending our allies. That they fired the first shot, and we just responded."

Obviously, I needed to be the brains in this outfit. Too many problems and not enough solutions.

"Hmm... not a bad idea. I can work with that. Just have to see if we can get them to come after us in a way that they fail. Give me some time. I'll get with my platoon and we'll do a little brainstorming. Got some pretty smart dudes working for me. Bishop taught me to take advantage of their help. Work together. We'll figure it out, if anyone can."

"Thanks, Sam, Michelle. Knew I could count on you two. My

only requirement is that we don't put our rangers too much at risk with one of your crazy schemes. Don't want anyone else in the infirmary, or worse. Let's go see how the tech teams are doing."

Now I just needed to come up with a plan to defeat a major power's naval battle group with two ranger platoons, an LCS, and maybe a Filipino commando force. Plus, convince them to start it.

No problem...

Raven had finally done something right. Heroic even, returning to help Sam.

And really, really, stupid.

At least Omar was in the destroyer's infirmary, if the Chinese hadn't killed him yet.

If only she hadn't listened to her crappy professor. She'd be back in Texas right now.

As she'd discovered, there were worse things out there.

Chinese naval ships didn't contain a lot of spare space for the highest of the high. She could almost stand all the way up in her prison for the lowest of the low.

Pahk, Omar's supposed benefactor and friend, peered through the plexiglass window in the door.

A star pattern of five circular holes allowed air and speech to pass through.

"Are you sure you don't prefer to be chained in my stateroom? The accommodations are much nicer there, you'll find."

She bent her knees in order to hold her head high. "This bucket of rust is nothing compared to the American navy. Give up now. They'll be coming for me."

Pahk laughed. "First, the imperialists won't risk war over a terrorist woman. Perhaps they'll negotiate for your release in a few years and be grateful for whatever condition you're in."

Would they leave her to rot in Chinese jails?

He ticked each item off on his fingers. "Second, their only nearby ship is outclassed by this destroyer, China's largest and stealthiest, with one-hundred-twelve vertical missile launch tubes. Anti-ship and anti-air missiles. Could take out an enemy fleet by itself.

"Third, our battle group also contains two frigates, a replenishment vessel, and anti-submarine aircraft. Face it, even if the Filipinos helped them, hardly likely, the imperialists wouldn't have a chance before we destroyed them. Especially if you're on board and they don't want to kill you by firing at us."

He dropped his hand. "No, their best bet is to hope for negotiation, not war. It's too late for that. So, care to bring the spoils to the victor?"

Raven slumped. "Maybe you're right about the navy, but you'll need to drag me kicking and screaming to your room, if that's what you want."

She'd had enough of men like Omar. Never again.

Pahk grinned as he stared through the cell window. "We don't have time for female histrionics, but I'll visit later. We'll see if you ever want to straighten your body again. Seems such a waste, to me."

He winked. Turned and strolled down the passageway.

Raven allowed herself to sob, now that there were no witnesses beyond the protected security camera blinking in the ceiling's corner.

If she stuffed her shirt in the window holes, blocked the only source of fresh air, would she pass out before they came to stop her?

Was she that desperate yet?

Chapter Thirty-Two:
Disinformation Solutions

Schnier sat in the sand, just outside the wave's reach. Elbows on his knees, he held his head in his hands.

Stared at sand-bubbler crabs scurrying into their burrows to avoid the water's destruction.

At least they had a home.

His used to be the rangers, but now he belonged with Raven, trapped on a Chinese destroyer.

Pathetic. Disgusting. Sad.

But what could he do about it?

Sam dragged Larrikowal across the beach toward Schnier, pulling his arm.

Schnier looked up and around. What was he so excited about? Some nerd news?

When they arrived, Sam just thrust the Filipino officer forward. "Tell him!"

Hmm... he wore major's insignia. Schnier could've sworn he was only a captain before. "Congratulations, Major. Tell me what?"

Larrikowal cleared his throat. "Thanks. My tech team, using the trained expert system your analysts provided, and their internal access to the system's records, found something interesting."

Schnier was already depressed. Now they wanted to bore him as well?

Sam bowed his head. Shook it. "Not like that. He doesn't care about the details. Give him the bottom-line, like you'd tell your Defense Secretary."

"Umm... yes, of course. We found two items of interest related to the Chinese. Regular communications between our President and Admiral Hu, the PLAN political commissar—"

Schnier snorted. "I know who Hu is. What's the point?"

Sam didn't wait for the SAF officer. "We've confirmed their President arranged with the Chinese for the sniper attack. Rigged it through multiple cut-outs to make the Speaker out to be a hero."

"We knew that already."

"No, we suspected it. They've confirmed it."

"So?"

"So tell him the other thing."

Larrikowal hung his head, as if he wanted to avoid further embarrassment.

"Spit it out, sir." That last word may have not conveyed all the respect Schnier would normally have included in it.

"You're not the only ones who've infiltrated our communications. With access to all the data flows in and out of the Philippines, we've spotted massive exfiltration of government data to China as well. Illegal flows of secret information."

Schnier shrugged. "Good to know, I guess, but I don't see how that helps us get Raven back. Besides, how did you pull that off so quickly? Sam's men have been pouring over that data much longer than you."

Sam pulled Larrikowal back. Stepped forward. "Besides access to our fully trained parsing model, they all speak Tagalog. We had to rely on translations of anything which looked interesting. But lucky for you, I do."

"Do what, speak Tagalog?"

"See how that can get Raven back, you idiotic captain, sir."

Could he really have a plan? If so, he'd forgive the disrespect in front of their ally. "How?"

"Disinformation. Comment Crew doesn't know that we know about their infiltration and the President's shadiness. They've been negotiating over government concessions in exchange for funding his post-government retirement. He needs the speaker elected to continue to cover up his corruption, but he also needs a big score from the Chinese between election day and when he leaves office."

"So?"

"So we take over the negotiations. Dangle in front of Admiral Hu the greatest political coup in his career. Control of a new port in the South China Sea."

"West Philippine Sea." Larrikowal corrected.

"Tilik Seaport becomes Tilik Harbor, or whatever the Chinese want to name it. Right on Lubang Island. Offer Hu a contract for economic development. An expanded fishing port. An unspoiled tourist attraction. Give them a contract to build the new harbor and a lease to run it afterward, in exchange for a substantial bribe to the Filipino President."

Would that work? Schnier had his doubts. "They'll never go for it. Too good to be true. The Chinese could use that to dominate the area. Run disguised spy trawlers in and out. Service their navy. Expand and support their economic claims."

"That's where Comment Crew comes in. If the President was suddenly much more willing to make the deal of a lifetime, Hu would wonder why. But what if his hackers inside their government found all the right evidence? Minutes of feasibility meetings. Off the record notes of legal discussions. Internal complaints and formal protests from officials about the very idea. If everything they know, all the intelligence they have, points to the same conclusion, could Hu risk not accepting?"

"Can you do that?"

"Well, no. It'd take a bunch of work. Lots of Tagalog speakers. Intimate familiarity with the inner workings of the government. We couldn't do it."

Of course not. "So again, what's the point?"

"Larrikowal could. His SAF team has everything we need to make it look real."

"How does that get us Raven back?"

"If the mountain won't come to Muhammad, then Muhammad must go to the mountain. We can't go get Raven, but that doesn't mean Hu can't bring her to us. I'll get with

220 | Thomas Sewell

Michelle and your supply clerk, but if we know exactly where and when they're coming, we just need to set the right trap."

Behind Sam's babble of nonsense, Schnier sensed something serious. Hope.

"You're always optimistic about your crazy schemes, and then someone gets hurt and I have to come bail you out. You can't risk my platoon to pull this off."

"Don't worry, dude. I'll have it all figured out by the time Larrikowal gets approval from his chain of command to put it all together. Might even find time to go surfing. Trust me. This is our opportunity."

Schnier's heart was ready to burst, but he couldn't let his emotions rule his head. He had responsibilities to his men, not just to Raven.

"Don't mess with me on this. You better be right."

But what if Sam *was* right?

Major Larrikowal hung up his secure connection to Dorenza.

They had approval!

He'd also been interested in the election-related possibilities, but no need to share that with their American allies.

Besides, the President's Party had already cheated to make the Speaker appear as a martyr. Ended his sergeant's career.

Blown his arm off in the process. Larrikowal would expected payback for that.

He fired off a coded message to his technical team. Pre-arranged wording to order them to implement the solution Sam and he had hashed out overnight.

They were prepared. He hadn't waited for approval, but instead gotten everything ready for when it arrived.

His message was simple. "Approval received. Execute operation Disarm."

They'd do the rest in the virtual world, which consisted only of data packets pretending to be real communication. Inject communications for the enemy to snare.

For now, he needed to call Maria. Gather his physical force at Lubang Island. He'd need them to pull off the rest of the plan.

He rubbed his hands together.

Even as a major, he still got to fight in the field. No need to tell Sheila.

Just another routine training exercise.

Chapter Thirty-Three: Island Prep

While the SAF tricked the Chinese, I told Schnier and Michelle I was going surfing off Lubang Island to check out the new port location.

So I put Hyo-jin out of my mind. Focused on the here and now. Broke out the eSurfboard.

My favorite type of reconnaissance. I stood on the front of the board. The slight upward angle of the underwater foil pushed it, and thus me, a foot above the waves.

I pulled the trigger on my wireless controller to increase the speed of the electric propeller.

Soared through the air, king-of-the-world-style.

Downhill from the jihadist's mountain camp, along the northeast side of the island, Tilik Seaport lay inside a U-shaped bay with a half-klick wide mouth.

Enough space for two super-tankers to pass each other, so no problem getting a Chinese destroyer and it's escorts to fit through.

After a bit of intercession by the SAF's Sergeant Maria, the local customs dudes even let me set my equipment up on the concrete pier once I'd apologized for their earlier failed pursuit.

First, I circled the bay. Noted landmarks.

Besides the concrete pier and the town with sea walls in backyards, the jungle overgrew about half of the edge of the water, while sandy beaches covered the shore's other half.

I measured the widest portion of the bay at about a klick across. The water next to the pier was plenty deep, but a shallow underwater island rested 250 meters away in the center of the proposed harbor.

Hu's ships would avoid that shallower area, of course.

I surfed from the calm waters inside the bay's mouth to the rougher waves outside. The sea quickly deepened. My vision turned from a clear view of the bottom into an inky depth with no end.

All the action would need to take place inside the harbor.

I took the opportunity of deeper water to test my eSurfboard's latest update, which included a stealth mode. The SEALs had asked for an underwater option for greater flexibility, even if the board ran slower.

A knob on the controller angled the underwater foil. The V-shaped wing could alternately lift the board itself into the air for less drag and more speed, or drop it below the surface for a much slower, but stealthier ride.

I dropped to my knees and then lay flat on the board. Held the edge of the side. Released the trigger to slow the motor.

My eSurfboard sank to the surface of the water. Bounced over wave crests instead of cruising above them.

I dialed the foil's angle of attack downward.

The front of the board dipped into the water. At first, waves just crested over the top, splashed me in the face, as it resisted upward pressure.

Then I held a deep breath. Accelerated again.

Not a lot, just enough to pull the board underwater, with me on it.

Too fast! The water pressure on my face and shoulders became an intense pounding. Like a continuous wipe out into the depths of a wave, with no hope of surfacing.

I released the speed trigger.

Pressure reduced to nothing as the board stalled its forward momentum. Popped to the surface now that water wasn't running past the underwater wing at high speeds.

I took a breath.

To make the stealth mode really work, I'd need additional equipment and preparation. Perhaps a Velcro strap to secure my waist to the board.

Definitely at least a rebreather and goggles.

All doable, so scraping past the PLAN ships as they entered the bay was workable.

Good. Raven's life, Schnier's platoon, and the SAF troops supporting us would depend on it.

Not to mention my own minor interest in survival.

Pahk stood with head bowed in the flag cabin's open hatch. "Admiral?"

"Enter."

The PLAN crew member who'd escorted Pahk nodded and departed to leave him with the Political Commissar and his senior aide.

Pahk stepped into the room dominated by the Admiral's table. No tea tray this time.

All business.

Hu sat at the head of the table. His senior aide typed away on a laptop on his right. Hu gestured for Pahk to join them on his left.

"Pahk. Welcome. You've read the President's offer?"

Pahk stepped over to the table and took his indicated place. "Yes, sir. It's quite the opportunity."

"I don't trust it. Too easy. Convince me otherwise."

"Sir. We know from our infiltration of the Filipino's systems that his cabinet, even those who have been friendly to our interests in the past, also don't approve. Surely, what they find as too much of a concession must be good for us?"

"Continue."

"Also, we know the Filipino President's incentives. To continue to cover up the previous rewards we've given him in exchange for many of their government contracts, he needs the Speaker to win. He's already gone so far as to accept as payment from us my arrangement for Omar to fake an assassination attempt. So clearly, he's been desperate."

"How is Omar's health?"

"The ship's surgeon reports he is out of critical condition. Now, he just needs continued rest and recovery. We could return him to his people, if that was your decision."

"We'll see. Your next point?"

Pahk nodded. "According to the communications from his political advisers, which Comment Crew provided, the assassination attempt wasn't enough. Dorenza's SAF received some of the credit in the public's mind when they risked their lives to protect the Speaker. So to win their election, the President needs something decisive. The two Parties differing views on our assistance and cooperation are one of their major points of contention."

"So?"

"If he can hold a press conference with you. If rather than being seen as opponents, he can present their people with the accomplished fact of peaceful partnership with us for their benefit, he believes that will guarantee the election."

"Their voting is obnoxious. He should have their election officials report whatever it is he wants them to report. But I suppose it works to our advantage, because he cannot truly consolidate power."

"Of course, Admiral. And beyond the election ploy, the Filipino President will certainly benefit personally, with the amount of gold we'll be delivering to him."

"*I'll* be delivering to him. I'm not sure I want to be as personally involved as he's requested."

"He needs to be seen to have a high-level counterpart on our side. You're the highest available on short notice. Besides, the Filipinos are hardly going to attack us or our ships. That would give an international justification for war and the immediate loss of his Party's power."

"Small comfort, if we are dead. But as you say, their incentives line up. Very well, we shall commit to the agreement. Permanent dominion of the South China Sea is too good of an opportunity to pass up."

Hu's senior aide typed notes of their discussion. "I'll record the decision and send out your orders, Admiral. Our legal team has reviewed the 99-year lease agreement and the corresponding exclusive economic zone rights and provided their approval as well."

"Good. Pahk, arrange for Omar to be ready to visit Lubang

Island, even if in a wheelchair. We want to make clear to the natives, including his soldiers, that we'll be in charge as soon as we sign the lease. It's only for the extended port area, but there are no other power centers within the island's population. I expect to quickly gain control of their tourist trade and lock down the import/export of food and other goods. After all, it must flow through our new port, even before we've built the agreed upon facilities."

"You asked me for the positive case, Admiral. May I make one more point?"

"Go ahead."

"On the negative side, we'll be exposed, with your task force constrained by the harbor. At least take some precautions. Keep the torpedo boats on patrol around the entrance. Require the Filipino Navy stay out of range. No joint naval forces as they've requested, just civilian craft. After all, this is a civilian agreement on their side, so why should they need comparable military forces?"

"A good point. We'll include that in our agreement memo. You're dismissed."

Pahk stood. "Admiral." He departed.

After helping the Chinese Navy accomplish their long-term goals in the South China Sea, his rice bowl would eternally overflow. His mother and sister were set now in China.

As long as everything proceeded smoothly with the lease signing ceremony. He'd ensure Omar understood that.

Major Larrikowal admired his new insignia in the Ports Authority 4x4's giant side mirror. He hadn't expected promotion for at least two more years.

His driver pulled over to the side of the gravel road in front of Tilik Seaport's wide concrete pier.

Not much, but sufficient to dock a Chinese destroyer. All of Tilik only held about twelve-hundred homes and businesses. Barely managed a handful of solar streetlights near the dock.

The big city, it was not.

Still, they had a nice protected waterway, which made their proposal to Hu plausible enough.

The Chinese had been invited for an early morning ceremony. Dawn of a new day in relations between the Philippines and their sometime antagonists.

So this afternoon, Larrikowal had a lot of work to get done to prepare for the meeting.

Or rather, his men and the locals did. He'd supervise.

First, he needed the SAF present, but not visible. The closest cross-street from the pier held businesses with corrugated aluminum walls.

Sergeant Maria directed the locals to install giant hinges on those walls. Stack sandbag forts behind them. They looked normal and impassable, but on signal, would lift quickly to create an urban firing position.

Schnier's rangers were used to being less intrusive. They posted sniper hides on balconies and multi-story rooftops. Whatever high ground they found. Encouraged building occupants to relocate for the day.

The rangers would rain death on the Chinese forces if the meeting went south.

Larrikowal was most worried about the press and Dorenza. The Secretary of National Defense decided he'd personally greet Admiral Hu live on the morning news.

Dorenza would arrive shortly in an official helicopter so the Chinese would track his flight. According to internal government communications, it was the President and a media contingent.

They'd stay overnight in the five-story hotel adjacent to the concrete pier. Tallest building in town.

If everything proceeded as planned, then great, they'd expose both the Chinese and the President's Party.

But Larrikowal remembered the most recent televised political event he'd provided security for. His partner from that event remained in the hospital.

He stationed the town's thirty-year-old military surplus ambulance nearby.

At least Dorenza wasn't tying his hands. Quite the opposite, he'd given an unusual level of freedom to the SAF and the Americans.

The other wild card. Their motives may not completely line up with the Filipinos. He'd have to keep a close eye on the Americans. Make sure they didn't do something to jeopardize the SAF's objective.

Humiliate the Chinese and ensure they never returned to the West Philippine Sea in force.

I chatted with Michelle on the radio while setting up my equipment.

Schnier's Explosive Ordnance Disposal (EOD) tech and one of my analysts who had scuba experience worked with me. We stacked command-detonated limpet mines under a flipped over boat on the beach north of Tilik.

The mines were shaped like an Apollo space capsule, except about the size of a lobster pot.

Internally, the base contained magnets strong enough to hold each mine to a ship's hull at any reasonable speed. The rest was split between electronics and explosives.

Water resistance outside the mine turned each into a shaped charge, capable of blowing twenty foot ring out of a battleship. Without the ability to lock down discrete compartments to prevent flooding, even one hit could sink a normal ship.

The boat wasn't to distribute them. It was to hide them. Couldn't have the PLAN ships get suspicious as they entered the bay.

Any I missed as they traversed the narrow northern opening, I'd need to tag closer to the pier.

We set the meet for early morning in the hopes they'd arrive overnight. Give me an opportunity to approach the hull underwater without easy detection from above.

So far, so good. Scheduled to arrive any time now.

Michelle spoke into my ear. "I'm worried about Schnier. He's always been a hothead, but he's under more stress than usual lately, with our break-up and this independent command."

"Not sure he'll listen to me, if it comes to that, but I'll keep an eye out. Try to talk him off any ledges."

"You're the best, Sam."

I grunted agreement as I stacked a mine on one of my two

eSurfboard prototypes. "Tell me that again once this is all over and we've succeeded."

"Nope, one per customer per year. Sorry."

"Typical. ETA?"

She mumbled something about estimates to the sailors in the background of the ship's wardroom. Waited for a response. "Half an hour until the lead missile boat enters."

The LCS Johnbee's surface radar tracked the Chinese task force for us. One missile boat led the destroyer, then their replenishment ship, with the second missile boat covering the rear of the formation.

At least Michelle would be safely out of harm's way. Unless, of course, we started a full-on war with the Chinese.

"I'd better get these mines strapped down to my backup board and then get my underwater gear on. I'll let you know once I'm in position to get a final update."

"Good luck, surfer."

Dude, I needed that luck.

Chapter Thirty-Four: Island Confrontation

My first attempt went poorly.

I loaded a pair of mines on my secondary eSurfboard. Slaved its controls to follow mine and keep a standard five meter follow distance.

Apparently two strapped on limpet mines are heavier than one surfer dude.

I left my two helpers, dressed as tourists, behind. I wore a shorty wetsuit complete with a rebreather for air and a mask.

Sped off to an intercept location in the bay's entrance. The second board gradually fell behind.

Way behind.

Good news, it also sank a bit. Floated under water, with only occasional peeks above the two-foot swells.

Once I stopped, it caught up to my lead board, but that wouldn't work when we needed to pace a moving target like a missile boat.

Reluctantly, I dropped one of the mines off here in the shallow water. We could retrieve it or deactivate it remotely at a later time. It wouldn't move on its own or anything like that.

No, limpet mines needed to be hand attached to a ship's hull.

Usually, that happened while the ship stood still, but the PLAN would surely have an anchor watch. In this clear water, during daylight hours, there's no way bored Chinese sailors wouldn't notice someone approaching, even under water.

Nothing to help it. One attempt per customer for the enemy

fast movers.

Michelle interrupted my recriminations and re-planning. "Surfer, first missile boat is in the slot."

"Roger that."

I plugged my mouth with a mouthpiece and turned the connected air valve. That'd keep me underwater.

Lay on my belly. Wrapped a strap around my waist, similar to the ones holding now just a single limpet mine to the secondary board.

Programmed the underwater wing's angle to pull me under the water until the board's buoyancy counter-acted it to keep us only a couple of feet down.

Accelerated. Glanced back at the other board. It followed.

Sunk under the waves. A dark shape beneath the sea, without sunlight overhead.

Water rushed past my face-mask. Pounded on my shoulders. But we stayed below the surface.

It worked!

The approaching ship was obvious. Two great disturbance in the water ahead, corresponding to its pair of undersea pontoons, each followed by a jet of water.

I banked and turned in a curve to the right. Sped up to match its speed. Almost too fast for me, but they'd slowed in the shallower water.

I lined up directly in front. Let the boat overtake me while I brought my secondary board closer and angled both deeper.

As long as I hit near the center, even above the water, the PLAN Houbei class has several feet of clearance.

If a pontoon smacked me in the back at high speed, that'd be a different story. So no sharp turns, please.

Just before the ship arrived, I unstrapped the limpet mine. Grabbed it with both hands. Lay on my back. Held on with my feet tucked under my board.

Activated the magnets.

As the ship passed over me, I thrust my arms out. Tagged the hull.

Clang!

Hoped no one heard that, or if they did, mistook it for a

random piece of flotsam.

The mine attached itself. The boat yanked it out of my hands.

One set.

I flipped over on my belly. Strapped myself back in.

Once the rear of the boat passed over me, I got the wash of the twin pumped turbojets. The edges of two giant fountains propelling the missile boat forward.

Spun me sideways. High-speed impact against hard water as my prop and foil faced the wrong direction.

The worst kind of wipe out. Tumbled. Slammed into waves. A sudden stop on my face.

I stopped. Surfaced. Couldn't help it. My board was dead in the water.

My secondary eSurfboard dutifully crashed into the back of the one I was clinging to. By flipping sideways, I'd stopped faster than just killing the electric motor could halt me.

So there we sat on top of the waves. Fully exposed.

I guess the missile boat's rooster tails were tall enough to hide both boards from view. Or else no one on board bothered to look back, not when their destination was coming into view.

Got lucky.

Sometimes better to be lucky, then good.

I checked my rebreather status. Turned my board. Tightened my strap.

Pushed the accelerator and sunk once more. Headed for the beach for replenishment.

They'd need to be NASCAR fast to prepare for the destroyer next.

As an indicator of his higher status, Pahk rode in the cabin with the boat driver bitch.

The six midnight-blue uniformed PLAN Sea Dragon assault team members didn't fit. They rode outside on the deck. The cabin protected them from wind, but not always from waves, especially at the high speeds the missile boat achieved with a lunatic at the wheel.

Admiral Hu sent them ahead with Pahk, the only one on board who'd landed on this island before, to scout the dock and setup a security perimeter.

That marked them as expendable. Or at least, easier to risk than the Admiral's own hide.

The Sea Dragons were the PLAN Marine's answer to the imperialist Navy SEALs. Dragons eat seals, right?

The rising sun in the east highlighted the beaches and buildings of Tilik on the west side of the harbor. Gave Pahk an excellent view. Put the sun in the eyes of anyone watching them from shore.

Clang! Something impacted the bottom of the boat. He looked over at the pilot, but she just ignored him. Minor hull impacts must happen all the time, especially close to shore like this.

He wasn't about to worry about sinking if she wasn't.

Mostly local Filipinos watched their entrance, dressed in their usual jeans and cheap branded shirts.

Could almost be a parade.

A pair of tall, white, military-age men sat on an overturned outrigger canoe and stared.

Tourists? Military?

If so, there was nothing they could do to the Chinese task force without weapons larger than hidden side arms.

Still, suspicious.

Pahk scanned the rest of the seaside village as their boat driver brought them alongside a wide concrete pier. Their boat slid sideways into a group of old tires hung from the edge to buffer impact.

A crew member jumped ashore. Another tossed him a line, which he made fast to the pier.

They'd arrived.

Pahk left the cabin. Motioned to the Sea Dragon Squad Leader. "Follow me."

They trailed him off the boat and on to the pier. A pair of port authority flunkies stood in bursting powder blue uniforms and saluted as they arrived.

The locals grew fat, even here in the rural boondocks. Perhaps after Hu took the place over, Pahk could bring his mother and sister here. Get them good jobs at the new port facilities while he liaised with Omar and the other locals.

Something to daydream about later.

The Sea Dragons behind him ignored the local officials. They weren't here to meet and greet, but to protect the Admiral.

The special forces soldiers split into two groups. In order to not escalate the situation, they allowed their rifles and pistols to dangle from their plate carrier harnesses.

Three swept left. Took position along a railing with a boathouse to protect them from the land. The remaining three spread out more to the right. Took over the base of the pier. Watched the nearby hotel and other buildings suspiciously.

Still, nothing out of place in the open, so both teams gave Pahk a thumbs up.

He stepped up to the local bureaucrats. "I'm in charge of Admiral Hu's advance security detail. Where will the meeting take place?"

If they were offended by his dismissal of them as inferiors, they didn't show it. One even bowed before speaking. "Sir, we will have the formal diplomatic exchange in the open space at the end of the pier. Afterward, if the Admiral consents, we'll move inside to our delegation's hotel for refreshments."

Pahk wasn't sure he'd have allowed enemy special forces within range of his President if he were in charge of Filipino Security, but clearly they didn't consider the Chinese a serious threat to his health with this setup.

"Good. I'll report back. These men will stay and monitor the area for the Admiral."

The Filipinos nodded, so Pahk turned on his heels and returned to the missile boat.

He ignored the driver and picked up the radio. "Pass word to the Admiral. All clear on the pier. We await his arrival."

After confirmation of his report, he turned to the boat bitch. "You can patrol the bay, now. Make room here for the destroyer to tie up. I'll wait on the dock."

She frowned, but nodded. What did she call him in her mind?

Perhaps he'd see if whatever rotgut liquor the locals provided loosened her up at the celebration later.

He hopped back onto the pier. A crew member released the missile boat.

Pahk waved to the driver as the boat sped off in a double-curl of water spray to scope out the rest of the bay.

Closest thing he had to a female friend out here right now, anyway.

My rapid replenishment went well. I pulled up to the beach with both boards on top of the water and together they carried another mine down from the stockpile we'd created under the overturned boat.

"This'll do. One mine at a time now."

The two ranger tourists adapted to the change in plans and returned to pretend they were beach bums.

In turn, I sped back out into the bay with my belly on my lead eSurfboard, with the secondary set to automatically follow closely.

Unlike the missile boats, I really needed to get two mines on to Hu's destroyer. I also wanted to avoid placing an explosive right next to wherever they held Raven aboard.

Complicated.

Along with my platoon's analysts, I'd examined 3D plans of the type of destroyer we faced. The center of the ship held the populated areas. The kind of spaces people would inhabit.

Machinery filled the bow. Both sensors, and to rotate and reload the deck gun. Just behind that, their vertical launch missile tubes.

But no storage space for humans, so my first target became as close to the ship's front as I could plant it.

A hit there would also kill any ability for the destroyer to move forward without more water pressure.

The ship's tail held a single helicopter landing pad, with storage and mechanical space underneath. The propeller and rudder flowed beneath the sea there as well.

So the tail was my ideal location for a second mine. Anything which wrecked the ability of the ship to move or steer would be a mission-kill type of blow.

The tail was most dangerous, though. Getting clipped while the propeller pushed the ship through the water would be lethal.

"Destroyer inbound."

"Roger, ball-breaker."

Given the deeper draft of the destroyer, I pushed the depth of my devices. Moved slower, but deeper.

Circled around underwater to intercept at an angle. Dude, no need to risk getting run over!

Just below the waterline, the destroyer transitioned from gray to red paint.

I slid in next to the front of the target.

The rush of water across my face and back shifted as the bow wave from the destroyer tried to push me off target.

I adjusted my prop's steering to counter-balance the sideways water pressure.

The interaction between them bounced me in and out. Toward and away from the hull. The bow wave just wasn't consistent enough to hold in one place without adjustments.

I'd have to risk a minor collision. No other way; I was running out of real estate.

I unstrapped the mine. Pulled it off the secondary board.

The additional drag immediately slowed me down. Allowed the destroyer's nose to pull ahead. It also caught more of the bow wave, pushing me away.

I leaned toward the ship. Tilted my board just enough to catch an angle and redirect the water pressure.

Which, of course, flung me out of control toward the hull.

I hit the activation on the mine. Slammed it onto the hull just before I made contact myself.

The magnets locked on. I released it.

The push off from hitting the hull with a mine slowed my approach. Like flexing your knees to absorb a drop.

Without the mine in my hands, I tilted my board away from the ship. My lower profile didn't resist the water as much.

The boards and I angled away underwater, as if we'd never been there.

That was close! What if I'd hit my head?

I couldn't wait to try the same trick next to an active propeller. Just its prop wash would be scary, let alone an impact.

Returned to the beach, but couldn't surface. The destroyer remained too close.

"By the time I can get another mine, the destroyer will be too far away."

"Target the replenishment ship next, then. See if you can mine the destroyer again while it's docked. Stopped."

I sucked a deep breath through my rebreather's mouthpiece. "Water's too clear for that. But I'll work the problem mentally while we take care of the final two ships."

"Surfer, focus on what you're doing. I can get some of the boys back here to brainstorm alternate ways of reaching that destroyer again."

"Roger that. It's far enough away now. Surfacing briefly for my next rapid replenishment."

"It's just a mine, Surfer."

I rose to the surface next to the beach. "Still sounds more official that way."

My men were already knee deep in the water with a mine. They'd carried it out and then dunked it to keep it out of sight.

"Excellent initiative! Drag a couple of replacement batteries down with you next time. Don't worry, they're water proof. These won't have enough of a charge to complete the mission."

I helped them strap the next mine into place on the secondary and then took my leave.

Back into the sea.

The replenishment ship was more like a freighter. Slow, deeper draft, not much of a danger, except from too much rust flaking off and getting into my eyes.

One more rapid reload of both my stock of mines and fresh batteries for the board, and I took on the final ship. Another missile boat.

This time, I slipped the mine gently into place, without a telltale clang, and then dive deep to avoid the dual-jet's turbulence.

I was getting better at this with practice.

That final escort boat handled, I returned to the shore for one more mine.

"Any ideas on reaching the destroyer again?"

"We've decided you need a distraction?"

"Whose life are we risking for that?"

"The two rangers there with you. They'll flip the outrigger and put it into the water. Paddle past the line of Chinese ships. The sight of two obvious observers will focus everyone's attention on them. Meanwhile, you can just sneak up and plant the last mine."

"Just sneak up, huh? Let me ask these two about it."

The EOD tech and my analyst met me at the edge of the water with a mine again.

"How'd you dudes like to go for a boat ride?"

I explained the plan.

Of course they volunteered. They're both rangers, after all. Every ranger starts as triple volunteers, every one.

Volunteer for the Army, then for Airborne, then for Ranger Selection.

Every one of us dumber than a rock, but these guys were braver than a sea lion.

Michelle's voice updated me over the radio. "The ships all docked. Now is your opportunity, before the reception on land gets too far along."

"Roger that."

Just one more trip to sneak high explosives underneath the nose of a Chinese naval task force.

Chapter Thirty-Five: Island Fireworks

Schnier and his spotter lay beneath a sniper hide on the fourth floor balcony of the Tilik Hotel. Near the junction of the port's pier and the main road, their height gave him a perfect view as the enemy's ships docked.

A roof overhang protected the two rangers from overhead observation.

A radio tower was the only nearby taller structure, but its platform was made of aluminum beams, open and exposed.

The rest of his platoon were scattered around the seaside town. One team to hold the base of the hotel, the others holding additional sniper hides.

If it came time to bring it, the Chinese wouldn't know what hit them until it arrived like a raging bull.

Earlier, he'd spotted Pahk and half a dozen PLAN spec ops take up laughably inadequate positions along the pier's external concrete walls.

Sure, they'd be somewhat protected from direct small arms fire at ground level, but the single wall didn't prevent Schnier's plunging fire from reaching them, nor the crossfires from at least two other sniper teams from flanking them.

A second group exited the destroyer. The little Pahk inside Schnier's zoomed in glass strode across the pier. Saluted. Pushed a bearded man in a wheelchair.

Omar!

After what Sam relayed from Raven about her experiences as Omar's wife, Schnier should've finished him when he had the opportunity.

His inner bull raged, but Schnier tamped the fires of hell down. Calmed his breathing. Sighted on the group.

No Admiral Hu, but Omar, Pahk, what looked like a senior aide, plus another half-dozen bodyguards.

Much good it'd do them, if Schnier decided to pull the trigger and unexpectedly end any of their lives.

He took another deep breath. Deliberately focused off Omar, and on to the other members of the group. As tempting as firing now was, he needed to give their plan time to work.

However, the moment it looked like the rodeo was ending prematurely, or they're cottoned to the trap, there'd be one less emir and then shortly afterward, one less North Korean alive.

Schnier's inner bull raged on.

Larrikowal stepped forward in his dress uniform with the rest of Dorenza's delegation. They stood on the wide concrete pier to greet the Chinese would-be invaders.

He kept in touch with his force and the rangers with an ear-piece radio. Back where he'd began, on protection duty for a politician.

Admiral Hu strode down his destroyer's gangway. His gold-trimmed deep blue uniform and matching tie sported a six-row-tall brick of ribbons over his left chest.

Based on the uniform chests of his naval officers who followed him down the ramp, PLAN and the CCP sure gave out a lot of awards.

For the ceremony, Dorenza wore a western-style tailored suit with a blood-red tie. He smiled a greeting for the cameras.

The pair of camera crews from ABS-CBN News transmitted from the south side of the pier. A government TV News crew recorded the opposite angle. Between their pooled video, they gave the entire nation a live view of the historic event.

We'd flown the media over in secrecy. Told them Dorenza had an announcement related to the Chinese fleet occupying the Spratly Islands.

Larrikowal laughed at their obvious shock when that PLAN fleet cruised up to the Port of Tilik. They couldn't record video fast enough.

Honor guards, really more bodyguards in disguise, carried the Philippine and Chinese flags. They followed their government officials to make each side of the negotiations clear to observers.

The SAF's technical analysts made sure the Chinese believed Dorenza was simply here for the initial greeting. To be humiliated by witnessing his rival's triumph.

They'd convinced Hu that the President, sensitive to his high rank, would only arrive with the Speaker once the Chinese naval delegation waited for them on the pier.

A young officer with short black hair in an awkward fitting army uniform pushed a bulky, bearded man in a wheelchair.

From his sniper perch, Schnier identified them on the radio. "Pahk, pushing Omar. Odd that Hu brought them here, putting his support out in the open."

Michelle added her interpretation, "He's making a statement. Telling the locals how he expects to run things. Might even make Omar a local representative. Co-opt his men even more. Remember, they have no idea we've destroyed his forces as a fighting unit."

Schnier snarled. "I can take them both, anytime you give the word. I know the plan, but we can't let those two walk out of here."

Larrikowal refrained from pointing out that Omar didn't appear to be capable of walking anywhere just now.

"Stick to the ROE. No shooting without an immediate threat. If there *is* a battle, and I hope there isn't, we must have on camera that they caused it. Otherwise, we'll be at war with the world unwilling to step in on our side."

Had he made a mistake in siding with Americans? In convincing Dorenza to agree to Sam's crazy plan? Letting the rangers bring arms to this meeting, rather than limiting it to his SAF?

Their country wasn't on the line. Not like his.

Dorenza took another measured step in order to distinguish himself from the Filipino delegation. He extended his hand for the benefit of the cameras.

Hu similarly stepped forward. Took his hand.

They performed a politician's shake, each wanting his good side to the camera. Dorenza won the dominance fight. Placed his hand with his palm away from the main camera and grabbed the Admiral's elbow to pull him awkwardly forward.

"Welcome to the Lubang Island, Admiral."

"Thank you, Secretary Dorenza. This is a historic occasion."

Dorenza turned more toward the cameras than toward Hu. "Admiral Hu, you're the political commissar of the Chinese task force haunting our islands recently. You're here because you've negotiated an agreement with the President to purchase this port and build it into a Chinese-owned and run facility. That, as you called it, historic agreement, includes a 99-year lease with control of the associated exclusive economic zone, correct?"

Hu raised his eyebrows at the unexpected statement of the obvious, but humored Dorenza. "Correct. That is the essence of our agreement. We have the appropriate treaty and legal documents your government sent over. They just need my signature and that of your President. When will he arrive?"

Dorenza took a half-step back. "My department has put together a press package describing the deal and your role along with the President's role. As you stepped off the ship, we released it to the national and international media."

"And the President?"

"He isn't coming. All treaties require the consent of two-thirds of our Senate. No such treaty has been submitted for ratification. In fact, I doubt even the President's own party members in the Senate would vote to give China such an advantage in this area."

Hu's neck turned a violent red to match Dorenza's tie. "This treatment is an outrage! I demand to speak with the President immediately and directly."

From down on the dock, Larrikowal couldn't see the reason for sudden shouting and wolf-whistles on the other side of the docked destroyer, but something had distracted their crew.

His earpiece erupted with Schnier's languorous voice. "Uh... Surfer, this here is a delicate moment on the pier. What exactly are those two idiots doing?"

"Providing a distraction. Now leave me alone. I need to get back under water and plant this last mine."

"Nude? In an outrigger?"

Michelle spat out, "They're what?"

"Only way to guarantee everyone on that side of the ship would watch them. Now leave me alone before their diversion ends and I have to come up with something more extreme."

Larrikowal gave a tiny shake of his head. At least their expedition would be off camera.

Dorenza gave Hu a wolfish grin. "Our media package included the evidence of your current and past corrupt dealings with the President. There isn't time to impeach him before the election, but I don't believe the Filipino people will be pleased with his record. We could arrest you for bribery, but technically, you have diplomatic immunity."

Hu gestured to his dozen commandos stationed for security around the perimeter of the dock. They reformed into a tighter group, facing outward. Backed toward the gangway to the destroyer.

"I don't know what you hoped to gain from this, but I'm not amused. We'll be leaving now."

"Three more points." Dorenza pointed at Pahk and Omar. "First, I must insist you leave those two here. They're on our soil and we have arrest warrants for them. Terrorism, Murder, attempted assassination, and a few dozen more charges. Second, you have an American woman on your ship. I've been told she's held against her will. Consider it a customs inspection. If you don't produce her where she can choose to stay or depart in front of my customs officers, we will prevent your ships from leaving this harbor."

"Ridiculous. We aren't subject to your laws." Hu turned to his delegation. "Let's go."

They marched toward their destroyer.

Except Omar. Larrikowal strode out like a fencer. Grabbed one of Omar's wheelchair handles.

Prevented Pahk from moving him.

Pahk pushed. Strained.

Larrikowal held on with both hands.

The dozen Chinese Special Forces broke apart as they swept past Dorenza and the others. Only a few feet of concrete pier remained between them and the wheelchair tussle.

Schnier spoke in his ear. "You can't hold 'em. Fold up and I'll take 'em down on the way to the ship."

Was the American captain that clueless? Just shoot the men on live television?

"Hold on. This isn't worth starting a war over."

Pahk evidently believed Larrikowal's words were meant for him. "You're the one about to start a war. Just let him go."

Larrikowal shook his head. "He's a murderer. A terrorist. And he shot my partner."

"Let the diplomats sort it out."

The Chinese soldiers arrived. They didn't assault Larrikowal directly, but two of them added their weight to Pahk's push.

Omar grinned as he began sliding and rolling toward the gangway.

Three were too many.

Sam, dripping seawater from a wetsuit which barely reached his knees, climbed up over the three-foot metal pole fence on the side of the dock. Stepped over to where the end of the gangway reached the pier.

Pahk released the wheelchair. Clutched his throat. Shook his head violently at Sam's appearance.

The two Chinese soldiers ignored Pahk. Pushed Omar behind Hu and the rest of the delegation.

Sam held up a pair of controllers. In his left hand, a trigger-looking handle for his eSurfboard. In his right, an open red plastic box of electronics with a dial and a set of uncovered switches.

"Admiral, don't you want to know what Secretary Dorenza's third point was?"

Chapter Thirty-Six: Island Fall

I sent my replenishment rangers ahead of me in the outrigger canoe from the beach. Told them to parallel the shore, but move far enough away to pass the Chinese destroyer a good fifty meters on the outside.

Wouldn't want to make anyone nervous that they were attempting to board. Someone might shoot.

Of course, I also explained that once in sight of the destroyer, they needed to do a striptease.

"Think of it like being a streaker at a big event, but on water."

My intel guy was more comfortable with my lunacy. "Whiskey Tango Foxtrot, sir?"

We dropped the excess limpet mines into the water as a temporary hiding place. I kept one more for my use.

"You're a diversion. A distraction. Ever learned a magic trick before? You're the hand the audience focuses on trying to figure out the meaning of. Can't do that if they just dismiss you with a glance. The Chinese need to wonder what you demented dudes are doing."

Schnier's demo dude reached down to flip over the outrigger. Slide it across the sand to the water. "This is the weirdest ranger assignment I've ever had."

We gave him a hand with the boat. Floated it next to my eSurfboards. I handed him a paddle.

"Just think of how many drinks you'll get by telling this story in some ranger bar outside Fort Bragg. They'll lap it up."

"If you say so, sir."

I listened in on the general inter-unit comms channel. Michelle piped in the media's audio of the meeting to replace any silence amongst our team.

Helped everyone out of sight to maintain situational awareness. Know what was going on over at the pier.

Once the two rangers reached the point I'd mentally designated as close enough, I checked my rebreather and dove under water on my lead board.

Flew beneath the sea toward the destroyer.

Docked, its propeller would no longer be a danger. I wouldn't even need to match speeds.

Of course, in shallow, clear water, their deck watch should spot me beneath the waves as soon as I got close.

Unless they watched the shows instead. The international events on the pier, or the stupid strippers on the water. I didn't really care which, as long as they didn't notice me.

Overload their observation function and they couldn't properly orient to me as a threat, let alone decide and act in response.

Their burlesque act must've been good. No machine gun fire found me underwater. I placed the mine on the rear rudder, just behind the propeller. With luck, it might take out both in one blast.

If so, mission-kill. Dead in the water without dead on-board.

To limit my exposure, I dove deeper. Beneath the broad hull. Out of sight.

Needed to stay out of the space between the destroyer and the concrete dock. Some tires hung on the dock reduced the ship's impact, but each incoming wave slammed the 7,500 ton ship into them.

Gently, not much speed, but enough mass to crush anyone in the way.

My board reached the bow. Didn't particularly want to stream back out into the open water. Made a right turn at the end of the pier instead.

Now the concrete pier blocked any direct line of sight from the destroyer, so I surfaced.

Listened to the progress of the negotiations. Dorenza was

really giving it to Hu.

I floated to where I'd dove over the railing to escape Filipino customs. As close as I could get without revealing my position.

Listened to Dorenza's first two points. Heard shouting as the Chinese retreated. Something about a wheelchair and a war.

Sounded like my cue.

I extracted the portable mine control console from my board's watertight compartment.

Stood on the board. Set the controllers on the concrete pier beneath a yellow-painted railing.

Grabbed the lowest pole of the barrier. Pulled myself up. Climbed over the top. Retrieved my devices.

Dripped water on the pier. Guess the cameras wouldn't get my best outfit.

I stepped over to where the end of the destroyer's gangway reached the pier. Intercepted the Chinese delegation. Uncovered the detonation switches.

"Admiral, don't you want to know what Secretary Dorenza's third point was?"

Hu stopped. His escort raised their rifles to ensure I understood they'd fire if physically threatened.

"Who are you?" Hu obviously still reeled from Dorenza's revelations. He should've ignored me.

I doubted they wanted to start a war without authorization, but open rifle barrels do promote an adrenalin rush. I took a deep breath.

"The man holding the switches. Pahk over there can vouch for me, but please allow a demonstration."

I flipped a switch. The one for the mine I'd originally dumped in the channel. Needed to clean it up, anyway. Can't leave unexploded ordnance around.

Boom! Everyone's heads turned toward the sound. A geyser of water spouted thirty feet into the air. Spread out in a cloud as it sank back to the sea.

I put my hand over the rest of the switches. "Don't make any sudden moves. Wouldn't want an accident. There's one of those attached to each of your ships. Two for the destroyer."

Pahk caught up with the Admiral.

Just in time to receive Hu's glare. "What's the meaning of this? He knows you?"

Pahk gulped. "We met in Seoul. An imperialist ranger lieutenant. The one Omar held prisoner."

"So you can see," I pointed at Omar in his chair, "why I can't allow you to take these two with you. They aren't even Chinese nationals. The international media might be interested in learning from your country why you allowed them on board after the Filipino police informed you of their charges against them."

Hu waved at his security detail. "Let the locals have Omar. He's become a liability. Pahk will return with us. As far as those cameras are concerned, he's dressed as a member of our military and is a Chinese citizen. So we'll board together and leave this *two-fifty* place."

Pahk pushed Omar's chair behind him. "Thank you, Admiral."

Larrikowal stepped up to take Omar's chair. Gave me the evil eye. Mouthed, "Don't start a war."

Omar tugged at a strap across his lap. "I kept my bargain. You promised! This doesn't end here."

Hu glared at Omar. "Prove it. As far as I know, you're just an acquaintance of Pahk's, who asked for a boat ride as a favor. We owe you nothing."

I compromised, despite it being against my nature. "We'll give you more time to mull over Pahk's fate. Something you should know before you depart."

Hu paused at the top of the ramp. "What?"

"Dorenza's third point was to tell you about the limpet mines, like the one I just detonated harmlessly in the water. They each contain an anti-tamper detonator, so I wouldn't advise messing with them outside a full shipyard. They're command detonated, either locally as you've seen, or via satellite radio signal activation, good anywhere in the world."

"Your reason for this act of war?"

"It's only an act of war if we actually blow you up, but you can still avoid that fate. You have until noon to return your guest, the American citizen, Raven, to this pier. I'm sure you wouldn't want to illegally detain her, as we rangers take leaving one of our own behind very seriously. You can drop Pahk off for extradition at the same time."

"And if we don't? Make your threat explicit."

"Then your ships won't leave this harbor. They'd make nice artificial reefs, don't you think? Something for the tourists to scuba dive through and admire your advanced technology?"

Hu stared at me. "You won't get away with these threats."

I ignored his bluster. "Until Raven and Pahk are here to stay, don't leave the harbor. We wouldn't want to think you're planning to take them outside Filipino jurisdiction and thus need to slow you down."

"I'll verify your words and consult with my headquarters." Hu turned to complete his journey up the gangway.

"You do that, but remember. Noon."

Hu's men followed him up the ramp as Larrikowal and the SAF took Omar into formal custody for terrorism.

Dorenza and the rest of the SAF retreated to the base of the nearby hotel. Out of any inconsiderate Chinese retaliation.

My two rangers, tourist clothing restored, docked their outrigger canoe near the shore at the end of the pier. I remotely navigated my surfboards over next to them, where they could pull them out of the water for me as well.

Watching them work from above, I heard a scream. Turned.

Pahk held Raven at the destroyer's railing. Ready to push her over. Into the crushing space between the ship and the dock.

I sprinted toward the hull, head craned back to watch.

Damn that Pahk! Should've taken him out of competition in Seoul when I had the chance.

From his sniper perch, Schnier identified Admiral Hu's unexpected guests. They'd brought at least two of their demands to the party.

He toggled his mic. "Pahk, pushing Omar. Odd that Hu brought them here, putting his support out in the open."

Michelle chimed in with her typical people analysis, always concerned with motives instead of deeds, "He's making a statement. Telling the locals how he expects to run things.

Might even make Omar a local representative. Co-opt his men even more. Remember, they have no idea we've destroyed his forces as a fighting unit."

Schnier's good old competitive spirit pushed itself forward. A man had to have at least some pride.

No way he was about to let Omar and Pahk get away. Not ever.

He focused his rifle scope high on Omar's chest. They were bulls in *his* pasture now.

"I can take them both, anytime you give the word. I know the plan, but we can't let those two walk out of here."

Easy enough from less than 100 meters to put a high-speed 7.62 round through Omar, the back of the wheelchair, and into Pahk.

Knock 'em so hard they'd see tomorrow today.

"Stick to the ROE." Larrikowal quenched his fire. "No shooting without an immediate threat. If there *is* a battle, and I hope there isn't, we must have on camera that they caused it. Otherwise, we'll be at war with the world unwilling to step in on our side."

Fine. He'd resist his instincts. Follow orders. Keep the world out of war.

For now.

Schnier listened to the news feed. Watched for an excuse to defend the delegation as Dorenza greeted Hu. Humiliated him on TV. Threw shade on the Filipino President.

Had to admit, Hu's expression when he learned they'd set him up was pretty satisfying.

Dorenza demanded Omar and Pahk remain. Good.

Larrikowal made a grab for Omar. The little SAF major had big brass *cojones*, for sure.

Schnier spoke in his ear. "You can't hold 'em. Fold up and I'll take 'em down on the way to the ship."

Larrikowal just kept tugging. "Hold on. This isn't worth starting a war over."

The rest of Hu's security detail caught up. A couple of them Pushed Omar's chair. Made progress toward the ship.

Schnier shifted his crosshairs to Pahk. "Give me a range and wind adjustment!"

Before his spotter could respond, Sam appeared. Interrupted. Blew up some seawater. Just like the little Tasmanian devil-surfer to destroy everything he came across.

Came in handy sometimes.

Pahk left Omar behind, but Sam allowed him to leave with Hu.

The SAF forward element caught up. Took Omar away. One brought to justice.

After capturing the end of the argument, the camera crews on the dock continued to film the Chinese ship.

Schnier settled himself down with a sigh. He'd keep his job as a sheepdog intact. Not begin a war over his pride. Look at the bigger picture.

At least this once.

Not likely to be much action until closer to noon, anyway, so he and his spotter alternated watching the destroyer.

His spotter saw it first. "Sir, looks like an argument on the ship."

Schnier focused in on the deck. Raven sitting on the ship's railing above the dock. Pahk shaking her arms.

"On glass. Imminent threat. Target, man at railing, risking HVT's life."

His spotter's training kicked in. "Check level. Hold over, six point 2."

Schnier made a minor adjustment. "Ready."

"Wind left point 3."

A quiet atmospheric day. Tiny shift in aim-point.

Sam sprinted into view below them.

Schnier toggled his mic. "Taking Pahk out."

Larrikowal was quick to respond. "Negative. Maybe this will end well. Pahk's obviously upset, so Hu might give her up to us."

"He's a clear threat. It's on camera that her life is in danger."

Michelle chimed in. "We can't impact the locals like this. This is their country. Their decision. We're just guests."

Their love wasn't on the line. Not like his. What if Pahk pushed her over the side?

Sam peered up at Raven from the edge of the concrete pier below them. Hands full of electronics.

Didn't have a firearm.

Schnier paused his breathing.

Raven scuttled away from Pahk. Stood on the top railing. She'd been a gymnast in college, but that wasn't a regulation high beam. Too round and narrow.

Schnier tracked Pahk as he followed her movements. Kept her off the deck.

She moved to the side. Played keep away with her body.

Was Schnier the sheepdog, or the bull? Would he protect her or start a war?

Or both?

He wanted to pull that trigger bad, but he resumed his even breathing. Tracked Pahk, just in case.

Pahk jumped at her. Tried to grab her.

Raven dodged back. Bent in the middle to avoid him. Her feet slipped off the top rail.

She fell.

Grabbed the bottom railing. Her feet and chest banged against the side of the hull.

Schnier's breath stopped.

The space below, between the hull and the dock, opened up as if to welcome her if she dropped further.

Pahk lifted a boot heel to stomp her hand.

No war now. Schnier eased his trigger back.

The round exploded from his rifle barrel with a flash of consumed powder.

His active hearing protection ear pieces canceled most of the sound, but the pressure wave still pounded him in the head as the rifle butt slammed into his shoulder.

Sam's voice from the radio overrode his noise canceling earpieces, "Take the shot."

Too late.

Pahk slammed his boot down on the railing.

Raven released her hand. Narrowly avoided being crushed.

Schnier's bullet blew open Pahk's upper chest. Exploded out his back. He fell back. Crumpled to the ground.

Instant demise.

She hung from the railing with one hand. Swung her other to get an additional grip.

Missed. Couldn't reach.

Schnier flung his rifle down. Dashed to the balcony door. Raced down four flights of stairs, barely touched every other one.

Sprinted across the road. Down the pier.

Raven hung in there. By only one hand.

Raven huddled in the corner of her cell in the Chinese brig. Would love water. Food.

Even plain rice again.

She'd heard a distant explosion earlier. Training?

No one came to explain. She hadn't seen anyone since the ship stopped moving so much.

Pahk peered through the plexiglass window. "Good. You're awake."

He undogged the hatch with a clunk. Pulled the bulkhead door open. The three hinges creaked.

She stood. Tensed. Ready to fight if he assaulted her.

He grinned. Stretched out his hand. "Come with me."

"And if I refuse?"

"Admiral wants to see you. Pass judgment himself. His task force. Pretty much gets what he wants, when he wants it."

"I'll follow you."

He retracted his arm. "Don't make me restrain you. Walk in front. Better view that way."

She inched out of the hatchway, back to the side, so she could keep as much distance as possible.

"What about Omar?"

"Don't worry about Omar." He winked. "He's no longer in the picture."

Died from his wounds? Did Pahk kill him? Or did they just let him go?

She certainly couldn't trust Pahk. Was she capable of trust for anyone, any more? After Omar?

The deck remained relatively still. Not much of the swaying

of sea travel. Why was the shipped stopped, anyway?

Would Pahk tell her?

"The ship stopped." Couldn't get mad at her just for making a statement.

Pahk grunted. Pointed down the corridor to a ladder leading up. "We're docked."

Docked? Too soon to be out of the Spratly Islands. Maybe the island China built up and stuck a barely usable runway on?

She walked in front of him. Conscious of his stare on her backside. Climbed the ladder, really just a steep staircase with minimalist metal steps.

He stayed close. Fixed his focus on her, right above. Had he no shame?

She stiffened her neck and back.

Two switchbacks, and then they arrived on deck next to a square building with a tower on top. A wire contraption made of four old-fashioned TV antennas spinning on a ball was like a Christmas tree topper on the tower.

Made a humming sound as it turned.

Pahk reached the deck. Poked her in the back. Pointed forward; to a larger deck construction. Some kind of control tower, even taller than the area they'd come up through. Four stories?

The terrain next to the ship distracted her. She knew this dock. Had seen it several times from much closer to the ground and water.

Lubang Island!

The Chinese destroyer brought her back. Why?

Filipino soldiers on the other end of the pier. A gangplank led down from this deck, it's head only thirty meters distant.

Four Chinese marines guarded the entrance. Might as well have been a mile away.

She ignored Pahk's unspoken command. Looked over the railing. The blood red waterline of the ship only fifty feet below her. Slowly moved back and forth. Impacted the pier's tire buffers.

Just above that, maybe ten feet, the raw concrete edge of the dock.

Freedom.

Was that Sam on the other side of the pier? Back turned? Looking down at the water?

Pahk seized her arms just above the elbows. Smashed her into the railing from behind. "Let's go. Back inside. Admiral Hu will decide."

Raven couldn't help herself. She screamed, "Sam!" It came out of her parched lips as more of a screech.

She got her left arm free. Spun. Elbowed him in the jaw.

Shorter than her. Surprised at the resistance. He let go. Collected himself. Faced her.

"There's no place to go."

Would death be such a bad destination?

She climbed backwards up the railing. Three rungs. Used her height. Sat on the top. Rested her feet on the middle.

Pahk dashed forward. Grabbed for her arms again.

Obviously didn't realize that as a former gymnast, she could also use her legs.

She kicked him in the chest.

No real damage, but pushed him back.

She climbed up higher to avoid him. Stood on the top rail. Just like the balance beam, except narrower and rounder.

And four stories higher.

Pahk grabbed at her legs. "Come on! Do what you're told."

She slid her feet to the side. Too fast for him.

Too high.

"I've done that too much already, recently, and I'm not even married to you!"

She'd rather die than give one more inch. Make one more compromise to survive.

He shifted tactics. Jumped up. Grabbed at her waist.

She instinctively dodged back. Sucked her stomach in. Bent her back to avoid his grasping hands. Realized she needed to keep her feet on the bar.

Failed. Slipped off.

Fell.

The railing became a blur. She straightened. Reached.

Grabbed.

Held on to the bottom of the three railings with her hands.

Momentum slammed her chest and legs into the gray-painted steel hull. Oof!

The ship moved with the harbor's smaller waves. A gap opened below her. Three feet between the hull and the pier.

Snapped shut again, like an alligator's jaws.

She wanted to live. Don't look down. Look up.

Climb up.

Pahk had other ideas. He raised a boot. Lined it up with her hand on the railing. Stomped down.

She let go. Kept her left hand unbroken. Swung from her right.

A wet splat above her. A sharp crack far behind her. A splash of blood.

Focus.

She swung like a monkey. Remembered her days on the horizontal bar. Reached.

Missed. Too far.

Pahk slumped backward to the deck. Lifeless eyes.

The ship shifted back and forth in the waves. Bounced her in and out in response. Made it difficult to get side-to-side momentum instead. To grab back on with her other hand.

Two of the Chinese marines who guarded the gangway jogged down the deck toward her and Pahk's body, rifles at the ready.

The other two scanned the town for where the shot had come from.

Forget climbing back up. Raven could barely hold on against the rolling of the waves.

Should she pick her moment to let go? Try to hit the pier? Avoid the crushing gap?

Four stories. Forty feet. Concrete. Might break a leg. Her head if she fell wrong.

No good solutions.

Sam stood at the bottom. Another American soldier sprinted across the pier.

Schnier!

A Filipino officer chased after him. Carried a small sail.

The Chinese marines arrived. Checked Pahk. Dead. Pointed at her. Alive.

For now.

They argued. She didn't speak much Mandarin, but from their body language, neither wanted responsibility for her.

Too much risk.

Schnier arrived below her. Shouted up, "Raven, hold on!"

Master of the obvious. "Not as easy as it looks."

Another wave knocked her into the side of the hull. She got her off-arm onto the ship's deck.

Nothing to hold, but she pushed up.

Grabbed.

Both hands on the bottom railing again!

Progress. She balanced her feet against the hull. Almost stable. Glanced down again.

Schnier and Sam held up their arms, as if to catch her. Forty feet? Not a chance.

The two marines came to an agreement. Slung their rifles. Advanced toward her.

She didn't want to stay on board, either.

Could they catch her? Keep her from the deadly drink?

The Filipino officer arrived. Handed Sam and Schnier a corner of his sailcloth. Pointed.

They spread out. Sam and Schnier moved right up to the edge of the pier. Leaned out over the tire buffers.

The Filipino stepped back. Stretched it into a triangle of cloth.

Schnier looked up. "Jump! We've got you."

Okay, maybe there was still one person she trusted completely.

The two marines coordinated their lunges. Grabbed at her wrists.

Before they reached her, she let go of the railing. Pushed off of the hull. Let her tumble turn into a back flip.

One rotation over forty feet.

Landed in the sailcloth on her back. Dead center. Maximum flat contact area.

Her parents and coach would've been proud.

Each soldier held a corner high. Allowed the cloth to give

258 | Thomas Sewell

downward as she hit. Slowed her momentum. Turned her fall into a pillow compared to the concrete pier.

They lowered her to the ground.

Sam grinned. "Thanks for dropping in."

The other two groaned.

She eased her way to her feet. Checked everything still worked.

It did.

Grabbed Schnier with one arm. Sam with the other. Pressed them together to crush the Filipino man.

Schnier let her move him, but squeezed her tight. "Raven, this is Major Larrikowal of the SAF. Quick thinker with that sailcloth."

"Glad to meet you, Raven. Heard a lot about you from Schnier these last couple of days. Almost caught you in my boat, but that didn't work out. Glad you made it."

Relief and exhilaration overwhelmed her. She laughed. "Thank you for the timely landing pad."

Schnier obviously had enough. He pushed the other two men away. Held her in both arms.

Kissed her.

She laid a fierce one on him right back!

A few moments later, he took enough of a breath to whisper, "I've been an idiot, but I still love you."

"I know, idiot. Me too. I mean, I love you too, but I've also been a muttonhead."

They kissed again.

Sam stood there with a grin plastered on his face. "Finally, I've been trying to get you two dudes together for days!"

Larrikowal waved cheerfully at the helpless marines staring down at them from the destroyer's deck.

Chapter Thirty-Seven:
Island Rest and Relaxation

Major Larrikowal, head of the SAF's new electronic counter-intelligence agency, rubbed the velvet box in his dress-uniform's pocket.

Dorenza's election night party at his campaign headquarters should be a validation of his victory, not knock-kneed nervousness.

But he still had to explain it all to Sheila. Worse than kicking down a bunker door.

She stood with her arm in his, sipping sparkling wine. Always did love the finer things in life. That's why he'd thought tonight was the best night to be on her good side.

Instead, he talked about work. About why Dorenza invited them to the party.

"Hu's sailors confirmed the presence of the American limpet mines, so he folded quickly. Had nothing else to do except go home, anyway."

Sheila shook her head. "So you weren't ever really in any danger, huh? What if he'd fought instead of run? Then what?"

"Then his ships go boom. No, he sailed home with his tail between his legs and quietly got them cleared by an explosives expert at a mainland Chinese port."

"Dorenza *nakagago* him."

"Yeah, he looked like an idiot to the world. Lost massive face. No matter what, his superiors are unlikely to be pleased with his results. Not after Dorenza's television broadcast from the pier."

"How's your retired partner?"

"Out of the hospital a few days ago. Resting at home, or else he'd be here, but he also needs to get used to life with just one arm."

She stared at his arms. "Uh-huh."

Quick, change the subject to something more positive.

"Tourism on Lubang Island is way up."

"Well, sure, all that publicity. You looked good on camera, even if you didn't tell me about your promotion yet. What a shock to find out that way, but I guess you wanted it to be a surprise."

He ignored her potential complaint. "Right, plus the elimination of the terror threat to outsiders."

She leaned deeper into his arm.

He swelled up his chest. "My unit accomplished both, of course."

She sighed. "Very talented."

He thought she was being serious, but wasn't completely sure. Was the time right?

A roar from the gathered crowd interrupted their conversation. At least 1,200 people attended Dorenza's "little celebration."

He stood on top of a raised platform with a bullet-proof lectern. Raised his hands.

The crowd cheered again.

"Thank you all! My opponent has officially conceded."

A roar in response.

"Couldn't have accomplished this without everyone in this room. Without the support of the Filipino people. I'm humbled to serve as your President. Enjoy the party!"

Cheers as he stepped down from the platform and returned to mingling with his supporters, foreign diplomats, and other guests.

Over the next few minutes of chitchat, he worked his way over to where Larrikowal and Sheila stood.

The Americans Dorenza invited gathered around the couple as well, including Watkins in his wheelchair, pushed by

Madsen, who had insisted that just because his foot was in a walking boot didn't mean he couldn't help his buddy.

Dorenza grinned at Larrikowal. Pulled a handful of cigars out of his pocket. "Well?"

"Umm..."

"Courage, Major. Faint heart ne'er won fair lady."

Sheila cocked her head at the exchange.

Larrikowal knelt in the crowd. Held up the jewelry box. Opened it to reveal his grandmother's ring.

She gasped.

"Sheila, my dearest one. Will you do me the honor of-"

"Yes. Oh, yes!" She put one hand to her mouth. Reached out to him with the other.

He slid the ring on her finger.

She lifted it in the air. Stared, delighted. Showed it around to the others. Lifted him up.

Dorenza clapped him on the back.

"Excellent work, Major!"

The Americans added in their congratulations.

Larrikowal felt like he'd fought his way across a jungle, then a mountain, and finally swam the ocean.

But he guessed he needed to grow up sometime.

Michelle watched Raven as Larrikowal's big proposal progressed. She kept glancing at Schnier. Snuggled into him.

Offered him meaningful looks of encouragement.

He'd need to watch that one, if he didn't want to end up hitched on a ranch in Texas.

But maybe he did.

After the congratulations died down, she grabbed Sam. Pulled him aside to a quiet corner of the party.

Out on a balcony, overlooking Manila's government quarter.

"We need to talk."

Sam tugged at his dress uniform pants, as if by messing with them, he could convert them into a pair of shorts. "We talk all the time."

She put her hands on her hips.

"I had to trade in a bunch of bureaucratic chips to get Schnier

262 | Thomas Sewell

off the hook. Pay for the down drones we sent after you. Allow my mission to expense those mines you gave to the Chinese."

He grinned. "Not to mention that resort you burned down."

Such a brat.

"That was you two obnoxious clowns, leading the SAF back from Manila. I just got stuck cleaning up your mess!"

"Thanks again, by the way. Wouldn't want to figure out the hard way what Omar planned for me next, even if technically I escaped on my own, just so I could save Schnier. Well, with Raven's help."

Obnoxious. And to think, she'd worn her thinnest black dress and the shell necklace he'd made for her in anticipation of this conversation!

"At least you still have your talent for destruction, everywhere you go."

"Seemed to work out alright. The Philippines has a new President inclined to work with America instead of staying busy collecting Chinese bribes."

She rolled her eyes at him. "The Agency and the Army are forming a new unit. Designed for physical infiltration of sites. To access data and equipment on isolated networks. Where we can't just break in from the Internet. Organization's most secure locations."

"What's this newfangled covert commando unit called?"

"Got a bureaucratic name. Designed to conceal as much as it reveals. Joint Army Unit Special Task Force - Urban Cyber Terrorism. Plan is to work out of Texas. Take over empty offices in the Johnson Space Center. Blend in with the geeks and the astronauts."

"Funny."

She lifted the necklace from her cleavage. Separated and clacked each black and white shell in turn. The action settled her spirit.

Not to mention, drew the eyes of male admirers.

"Anyway, I want us to be partners. To work in this new unit together."

He stared into her eyes, as if seeking some truth. "Partners? As in working together as friends on a joint venture, or the kind of partners with benefits?"

She actually blushed! Of course he'd take her statement that way. Was he serious about maybe getting back together, or teasing her?

So difficult to tell sometimes.

"Why, not sure you can handle me?"

"Have before, if you recall. Still sprint faster than you, also."

"I do recall you running away a lot, when it came to our relationships."

He laughed. "I'm not the one who fled sunny San Diego for brisk Berkeley."

"Well, this time, I'm not sure you have much of a choice, except to go chasing after me to the new unit."

"What do you mean?"

Had she blown it? He never liked to feel coerced.

She put her hands up in the air, as if to surrender.

"It wasn't me. I'm being roped into this by my management as well, but apparently Major Williams isn't your biggest fan. He's figured out a way to get rid of you. Donate you to the new joint task force."

"Don't you still have leverage in the Agency?"

She lowered her hands. Coincidentally, lay them on his shoulders.

"Used it all to pull Schnier's independent command out of the fire. No, I'm being voluntold as well. Langley isn't super-excited about all the stunts you guys pulled during my mission, however well it all turned out."

"I don't mind being with you, but when people are making me do something, I tend to resist, just on principle."

And what exactly did "being with you" mean in this particular context, surfer Lieutenant Sam Harper?

"I understand. Really, I do. I feel the same way. But that doesn't change the opportunity to do something great. Besides, my boss let me have some cookies for you."

"Cookies?"

She pulled herself closer to him using his shoulders. Whispered in his ear.

"Remember, it's a brand new unit. Not only can you recruit

just about anyone you want from the rangers, but I've been authorized to let you in on a little secret."

"Oh? I'd snag Madsen and Watkins. Have to consider which intelligence analysts to bring along."

She pressed herself into his chest. If this next didn't get him, nothing would.

"Your parents. You'll have clearance for the Agency's codeword-only file on what happened to them. In our spare time, between other missions, we'll be allowed to follow-up on what actually happened that day. Who killed them. Why they died."

"I went through what's known already. Nothing but dead ends."

"The CIA knows more about your parent's assassination than you think. As an officer in the joint task force, we can go after the perpetrators. Together."

He paused to consider. Looked down at her. Squeezed her in a bear hug.

"Okay. Let's do it."

Now, she just needed to tease out of him exactly what he meant by that. At least they'd have time together now.

She needed to teach him a little lesson in interrogation, that's all.

For series updates and free bonus stories such as the tale of Sam's *Ranger Selection*, email TR@catallaxymedia.com or visit https://books.bookfunnel.com/militaryheroes.

Terrorist Interrogator is next in this series.

Acknowledgements

Thanks to Christi Sewell, Michael Sewell, Larry Kowallis, Liza Wood, Mary Arnold, Jude Gries, and David Parker for their feedback. Special thanks to Clint Baker for pointing out cave clearance is a *bad idea* and thus almost getting Watkins killed.

www.ingramcontent.com/pod-product-compliance
Lightning Source LLC
Chambersburg PA
CBHW052040240626
47153CB00006B/2168